The
Vanishing
Child

BOOKS BY JENNIFER HARVEY

Someone Else's Daughter
All the Lies We Told

The Vanishing Child

JENNIFER HARVEY

Bookouture

Published by Bookouture in 2021

An imprint of Storyfire Ltd.
Carmelite House
50 Victoria Embankment
London EC4Y 0DZ

www.bookouture.com

ISBN: 978-1-80019-625-4
eBook ISBN: 978-1-80019-624-7

For Paolo and Helena with all my love

PROLOGUE
Jonathan Hutton, July 1972

I should have listened, Mom. I should have done as you told me. *You come straight home, you hear me? And don't talk to anyone.* How many times did you tell me that? And how many times did I promise you I would always do as you said. But I didn't stick to my promise. I didn't do what you told me to, and now... I'm so sorry, Mom. I'm so, so sorry.

Oh, and I wish so hard he would go away. I close my eyes and pray with all my heart to get out of here. To be back home with you. To be safe. I just want to go back in time. Just one day, that's all. Let me go back one day. Back to the moment I was walking up the hill.

Because then I'll just keep on walking, Mom. I'll just keep on pushing my bike up the hill. And when he comes up to me, I'll be polite, just as you always told me to be. I'll say "thank you" when he offers to help me. I'll say, "That's okay, I can make it home from here."

Yes, that's what I'll do. That's what I'll say.

I won't feel tired. I won't feel hot. I won't feel annoyed that the tire is punctured. Instead, I'll think about Dad and how he told me he would show me how to repair it. I'll keep my promise to him and wait so we can fix it together.

Honestly, Mom. I'll keep on walking up the hill until I get to the top, and then I'll freewheel down. And at the bottom, I'll walk the last few yards until I am home. I'll just walk in the door, like any other day. It will be like any other day. I won't stop to talk to him. I won't follow him inside. I'll just keep on walking. I'll come home.

And you'll ask me what happened, and I'll show you the tire, and you'll smile and make me a glass of lemonade and tell me to rest up, and then we'll wait for Dad to come home.

And after dinner, he'll ruffle my hair and we'll go out into the yard and he'll show me what to do. "A boy should know how to fix a punctured tire," he'll say. And I'll nod and hunker down and watch what he does and learn.

Make it happen this way, Mom. Please make it happen. Take me back in time. I'm praying so hard for it. Just one day. That's all. Please, please…

Because it's so dark down here. It's so, so dark. And I know he's going to hurt me. I saw it in his eyes. He wants to hurt me. Just like those other boys. He wants to do to me what he did to them.

Please, Mom, please… Take me back. Just one day. Let me come home.

CHAPTER ONE

The call came out of the blue. The voice on the other end of the line was professional, but gentle too, and sympathetic.

"Hi, I'm Suzie McColl," the caller said. "I'm a palliative care nurse at the Cascadia Hospice. I'm calling on behalf of your father, Robert Allen."

I had no idea how she got a hold of my number and didn't know how to react. I just muttered something like, "Oh, okay," too shocked to say much more because hearing Rob's name alongside the words "palliative care" hit me far harder than I expected.

Suzie told me she was calling to ask if I wanted to come and say goodbye to him.

"He's spoken about his family so often," she explained, "and I think he would like to have someone with him when the time comes."

When the time comes. I couldn't quite absorb that. I could tell from the tone of her voice that the thought of Rob dying with no family beside him upset her. It was clear she wanted to help him and that she cared about what happened to him.

I listened to her and couldn't help thinking she'd made a mistake. She had to be talking about someone else. Because my father wasn't the sort of man people cared about. At least, not enough to go to the effort of calling around and trying to gather his family together one last time. That wasn't the man I knew in any case. That wasn't my father.

If she knew our history, I thought, *she'd understand there was no chance of any of us going up there.*

But Suzie seemed determined. She had the key to his house, she explained. I could stay there while I visited him in the hospice. She could get the place ready for me, make up the guest bedroom, it wouldn't be a problem.

"My grandma is his neighbor," she told me. "And I've known Rob my whole life. It would really mean so much to him. To all of us really."

She spoke about him as if he were family, and I didn't want to tell her it had been fifteen years since I'd last spoken to him. But something about her voice, the kindness in it and the fact she didn't ask too many questions, convinced me that maybe someone should be there for him. Maybe the past was not worth dwelling on.

When I told her I would come up, I heard her sigh with relief and realized she must have called me last. Gina and Mom had already turned her down. This call had been her last shot.

And I found myself wondering, *How'd you get to know someone as nice as this then, Dad?*

"Listen, I just need a couple of days, to sort some stuff out, before I can make it up there," I explained. And Suzie thanked me and told me she was looking forward to meeting me. Everything so polite, and nice. As if he was a good man, an ordinary man, and not a father and husband who had long been estranged from his family.

It was only when I put the phone down that it hit me. The crazy coincidence of it. Rob, of all people, coming through for me when I needed it most. How ironic.

*

Will didn't react when I told him I'd found a new place to live and I wondered if he'd practiced containing his relief beforehand, making sure to stay expressionless, not realizing it was this very reticence that gave him away. A silent hallelujah. But a rejoicing for all that.

"I'll be out of here in a day or two, if that's okay?"

It was. "You need any help?" he asked. "I can help you move with your stuff, if you want."

So casual, as if I was just a friend who had stayed over for the weekend and not someone who'd shared a home with him for more than five years. This was how far we had deteriorated.

"Thanks, it's okay," I told him. "I'm heading pretty far, so what I can't fit in the car I'll need to leave behind. Is that okay?"

"Yeah, sure. Where you headed then?"

And I counted the distance in my mind, all the miles from San Francisco to Newcastle and wondered if it was far enough.

"North," I told him. And left it at that.

Newcastle. I had needed to look for it online after I'd spoken to Suzie; I'd forgotten the precise location. Rob rarely spoke about where he came from. It was as if his hometown, his childhood, had never existed; the past, something he preferred to forget.

I'd taken a virtual wander around the town and the surrounding wilderness, overawed by the beauty of the mountains and the sheer vastness of the forest, and the way it all gave way at its edges to the dark expansiveness of the ocean. It seemed strangely tranquil yet intimidating at the same time. Newcastle, some sort of in-between place, where nothing of any note ever happened. Anyone looking for excitement or adventure would need to head to Seattle or the wilderness.

Though my little internet excursion had thrown up a surprise. It seemed that Newcastle's biggest claim to fame was a series of child murders that had occurred in the '60s and early '70s, and for which the perpetrator had never been caught. Unsolved crimes that still had the power to intrigue the internet in 2018. It made me think that my dad did belong there after all. He contained those same dichotomies. That superficial tranquility harboring terrible secrets. In the same way the ocean, the mountains, the forest could be a source of horror as well as wonder, Rob was a man who could dish out affection as easily as blows.

It seemed strange to think that I was about to leave the easy, golden sunshine of California for this seemingly unknowable place.

North. Why couldn't I just tell Will where I was headed? But it felt like a defeat, for some reason, to admit I was headed to my dad's house. As if I was a child who still needed paternal protection. And besides, how could I suddenly explain Rob to him, when I had barely mentioned him in all the years we were together?

"Hey, that man I never mention? My dad? He's dying, and I'm going to see him one last time. Then I'm going to pick up the key to his house and take it from there."

No, it was easier to say nothing. Easier to walk away. Get in the car and drive. Just wave a goodbye. No explanations. Just how I liked it.

The hours on the road gave me time to start making some sort of plan for what I was going to do when I got to Newcastle. I had enough money to last a couple of months or so, but after that? All I could do was get the key from Suzie and then try and figure things out, maybe I could even make the place my own. Mom and Gina wouldn't mind. They'd be happy, I hoped. I could almost hear Gina say it, even. "You know, Carla, you could settle down here. Make a go of things." As if I hadn't spent the last five years trying. And failing. But this was a chance at something new and I had to take it.

And as I headed north, I felt strangely uplifted and uncharacteristically optimistic. I had a "new beginning" sort of feeling, and I had to keep reminding myself that I was headed there because my father was dying.

There was an end to deal with before any beginning.

*

Suzie turned out to be one of those people who are as friendly and sympathetic in reality as their voice on the telephone suggests. I liked her immediately. She'd given me her address and told me to come by and pick up the key to Rob's place. When she opened the door, her smile was exactly as I had imagined it would be—genuine, and warm. I could see she was the kind of person people went to when they needed help, because they knew she could be relied upon. When I'd spoken to her on the phone, I had imagined her to be in her late forties and it was a surprise to discover that she was around my age, but wiser and more responsible.

She drove over with me to Rob's house and helped me with my bags, then left it at that.

"I'll let you settle in first after your long journey," she said. "We can talk later."

And she smiled as she handed me the key and said, "You know, you look just like him," as if she wasn't expecting there to be any resemblance. It had been years since anyone had told me that and I was surprised to discover it no longer made me cringe. If anything, I was glad there were people here who looked at me and saw someone familiar. Perhaps it would make it easier for me to get to know everyone. I'd be "Rob's daughter," and not some stranger who'd rolled up from San Francisco.

I thanked Suzie for her help and told her I hoped she'd come over for coffee soon.

"Oh, don't worry about that," Suzie smiled. "This is the sort of town where neighbors look out for one another. I'll come by tomorrow when you've had a chance to get settled in and we can go to the hospice together if you like?"

I'd nodded and smiled and hoped that Suzie hadn't caught the look of uncertainty that must have crept across my face. Because now that I was here, I wasn't sure if I could go through with it. A piece of me was already thinking that it might be simpler to let him die alone or at least wait until he had slipped so deep into a drug-induced coma that I could avoid talking to him.

"Don't worry, he's still pretty lucid," she said. "The pain medication he's on at the moment hasn't affected him too badly yet."

"So he can still talk?" I asked her. And she touched my arm and nodded, not understanding that my question stemmed from panic. She just assumed the news he was awake and aware came as a relief.

"That was why he wanted someone to be here now, while he could still talk," she told me. And it was my turn to smile and nod. And again, I had to wonder. *How did my dad end up with friends and neighbors like these? People who cared so much?*

The more I thought about it, the less sense it made.

Settling in. Suzie made it sound easy, just a question of putting the key in the lock and turning the handle, but as soon as I walked inside, I began to fear that maybe I'd made a mistake and that it wasn't the place for me after all. Because my dad was more present than I'd imagined he would be.

It was stupid that I hadn't anticipated it, it was his house after all, and a few weeks ago, he'd still been rattling around in these rooms and living his quiet and isolated life. No family around him, but with friends who seemed to care and who took an interest.

Somehow, I'd convinced myself that living in his house would not affect me. That I'd just walk inside, and it would be like entering a stranger's house, a place I had no connection to. Instead, I encountered something else entirely.

It was a shock, when I opened the door and was confronted with a hallway lined with photographs. Me and Gina as kids, school portraits, family get-togethers. A studio portrait of my mom when she was young that I had never seen before. Every photo was framed and they were carefully arranged over both walls. It was like walking through an arcade of memories. And there was something strangely feminine about it too. A hallway lined with photographs, that was the sort of thing a woman would do to make a house a home, not a man who…

And a disconcerting idea crept up on me. That a change had come over him while we were all living our separate lives. He'd become better, in some way. Nostalgic, a little sentimental even. *No*, I thought. *That was impossible.*

I wondered if he would even recognize me if he walked through the door and saw me standing there. Would he know it was me? Would he call out my name—"Carla!"—surprised to see me, or would he stare at me as if I were a stranger?

The last time I'd seen him was fifteen years ago. I'd been headed to a new life, a new job, a new city, hoping for something better and unsure if I would make it. Within a year I'd be back in San Francisco. Fresh starts, it turned out, require more than just a change in location.

He'd been strong still. Healthy and vigorous and looking much younger than fifty-three, by at least ten years. He had looked like a man who would never decline and I think he believed this was true. He had always been aware of his physical presence and had never hesitated to use his powerful physique to intimidate.

We hadn't said very much that day. When it came to the time to leave, he'd leaned towards me expecting an embrace and when I flinched—a reflexive response not intended to be cruel—he nodded and pursed his lips. There was no need to tell me that it hurt, I could see it did. His attempt at affection had surprised me. But we'd left it at that, both of us knowing we would never get past this moment. We would never lean towards one another, never embrace. Too much had happened.

"You take care of yourself, Carla," he'd said.

"Yeah, you too."

"And call me when you get there, so I know you arrived safe."

Again, his concern so unexpected, so *fatherly*. I had turned away from him, because I didn't know how to react to this uncharacteristic affection, and I questioned it immediately.

"I will," I had promised him. But I had never intended to keep my word. I had forgotten the promise almost as soon as it was made. My father, just a vague presence in my mind as soon as I'd walked away. I wanted to forget him.

But those photos on the wall hinted at something. Maybe I had misunderstood him all along. And now, here I was, about to face him again. Or what was left of him. And I stared at the portrait of me as a kid that hung on the wall, and wondered what that child would have thought of her future self. That kid would never have gone to him. That kid would have run as far and as fast as possible in the opposite direction.

*

Suzie came by in the morning while I was rummaging around in the kitchen trying to see if there was anything in the house for breakfast, coffee maybe, or some cookies. But there was nothing in the fridge or the cupboards.

When I opened the front door, she was standing on the porch carrying a bag filled with some essentials, bread, milk and coffee, and she laughed when she saw the relief on my face.

"I only realized this morning that there'd be no food in the place," she said. "Sorry for not thinking of it yesterday. I got you a few things just to get you started. We can go to the store later, on the way back from the hospice, and get some supplies."

I motioned for her to come inside and thanked her as we walked to the kitchen. For the first time since I arrived, I felt relaxed, because Suzie was making the decisions and I wondered how she had managed to become such an efficient and organized person. We were around the same age, but she seemed far more in control of her life than I had ever managed to be. But it was a relief to let someone else take charge. We were going to the hospice and that was that.

In the kitchen, she set about making coffee and unpacking the groceries she had brought.

"Here, let me sort out some breakfast while you get yourself washed and dressed," she said.

It was only then that I realized I was still wearing my pajamas and that my hair was tousled, and I smelled a little funky. I smiled at her a little sheepishly and headed upstairs to get ready.

All night I'd been trying to think of some way to put off going to see my dad, even if it were only for a few days, but I'd been unable to come up with a reasonable excuse. After all, I'd come all this way, I'd responded to her phone call, so she had no reason to think I'd refuse to see him.

In the end, I found myself hoping we'd get to the hospice and find him too sedated to talk. I could sit by his bedside and play the dutiful daughter and feel good about myself without having to talk to him or confront him. I could even tell him things, safe in the knowledge that he couldn't hear me. It could be cathartic.

Though even that unsettled me. Because maybe it would be better to take this last opportunity to sort things out between us and really talk to him.

When I got back to the kitchen, Suzie was sitting at the table drinking her coffee. She immediately stood up and went over to the percolator, poured me a mug, then set it down.

"Here you go," she said. "I hope you like muffins with your coffee? It was all I could get at the store for now."

I had never been treated so kindly by a stranger before and I wasn't sure how to react. "Thank you," I said. "It's so kind of you. You really didn't need to do this."

And she looked at me as if what I had said made no sense, then said, "My pleasure. And anyway, it looks like you need it."

"Sorry?"

"I mean, it looks like you had a rough night. Did you have trouble sleeping?"

I shook my head and sipped my coffee and once again Suzie surprised me with her perceptiveness.

"Listen," she said. "If you're worried about how he'll be when we get there, then don't be. Like I said, he's still doing okay, all things considered. I mean, he can talk still and he can eat and drink unassisted and walk about a bit. Just as long as we don't stay too long and tire him out, he'll be fine. The worst that can happen is that he's asleep."

I didn't know how to tell her that this was what had kept me awake all night. Knowing he could still talk, that he was still conscious, was the very thing I dreaded. I had thought her unexpected call had come because he was close to death. The fact that he was apparently still very much alive frightened me, and I wondered if I would have come up here at all if I had known the true extent of his state of health. A part of me was still unsure why Suzie had called me. If he wasn't close to death, then why the rush? Or had he told her to sound so urgent because he knew we wouldn't come if we thought he still had weeks to live and not days?

"I just don't know what to say to him," I told her. "It's been so long since we saw one another and I'm not sure if I'll be able to find the right words."

She stretched her arm across the table and took hold of my hand. I let her do it, surprised by the gesture of comfort and how easy it was to accept this sympathy from her.

"If it helps, he spoke about you a lot, especially over the last few weeks. I think he's been thinking things over, you know? And he wants to see his family again while there is still time. Even if you sit there and don't say a word, that will be enough for him, I reckon."

I smiled at her and shook my head. "Maybe, who knows. Like I say, it's been a long time and there's a lot of baggage we never really dealt with, so…"

"Trust me," she said. "It'll be fine. You'll find the words. At times like this, most people do, and I know he really wants to see you. When I told him you were coming, he cried so hard."

I almost told her right then that I couldn't do it. The idea of my father crying and looking forward to seeing me… There was something about it all that pushed me back into the past. I was frightened that he was manipulating me. Feigning interest just so he could get what he wanted. And I worried that the photos in the hallway indicated nothing. He was still the same man, and men like him never change, they always get what they want.

But I was here now, and Suzie was not going to take no for an answer.

"Right," I said, as I swallowed down the last of my coffee and took the last bite of my muffin. "Shall we get going?"

On the drive over, Suzie chatted to me, but I couldn't focus on anything she said because the question that had kept me awake all night was taunting me over and over again: *What the hell am I supposed to say to him?*

I wasn't ready to face him and I should have been honest and explained to Suzie that I needed time, even if there was so little of it left. Because it was more than simply being scared of seeing him again after all these years. I was also aware that the question I had for him was too immense for a frail dying man to answer.

"Why did we mean so little to you?"

That wasn't a question for a deathbed. It was a question that should have been asked years ago while we were still capable of grappling with it. Because it contained a thousand other questions, and also my greatest fear: that he would answer it. Just look me in the eye and say: "Carla, that's just who I am."

*

The room was surprisingly beautiful. A large window overlooked a garden and light filled the room with a warm golden glow. It looked pretty much like an ordinary room. Framed watercolors hung on the walls, a small yellow sofa with matching cushions sat in a corner of the room, a burnt orange rug decorated the floor, and a coffee table lay strewn with books and magazines. Nice little touches that made the space feel warm and welcoming. It was a place for people to come together.

It was only as I approached the bed that I saw the equipment. A line leading into the vein on his left hand, connected to a machine which presumably controlled the dosage of whatever medication he was receiving. It was strange to see the thick veins protruding from the thin skin on his hands. Old-man hands. Hands that had once caused so much pain.

I walked over to the bed and looked at him as he lay there, a pale imitation of the man I remembered; his skin, paper thin and almost translucent and dotted with liver-colored age spots. His eyes were closed, and his lips cracked and dry because he had to breathe through his mouth. And thin. He was so, so thin. The shock of seeing him this way made me draw breath and Suzie took hold of my hand and squeezed it, then pulled a chair over to his bedside and gently settled me down in it. This was her domain, and her nursing instincts took over and began to calm me. And once again, as I gave myself over to her control, it was enough to help me compose myself.

He wasn't aware of me, and I wasn't sure if it was due to sleep or a result of the drugs, but it was a relief to know I could spend the first few moments with him simply watching and not having to talk to him.

"Can he hear me?" I asked Suzie.

"Maybe," she replied. "We haven't sedated him. But he sleeps a lot more now, so there was always a chance that he wouldn't be awake when we arrived. I'm so sorry."

"No, it's okay. I prefer it, to be honest. It gives me a chance to get used to seeing him like this. I mean, the last time I saw him, he was so…" and my voice faltered, on the verge of tears.

Suzie touched my shoulder and smiled, "Shall I leave you alone with him? I can go fetch you a coffee or something if you like?"

I nodded and waited for her to leave the room and close the door behind her before I took hold of his hand, relieved when my touch did not rouse him.

For a while I just sat there and listened to the slow and easy rhythm of his breath. It was calming and the quiet of the room lulled me into a sort of trance and made me wonder what Mom and Gina would make of this tranquil scene. I could see Gina shaking her head and turning away in frustration. She would think he didn't deserve to die this way, quietly and with a hand holding his. She thought he wasn't worth it, that our love and our care were better given to those who deserved it.

A few days ago I would have agreed with her. The thought of sitting with my father and comforting him on his death bed would have seemed absurd, impossible even. After what he had done to us, he deserved nothing. The way he had tried so hard to break us for no apparent reason. Why forgive any of that? Why offer him sympathy and comfort, even when he was dying?

No one would have blamed us for leaving him to die alone if they knew how much pain he had caused us. But sitting at his bedside, holding his hand, and seeing how fragile he was, how much of him had already disappeared, it was impossible not to feel some sort of compassion. I wouldn't have called it love, exactly, but it came close. I didn't want him to die alone, I realized. And it felt right to hold his hand and help him through these final days.

Though it didn't stop those old unanswered questions from resurfacing: "Why could you not love us? Why did you not try to love us?"

And, again, I could almost hear Gina admonishing me.

You know who he is, Carla. And you know he can never change. Don't put yourself through this. He's not worth it.

Maybe that was the best way to look at it. But his stillness provided me with a momentary burst of courage, and I whispered in his ear.

"Those photos on the wall. You thought about us all this time. Didn't you?"

"Did you love us after all?"

"Are you sorry? Would you have said so if we'd asked you? If I'd called you up, years ago, would you have told me: 'I'm sorry, Carla. Forgive me.'"

It was easy to ask him these things now that he was just an old man, asleep and dying in a hospice bed. No threat there. Perhaps just the hint of the man he had been, along the jaw. That strength which had terrified us all those years ago. But he was soft now, vulnerable, and incapable of violence.

As I sat there watching him, a strange feeling came over me. A hope that was both unexpected and disorienting. He had asked us to come up here and be with him in his final days, and I'd agreed without fully thinking it through. The need to get away from Will had clouded my judgment. But now I realized that maybe I was looking for something from him after all. This was his last chance to acknowledge the pain he had caused, and I wondered, if he did that, then maybe I could even forgive him too. I'd trade him comfort on his deathbed for an apology. A peaceful death in return for some honesty. It was a fair deal.

And if it didn't work out that way? Well, then I could always abandon him. Leave him to die in this pleasant room, alone and attended to by strangers.

"Johnny?"

His voice was faint, slurred from the medication and raspy with illness, but the sound of his voice so close to me made me jump. And again, he said it. "Johnny?"

"No, Dad, it's me. It's Carla," I told him.

And I saw his eyes flicker and start to open. And for the first time in fifteen years, I looked him in the eye. His watery gaze unfocussed, his delirium clearly in control of him. That name again, filling the heavy atmosphere in the room. "Johnny?"

"No, Dad," I repeated. "It's me."

He squeezed my hand and I heard him exhale, as if he was trying to speak, but this was all he could manage. It made me nauseous to hear it, because he sounded like someone letting out their final breath, and as he focused and tried to remember who I was, I felt overcome with dread. All I wanted to do was get out of the room before he had a chance to speak to me. It was cowardly, perhaps even foolish, but instinct took over and I fled, my name on his lips, his weakened voice, finally finding the strength, "Carla, Carla." But I couldn't turn back.

When I appeared in the corridor, Suzie was surprised to see me.

"Are you okay?" she said. "I was just coming to bring you this," and she held out a cup of coffee for me. I shook my head and made up some excuse about it being too much for me and told her I had to leave.

"The shock... I didn't expect him to be so thin, to look so sick," I told her. "He didn't know who I was. He was calling out for someone else and..."

"Hey," Suzie said, and she touched my arm and tried to comfort me. "It's okay, it's okay."

She offered to drive me home, but I declined, afraid that she would ask me why I needed to run away. But how do you explain to someone, that the sound of your name on the lips of a man who had hurt and humiliated you—even years later, when that man, once so powerful and strong, was now so frail and incapacitated—was enough to send a shiver of fear down your spine? How could I tell her that when I heard him say my name, my fear had mixed with loathing and a sudden urge to lash out? Because a piece of me looked at him lying there, helpless and vulnerable, and thought, *I could end this for him. I could end this, right now.*

CHAPTER TWO

Back home, I sat in the living room at the big bay window and stared at the front yard, numbed by what had happened and frustrated with myself for being so cowardly. I should have stayed in the room. I should have whispered his name in return. I should have picked up his hand and let him know I was not a hallucination. Provided him with the comfort he needed. *Damn*, I thought. *What am I doing here?*

When I called my mom, she picked up on the first ring. "Carla?"

"Hey," I said.

"Are you okay? You sound a little shaky."

"I'm in Newcastle," I told her, and the line went quiet.

"Mom? Did you hear me? I said I'm in Newcastle, it's Dad's—."

"I heard you, Carla. And I know where Newcastle is." I heard her take out a cigarette and light it, then take a drag and exhale before continuing. "So, that woman called you too then?"

"Suzie? Yeah, she did."

"And you actually went up there? To see him? Without telling me?"

"Yeah."

A pause again while she smoked and absorbed the news. "I see," she said. "Well, if that's what you think you need to do then I can't stop you. I just wish you'd told me."

"It just felt like the right thing to do," I told her. "Someone should be here with him, don't you think? And besides, you and Gina didn't want to do it, so I figured…"

"I hadn't made up my mind as it happens," she said, her voice sharp with irritation. "You don't cut someone completely out of your life just because you're divorced."

You don't? I thought.

It sure felt that way. Since the divorce, she had barely mentioned his name, even under her breath. Rob was out of our lives, as far as she was concerned. But this wasn't the moment to bring all that up.

"Yeah, I know," was all I said.

"So, have you seen him? Is he okay?"

"He was asleep when I saw him this morning. They've got him on a lot of drugs for the pain and it tires him out apparently."

"Oh, is he in a lot of pain?"

"Mom, he's in a hospice. He has round-the-clock nursing care, of course he's in pain. To be honest I'm not sure he was even aware I was there."

"I thought you said he was just sleeping? So what's the point in sitting with him if he's comatose?"

"I think I just came by at the wrong time. Suzie said there are moments when he's awake, and that I'll get a chance to talk to him. I didn't get the impression these were his final hours or anything."

"Really? Then why did she make it sound as if he was breathing his last when she called me?"

"Oh, Mom, I don't know. Maybe she knew we wouldn't come otherwise, if we thought he had weeks to live instead of days."

"Yeah, well, she'd be right about that. Anyway, you okay? You sound a bit down."

"I guess I am. It was just weird, you know?" I explained. "To see him so frail. I need to get used to the idea that he's dying."

There was a pause as she absorbed the news, and I waited and hoped she would leave it there. Because the truth was, now that I was over the shock, I realized that I had felt an unexpected sympathy for him. It was sad to see how ravaged by illness he was.

A piece of me thought he didn't deserve to suffer this way. But I didn't think that would be something she wanted to hear.

"Yeah, well, death is like that," she said between drags on her cigarette. "So, any idea when you'll be heading back?"

"I don't know. I mean, I have no idea how long this is going to take, it could be a few days, or maybe even a few weeks. They seemed to be a bit vague about it."

"Carla, you can't stay up there for weeks. You can't put your life on hold for him. You've gone up there and you've seen him. Surely that's enough? I mean, what does Will think about all this? Is he okay with you running off with no idea when you'll be back?"

"What does Will think of me being by my father's bedside when he's dying? Mom…"

"That's not what I meant, Carla. There's no need to talk to me in that tone of voice."

"Sorry. I know, I just… I'm here, okay? I'm here and that's all there is to say about it. And when he passes, well, there will be things to sort out then too, funeral arrangements, that sort of thing, so…"

I heard her sigh, not quite with exasperation; it was more a sort of weariness, as if she was tired of having to explain the ways in which Rob was not worth the effort.

"You know you don't have to do that, Carla. I'm sure, given the circumstances, they could find someone else to sort things out. It sounds like he has friends up there."

"Yeah, well, I'm here now, and, like I say, it just feels like the right thing to do."

She paused and it was almost as though I could hear her thinking of a suitable reply. Something neutral that would conceal her emotions and stop the tension from rising.

"Okay, if you're sure. But don't feel any obligation, that's all I'm saying."

I waited for a couple of seconds and didn't say anything. Just let the line fall quiet so that Mom would eventually figure it out. I wasn't planning on doing any of this on my own. I wanted her here with me. Gina too, even if it was only for a few days. They shouldn't leave me to say goodbye alone. It took her a moment to understand. "You really want us to come up there, don't you?"

"Could you? I don't think I can face it on my own."

"I don't expect you to, Carla, I just want to be sure you understand that you're under no obligation, none of us are," and I could hear she was struggling to contain the tension in her voice.

"Yeah, I know," I replied. "But you might even feel better if you come up here and say a last goodbye. I know I felt better once I'd seen him—"

"Okay," she interrupted. "I get it, okay? I get it."

"So, you'll come up?"

"Listen, if you think you need me to be there, then give me a call when you think it's getting close and I'll come up, okay?"

"Mom, I'm calling you now."

She was expecting me to offer her an opt-out. To tell her that I didn't need her there. That I'd find a way to sort it all out on my own. But I was in no mood for compromise. And besides, almost as soon as I had heard her voice on the other end of the line, it had hit me that I was going to need help at some point. We couldn't expect Suzie to do everything for us.

After a few seconds, I heard her sigh again, this time with resignation.

"I'll get Gina to come with me, okay? Then we can all say goodbye together." I picked up the snark in her voice, but decided to ignore it.

"You really think Gina will come? For Dad?"

"Don't worry, I'll make sure she does."

"Listen, if she doesn't want to, then don't force it. Honestly, Mom, it's no big deal."

"No. We're not going to do this without her. Anyway, get some sleep, it's getting late. I'll let you know when I can get a flight up there."

"Okay… and, Mom?"

"Yeah?"

"I… no, it's okay, forget it. We can talk when you get here."

The phone clicked and the line went dead, and I wondered how I was going to explain it to her.

"Hey, I split up with Will, so I'm thinking about staying on here. In Dad's house. What do you think?"

I could already imagine the look in her eyes. The confusion and uncertainty. The absolute impossibility of it. Because once Rob was gone, they would want to be rid of every trace of him. They would want nothing to remain or linger.

But I had no choice. I had nowhere else to go. *God,* I thought. *How the hell was I going to explain that to her?*

CHAPTER THREE

Those photos in the hall, every time I looked at them, I wondered how Mom and Gina would react if they saw them. I was sure they wouldn't like seeing a display like this, because it made Rob seem like some normal family man, and they had long ago decided where to place Rob in their hearts. They had made a little corner of the world especially for him and labeled it: "forgotten."

It wasn't that I hadn't done the same; I had, just not to the same extent. I wasn't as good at pushing people away, and pieces of my father would creep up on me sometimes. Memories. Questions. A stray emotion. I don't know how Mom and Gina managed to erase him so completely. Maybe they were just stronger than me, had more resolve.

But I'd gotten used to seeing them and had even started to wonder if the reason he had hung them there was simply because he missed us.

Gina would have a difficult time believing that, of course. It would take more than a few photographs hanging on a wall to convince her that Rob cared about us.

But my mom, I wondered about her. How she would react to seeing our smiling faces in the photographs? And not just posed smiles, fake for-the-camera grins, but real smiles. There had been moments when I had wanted to turn them to face the wall, because the sight of us playing happy families was too painful to acknowledge. But the truth was, there had been moments of happiness, however brief, and we couldn't deny it.

Forgiveness was something else, though, and I wasn't sure any of us were ready for that yet. But his house, and the way my dad was present in all the things around me, made me feel the possibility of it. For the first time in my life, I had a sense that maybe things which had once seemed impossible, were not so difficult after all. You just needed to know where to look. You just needed to open yourself up to it.

I took a beer from the fridge and headed out to the garden to sit and relax and think. The sun was starting to go down and the atmosphere was peaceful and calming, a nice antidote to my thoughts and mixed emotions.

Somewhere in the background the sounds of life and people thrummed. A car tooted its horn on the street, an airplane flew overhead, a radio blared in a house nearby. Distant sounds that didn't overwhelm the sounds of the garden. The proximity of wild nature here was something I would have to get used to.

I heard birds, the kind that sing melodiously as soon as the day begins to fall into dusk. The leaves in the aspen tree shivered in the breeze and sounded like tinsel, all Christmassy. Kids somewhere on the street were shouting and laughing, glad it was warm enough still to play out late. Sounds that let you slip into the moment and then take you away from it. Away and back to a warm, beautiful day pretty much like this one. Only years ago. I didn't want to remember it, but it persisted and so I gave myself over to it. A happy family? No, we were never that.

Back then, the days could shatter unexpectedly. Peace, calm, anything good, all of it could be disturbed in an instant, and for no apparent reason.

That day—though it could have been any day, take your pick—I was sitting with Gina in the garden, playing in the grass, chattering, giggling, Gina showing me how to make daisy chains. Not the sort of day that was worth remembering, because it was so ordinary, nothing special happening. Just another day. Until it wasn't.

When I looked back to it, when I asked myself what it was that made him rush towards us like that, what it was that made him shout, his face red and ferocious, there was nothing there. No specific thing. No triggering incident. Just him. Just Dad being Dad. Volatile. Angry. Never to be relied upon. Always disturbing the peace.

Perhaps we were being too noisy? Our laughter too shrill? Our songs too repetitive? Who knows? You never asked him for reasons. You just took the punishment and waited for it all to blow over.

When he came at us, we were stringing flowers together and laughing and then a shadow fell over us, and the flowers were plucked from our hands and there he was, looming and raging and making no sense, and telling us to, "Shut up! Just shut up!"

Dragging Gina. Pulling her up from the grass, slapping her head and yelling at her to "Get inside now! And stay there."

Then glowering at me, too small still, even for him, to be pulling at my arms. But his voice was enough to cow me and leave me whimpering.

"You too, Carla," he said. "Inside, now!"

But I couldn't move. The boom of his voice was too loud, too strong, too frightening.

"Did you hear me? I told you to get inside. Now!"

But I stayed in the grass and felt a familiar warmth spread between my legs. The shame of it. The fear that this would lead to a spanking.

And he came towards me, leaned over and was about to grab me, and I waited for it, the sting of the slap, only Mom was there. Coming between us. Alerted to the disruption by Gina.

"Rob! Leave her alone!"

I didn't see his face, all I saw was my mom's back. The pattern of her dress. Lilac with tiny flowers on it. Yellow they were, and delicate. Her summer dress. Black hair, glossy and flowing down her back. Loose for the summer. Barefoot and carefree. Save for things like this. Save for him and his voice and the size of him, the width of his shadow, the blackness of it. The presence.

Then the sound. Horribly familiar, and down Mom went, tumbling beside me on to the grass. And then down he came again for a second blow, then a third as she crossed her arms over her face, grabbed her head and tried to deflect the violence. Curled fetal and vulnerable as a newborn.

Though he never hit her face. I remembered that. The bruises were always hidden. Those delicate flowers on her dress hid deeper, darker shades of purple and blue. Yellows and greens, not of flowers but of battered skin.

And when he was done, he left us there in the grass, Mom sobbing as she caressed me and tried to soothe away a pain she knew she could do nothing to lessen. When I looked up, Gina was standing at the window watching us, hands pressed against the glass, her eyes black as onyx, as she watched Rob walk back to the house.

"Perhaps now I can get some peace," he raged.

But Gina's face suggested something else. She would never let him have it. She would make sure peace was the one thing he never achieved.

*

I'd spent years trying not to think about those things. Years hoping that my father's absence from our lives would somehow erase the memories and with it the pain he had caused. But that was a foolish thing to wish for, and as I sat in the garden thinking about the man who now lay dying in that hospice, I also understood that I'd be wise to never forget who he was. He was frail and diminished now, but that couldn't undo the pain he had caused.

And I wondered if that was really what this was all about. The real reason I was here. It wasn't just convenience, or even about trying to do the right thing and be with a dying man during his final days.

No, I wanted something from him. I wanted to hear him say "sorry." I wanted him to wake from that opiate stupor and talk to me with a clear head and an honest heart. For years, I thought our relationship was too damaged and beyond repair. But those photographs hinted at the possibility there was another side to him and I needed to try and edge a little closer, because if he did care about us, then I wanted to feel it. This was my chance, my last chance, and if I didn't take it, I knew I would always regret it.

CHAPTER FOUR

I decided I needed a few days before I saw Rob again. I had come up here assuming he was close to death but now that I knew he was capable of talking to me I needed some time to figure out what I wanted to say to him. I'd always thought that if I ever saw him again, I would still be too angry to want to talk to him. But when I saw him in the hospice, I had been overcome with emotions I wasn't prepared for. I felt sorry for him. I cared more than I realized. Despite everything, he was still my dad, and that meant something. I just didn't know what.

Suzie called me a few times asking if I was planning to visit again. I let her calls go to voicemail, then eventually sent a text message apologizing and letting her know that I'd call her when I was ready to see him. She replied with a short "Okay," enough to let me know she was disappointed with me. But she let me be, and I was grateful to her for that.

In the meantime I started to familiarize myself with the house and make plans for what I could do to make it a bit more comfortable.

His house was everything you'd expect for a man living alone. Sparse, I supposed you would call it. The essentials for living, but minimal when it came to comfort or any sense of home.

Those photos in the hallway stood out as one of the few personal touches. For the rest, no visible effort had been made to add some cheer or homeliness—no cushions or bedspreads, no doormats or pot plants, no art on the walls. In the kitchen, there was insufficient cutlery and hardly any cooking utensils.

That's what I went looking for. Some decent knives. I'd finally got my act together after almost a week of takeout and junk and had bought some fresh stuff to cook. But every drawer I pulled open revealed either piles of miscellaneous rubbish or knives so old and blunt they could barely cut through butter.

Something about his kitchen left me feeling down. It was the loneliness of it. Why have utensils if you're only cooking for one? I could see him sitting at the tiny table in the kitchen. Canned soup maybe, in a chipped bowl. Or a sandwich. Nothing fancy. Nothing homecooked. And the image of him in this house, alone, and eating only because he had to—there was no joy in it, no pleasure—left me feeling sad and emptied out.

Every time I looked at the table, I saw the way the Formica veneer had started to peel away at the edges, I saw the stains on the surface where he'd left a hot cup of coffee, the cigarette burns, and it was as if this was all his life had ever been. This solitary existence where it didn't matter if everything fell into disrepair because no one was looking. Nobody cared. It was as if the ghost of him had already started to manifest itself in the things he would leave behind.

Goddamn it, Dad! I thought. *Why'd you have to live like this? Why did everything need to be so pitiful?*

Then I looked round the kitchen and understood.

That's it, isn't it? All this, it's a punishment. You don't think you deserved anything better, do you?

And I wondered what Gina would say, if she saw me standing there in the kitchen, unable to move because of my rambling thoughts. Paralyzed by pity for a father we had all learned not to love.

"That's your problem, Carla, you always stare at things too long. You always think too much."

It was true, of course. I did think too much. That was the difference between us. A difference that seemed to ensure Gina stayed on an even keel while I drifted and never seemed to settle on anything, anyone, anyplace.

Maybe that's what I was really seeing there, in his house, the way it was possible to drift into things, to arrive someplace and stay there, not by choice, but by accident, because you're tired and you just need to stop.

But staying put is not the same as settling.

There you go again, Carla, thinking too much.

There was one last cupboard I hadn't tried. In the corner of the kitchen, it stretched from floor to ceiling, large like some old-fashioned sort of pantry. One of those cool spaces houses used to have before refrigerators existed.

More junk was what I expected, and sure enough when I opened the door, a mess confronted me.

Bric-a-brac piled up. What looked like gardening tools, pruning shears, a trowel, things that didn't belong in a kitchen. Piles of newspapers, yellowed and stacked higgledy-piggledy. A tray of knives and, for some reason, scissors, all bundled together.

I took one of the knives and tested the blade against the ball of my hand. Sharp enough to make an indent, sharp enough to make me pull it away, just in case. The only sharp knife in the house, hidden away like that in an overfull cupboard. Something he had no use for, but kept sharp anyway, just in case.

I was about to close the door, get back to the task in hand, when something caught my eye.

A wooden box tucked away in the far corner, the size of a shoebox, perhaps a little bigger. I'd have left it there, maybe noted it was something to look at later, but the sheen on it made me look twice, because it had a polished quality to it. It looked expensive. I imagined touching the wood and feeling something smooth, like marble.

I reached into the back of the cupboard and pulled it out. It was heavy. Not just the wood, but the contents. In the daylight, when I set it down on the table, it glowed, amber colored, with a deep-gold grain and chestnut whorls. Walnut, perhaps.

Whatever's inside must be precious, I thought. *An exquisite box like this left you imagining jewels or watches or polished gold coins. Something magical, a treasure.* And my heart beat a little faster when I looked at it, because it provoked a sort of childish anticipation.

When I touched the surface, it was even smoother than I had imagined, and the way it had been polished and buffed reminded me of a little pearl bead I'd had as a kid. I'd roll it between my thumb and forefinger when I was worried, its smoothness soothing me. I could feel the same thing there in my fingertips, that trancelike, soothed state as I stroked the surface of the box.

I didn't know then it would be the last small moment of calm for a very long time. Perhaps, if I had, I would have savored it a little longer.

Perhaps, if I'd known the trouble the contents of that box would unleash, I'd have left it unopened, placed it back in the cupboard, back in the shadows. Left it there, hidden away, dark as a secret.

*

I opened the box, expecting treasure. But there was no treasure. Just a tattered collection of papers that seemed unworthy of such an exquisite container.

Old newspaper clippings and notebooks in a beautiful box. It was strange. Strange enough to entice me. I sat down and began to take out the papers and read through them, not expecting to find anything interesting. Instead, I found a carefully curated documentation about those three boys I had read about on the internet. Adam Peterson, Danny McIntosh, and Jonathan Hutton. Seeing their names handwritten in those notebooks transformed their story somehow. It seemed more intimate, so personal.

It was dark by the time I finished leafing through the first of the notebooks. I didn't know how long I had sat there in the kitchen trying to make sense of it. When I'd started reading, I didn't even try to understand any of it. I just turned the pages, looking up now and then to catch my breath and stare out the window.

It had been sunny out when I started reading, but now I noticed the glow of streetlights through the window. A whole afternoon, gone, just like that. Filled, it seemed, with only one question.

"Why would he collect something like this? It was all so grim and macabre."

The notebook, the first of them I opened, was a collection of newspaper articles, cut out and glued to the page. There were hand-written notes in the margins. Rob's handwriting. A spidery scrawl that had fascinated me as a kid and taken me years to decipher.

The pages had stiffened over the years as the glue had hardened, and with every turn of the page, it made a sound like the scrunch of leaves underfoot on a cold autumn morning.

The articles were all about a boy, Jonathan Hutton, who had gone missing when he was eleven. I vaguely remembered his name from the old articles I'd found on the internet. The papers reported that he had been heading home after school when he disappeared. The last anyone saw of him, he was unchaining his bike in the shed, and nodding goodbye to his friend Peter.

"Hey, see you later." The last words anyone heard him speak.

And all of it happened here. In this quiet, nondescript little town.

When I'd first read about those boys it had seemed so improbable. A small, comfortable sort of town like Newcastle couldn't have such a terrible history. It seemed so safe and so peaceful. But, now that I'd been here for almost a week, I'd developed a sense that something wasn't quite right about this place. I felt it sometimes in the smile of the cashier at the supermarket checkout, something insincere. I felt it too in the stares as I walked down the street, an unspoken acknowledgment that I was a stranger. It was there in the eerie sort of isolation I encountered some afternoons when I went for a walk, the streets emptied of people and so quiet you could hear the squeak of rubber as your soles shuffled along the sidewalk.

I could imagine Newcastle as a town that could have produced such a story. As a place where those boys and the grisly manner of their deaths were entirely possible .

There was something about the way the wilderness encroached upon the unnatural perfection of those suburban neighborhoods that I felt made it possible. The well-ordered normality and the seeming regularity of people's lives was actually a form of protection—a protective barrier they put up against that wilderness, against uncertainty or some tendency within them they preferred to ignore.

And I had started to wonder if the quiet façade was something more—it was also a way to contain secrets and hide uncomfortable truths. To create the impression that there was nothing to see here, nothing to question or doubt. Everything was fine and as it should be.

And those old newspaper clippings were proof that my unease was well founded. This *was* a town where terrible things could happen. They *had* happened. That wilderness, it had found a way in.

NEWCASTLE BOY MISSING.

It was strangely subdued as a headline, the editors seemingly incredulous, because things like this didn't happen in a town like Newcastle. Not in those days, back in 1972. It felt as if they wanted to let the world know that this wasn't the type of place that allowed its children to go missing. There was an implication there that he would be found. That nothing more than this would happen. He was missing but he would turn up some place eventually. And I wondered about that, how it was they could appear so quiet and calm. Because they knew this wasn't the first child to go missing. They knew this had happened before. They knew that Newcastle *was* the sort of place where children were lost forever.

I looked at the date in the headline, Wednesday, July 12, 1972, the day little Johnny Hutton disappeared, and I wondered why my dad had clipped out the headline and glued it neatly into a scrapbook. Rob would have been twenty then and had already moved away. There was no reason for him to have any connection with an eleven-year-old boy. Yet the apparent care he had taken to place it there made me feel there had to be one, because why clip newspaper articles about a kid you didn't know?

Unless he did know him? I thought. And then I registered the name. Johnny. The same name Rob had whispered through his delirium.

Wow, I thought. *So you knew this kid? Shit.*

I stared at the photo that accompanied that first headline and tried to see if there was some sort or resemblance there. Family of ours maybe? Some cousin or other?

They'd used his school photograph. Hair neatly combed, a clean shirt, Johnny smiling for the camera, teeth a little crooked, a little goofy. The paper was grainy now, and the photo was fading. But there was nothing there I recognized. Nothing familiar around the eyes or the shape of the smile. Same with the name. Hutton. There were none in the family as far as I knew.

And I wondered if it were possible to see someone's fate in their face. Some subconscious awareness in the crease of the eyes, the breadth of the smile, the tautness of the brow; something that suggested they knew somehow; they knew something bad was coming. But there was nothing there, of course. He was a happy, smiling kid, unaware of all that was to come.

I stared at him and thought, *You will disappear one summer day, Johnny. And they'll spend years looking for you, but you'll never be found. This will be the last photo ever taken of you.*

And he stared straight back. A smiling boy thinking about summer and what he was going to do when school was out.

The article itself revealed very little.

The search continued today for eleven-year-old Jonathan Hutton who disappeared on Wednesday afternoon on his way home from school.

A pupil at Northwest Middle School, Jonathan was last seen cycling from the school premises at around 4 p.m.

When her son failed to arrive home at dinner time, Alice Hutton raised the alarm and neighbors joined the search of the neighborhood.

It is now two days since his disappearance, and Jonathan has yet to be found. This afternoon his mother issued a heartfelt plea.

"Jonathan is a quiet and studious boy, so very loving and kind. It is very unlike him not to come immediately home from school. We are all desperately worried and want him home with us as soon as possible. If anyone has any information as to his whereabouts, please contact us. If you saw anything, please let us know. Jonathan is so deeply loved, and our hearts are breaking without him."

At the time of his disappearance, Jonathan was wearing a red short-sleeved cotton shirt, tan-colored pants, and white sneakers. He rode a green push bike and was carrying a navy-blue backpack.

Police are asking anyone with information to come forward. A special hotline has been set up for anyone with information. Please call Newcastle 675- 2106.

I wondered what it was like, back then, to read something like this. More shocking than it felt now, I suspected, when stories such as this felt more commonplace. When papers and news stations seemed saturated with the latest breaking horror. No detail spared, no matter how intrusive or gruesome.

Reading it now, the mom's pleas seemed so polite. The way she talked about her son's quiet qualities, how good he was, how shy—it felt as though she wanted to create a good impression. Her son in the newspaper. She wanted to get it right, and let people know he was a good kid.

Did parents praise this sort of shyness in their children still? They probably did, but it felt like something from another era for all that.

Perhaps it was the yellowing newspaper, the crackling stiffness of the scrapbook as I turned it. I imagined Egyptian papyrus would make a similar sound. Old, cracked, almost unreal. The news printed there in those newspapers, something mythical, a history so old you could believe it had never happened.

If it had only been the clippings, then maybe I could have folded shut the pages and left it at that. Viewed the scrapbook as nothing but a quirky, inexplicable hobby Rob had one year. A little piece of shocking local history he felt needed preserving at the time, but that he'd since locked away in a box, the box itself then shunted to the back of a cupboard and forgotten, much like Jonathan Hutton himself. Did anyone think of him anymore? His parents, perhaps, if they were still alive. But anyone else?

But those notes in the margins puzzled me. The things he'd underlined. The seemingly random things he'd cut out and pasted into the book. Things I guessed made sense to him, but I just couldn't figure out yet. It was as if he was writing in code.

One note stood out because it was so different from the rest. *Down by Lake MacKenzie.*

That was all. Down by Lake MacKenzie. I turned the page, looking for an explanation and instead found another line of text.

Last one. Please, let this be the last one.

I read and re-read it, trying to absorb what it could mean. Something awful, I could feel it. Something unspoken and dark. Something Rob could never tell anyone about. These notebooks, they were more than a hobby, more than just diaries. They were something he had kept hidden in a box because he had this secretive side to him. He never let anyone get close enough to know him. I was sure, if I were to ask my mom if she had ever talked to Rob about those missing boys, she would know nothing about it. They had been important enough for him to keep that scrapbook. But they were not something he wanted to talk about.

It was the single most remarkable thing that had ever happened in this town, and surely the most unforgettable thing to have happened to him when he was a child. He cut out articles from newspapers, wrote notes in his diary, then tucked it all away in a beautiful box. It made me feel a little sad to think that he had always been this way. Unapproachable, full of secrets. A man, a child, who didn't want the world to know who he was. There was something lonely about it. A little damaged.

And I felt a little pang of remorse that I had never considered Rob in this way before—as someone with a story he felt unable to tell, emotions he could not quite express. Someone as damaged and human as the rest of us. Someone who cared enough about three boys who were strangers to him, that he had needed to document what had happened to them. And I imagined I could hear his voice, low and weary after the end of a long workday.

"I suppose you want to know why they were so important to me?"

JONATHAN HUTTON, JULY 1972

I was about half a mile from home. So close, I could have walked. Come home a little late. That's what you would have wanted me to do, isn't it, Mom?

But a punctured tire on a hot day. Pushing a bike up a hill. Sweating and thinking about how far I had to go. Half a mile is a long way when you're on your own.

"Hey, kid, looks like you could do with some help there."

He had a friendly voice, and it was a word I needed to hear. Help. He wanted to help me.

And I thought I recognized him, but I couldn't remember where from exactly. Though the reason I trusted him was stupid. He wore the same sneakers as me. I remember looking at the familiar red stripe that skirted the edges where the canvas met the rubber. It shouldn't be something to make you feel safe. But it was. I trusted him.

"You got a long way to go?" he asked me.

"No, about half a mile or so."

"All the way up there?"

He pointed to the hill. The sun was still so high, and it shone in my eyes, and it was so hot, walking up there, into the heat, the light.

"Yeah," I told him.

"I can fix that tire for you if you want? Have you on your way in no time."

And I should have remembered. What goes up must come down. At the top of the hill I could have freewheeled back down, ridden the hill to the bottom. Shortened the distance so that it was just a few blocks to go after that.

Or tied my bike to a fence and walked home without it. Collected it later with Dad. You'd have understood that, no?

But I got scared, Mom. I thought you'd get mad at me if I left my bike on the street. It was so expensive. We would count the coins in the jar each month, remember? A whole year of saving. A whole year of waiting and me asking you, "How much more do we need?"

Something so precious. You don't abandon it on the street.

"Here," he said. And he took hold of the handlebars and started walking with it to his house, like I'd agreed already that he could help me.

"Let me show you how to fix it. It's easy really. Come in handy for later too. A boy should know how to fix things, don't you think?"

I was going to tell him I did. We'd talked about it, me and Dad. About how we'd fix it together when the time came. It was going to be our project. He was looking forward to it. And so was I. I should have remembered that. I should have waited. Walked to the top of the hill. A half mile isn't so far really, is it?

I should have told him, "My dad really wants to show me how to do this. I promised him." I should have stood there and waited for him to wheel it back to me, saying, "Sure, I can understand that."

But he had the bike and had wheeled it into his yard. So, I followed him. Followed the bike. Kept an eye on it and didn't abandon it. I was careful with it.

Just not careful enough.

He turned it upside down and spun the front wheel, took off the outer tube and showed me the inner tube inside.

"Look, here, see? You got a great big hole here. What you do? Bike through some glass or something?"

I tried to think. Had I?

But nothing came. So I shrugged and said, "I dunno."

"Yeah, well," he said. "Let me get my tools."

He walked off towards his house, while I stayed there in the yard with the bike.

I could have changed my mind then. I thought about it. I thought, *Just take the bike and leave.*

But the tire was all loose and open and I didn't know how to get it back in. The inner tube, black as licorice, soft and flopping out like its insides had spilled.

When he got to the door he turned around.

"Hey, you fancy a lemonade or something?"

Did I nod? Did I say yes? I don't remember, Mom.

But he called me over. Gestured with his hand. Said, "I got some in the fridge. Real cold. Come have a drink while I find that repair kit."

I walked towards him. Thirsty. Hot. He held the door open and I walked right in. I walked right in, Mom. The one thing you always told me not to do. And I did it. I walked through the door.

And you're just a few blocks away. But you don't know it, do you? And I can't call out and tell you, "Here I am. Down here. I'm right here."

Because no one can hear me here. Nobody knows I'm here. Only him. Just him.

You always told me to take care. Don't talk to strangers. Come straight home. And I listened. I always listened.

I was on my way home, Mom. I promise you I was. And now you'll be worried and thinking, "Where are you, Johnny?"

And all I want to do is tell you, "I'm here. I'm right here."

But I don't say it out loud because I don't want him to hear me. I don't want him to come down here.

Stay away, stay away.

He keeps it dark all the time. Like a cave. Always night. Just a chink of light that shines under the door sometimes. The door at the top of the stairs. When he opens it, the basement fills with light and makes me cover my eyes. Because after so much darkness, the light is painful. I don't see him coming, but I hear him. Walking, step by step down into the cellar.

Stay away. Stay away.

But he never does. He keeps on coming. He keeps on hurting.

And here he is again. The key turns in the lock. The light shines under the door. The staircase is illuminated, and it hurts my eyes.

Thump, thump, thump on the stairs as he comes down.

"No, please," I say. "Please."

But he doesn't listen.

"Quiet!" he screams. "You hear me? I told you to keep quiet!"

CHAPTER FIVE

Mom arrived alone.

"Before you say anything…" Her first words when I saw Gina wasn't with her.

"It's okay," I replied. "I wasn't really expecting her to come."

Mom sighed and pulled a bag out of the taxi and heaved it over her shoulder. A small, overnight bag. She clearly wasn't planning on staying long.

"She'll be here tomorrow, actually. There were a few things she needed to arrange with David and the kids. We can't all just rush off when we feel like it, Carla."

A small jibe, but she caught it at least.

"Sorry, that came out wrong," she apologized. "You know what I mean."

"Don't worry about it."

She stood on the driveway and looked up at the house, appraising it.

"It's not as shabby as I thought it would be."

"Wait until you get inside," I told her.

She nodded, "Right, I see," then we walked up the porch steps and she gave me a kiss on the cheek.

"You know, I never could figure out why he came back here."

"Really?" I said, "Why?"

"He always said he hated this place. He said it had a *bad vibe*. Whatever that meant."

I was still familiarizing myself with the town, but I couldn't think of a particular reason for him to have hated it. It seemed like an okay sort of place to me. Small enough for people to know one another. Big enough to keep to yourself if that's what you wanted.

But that *bad vibe*, I knew what he meant because it did have that feel to it at times. I found the proximity of forest a little claustrophobic, the pines too tall, too dense and too dark for my liking. It was impossible to ignore the way they made their presence felt and the way the astringent scent of the trees mixed with the faint saline sea air, and permeated everything. Some days it felt as if the town itself was an illusion and that the wilderness was the only reality. *Bad vibe* was a pretty good way to describe it.

"Maybe when you've nowhere else to go, coming home makes sense," I told her.

"Oh, who knows? I gave up trying to figure out your father years ago. Anyway, let me get inside. We've got plenty of time to talk."

I looked again at my mother's overnight bag. In and out in a couple of days, by the looks of things. Her idea of plenty of time to talk was apparently different from mine. I followed her inside and saw her stop in the hallway, drop her bag to the floor, and stare at the photos lining the wall.

"Sorry," I told her. "I should have warned you. They had the same effect on me."

She didn't say anything, just walked slowly down the hall, stopping at each framed moment, leaning in close, then pulling away, as if the memories had her on a string. She had her right arm folded across her chest in a subconscious act of self-defense. Caught off guard but not wounded enough to fold both arms around herself. She didn't need protection from the things she was looking at. She just needed a moment to take them in. To make sense of them, and then move on.

"I suppose it says something about him," she said as she gestured at the wall.

And I wanted to say that I'd been thinking the same thing, but she picked up her bag and walked to the end of the hall and into the kitchen.

I heard her thump the bag down on the table, pull out a chair and sit down, and rummage in her bag. A second later, I heard a familiar click as she flicked open her cigarette lighter. She didn't ask if it was okay to smoke indoors. No doubt she assumed there was no need. It was Rob's house after all, so there was no need to ask me for permission.

I joined her at the table. "Listen, I haven't had a chance to cook anything. You okay with just a snack for now?"

She waved her hand and took a drag on her cigarette.

"I can wait, if you can."

I nodded and thought about asking her if she wanted to take a walk with me to the local store later, but then thought the better of it. Maybe it would be better to head there alone. It was hard to tell what sort of mood she was in exactly. Tired from the flight, sure. But she was also quieter than I'd expected. As if she was holding back on something. Either that, or she was waiting for me to begin.

"So, you convinced Gina to come up here?" I asked her.

She looked around for an ashtray and, finding none, flicked the ash into the palm of her hand and waited for me to get up and find one.

"A saucer will do," she said.

I rummaged in one of the drawers and found a small cut-glass bowl, the kind you'd keep sugar in, and she smiled when she saw how delicate and feminine it was.

"I never knew your father had such refined taste," she said.

And we both laughed a little. It was good to break the ice with something small and unexpected.

"Maybe she knew she'd regret it if she didn't come," Mom continued. "She knows she needs to put things to rest. You know?"

"Yeah? I thought she'd done that a long time ago."

"Well, you thought wrong."

I waited for her to explain, but she didn't take it any further. Typical Mom. Leaving things hanging just when you think you might be getting somewhere.

If you want to know your sister, ask her yourself, is what she meant. She wasn't here to try and explain Gina to me. Fair enough.

"Anyway," she continued. "What's the deal? You seem a little preoccupied," she asked me.

"Do I?"

"Yes, you do. So, come on, tell me. What's up?"

There was a slight brusqueness to her voice. The journey up here had left her jittery and impatient.

"It's just all this business with Rob," I explained. "I don't really know what I'm supposed to do."

She stubbed out the remains of her cigarette and sighed.

"Well, that makes two of us. And I'm still not convinced he deserves this, but I figured it wasn't something you should face alone. So, here I am…"

She gave a small shrug, her bottom lip pouting in resignation, but I wasn't looking to argue with her. We were here and whether that was the right or wrong thing to do, well, we'd soon find out.

She pulled another cigarette from the pack and lit it, took a long drag, and exhaled. "So, how long does he have exactly?" she said.

"His nurse says it's not long. But that was about all she could tell me. She's glad we're going to see him before he passes, though, I know that much."

My mom took another drag on her cigarette and looked at me as if what I had just told her was strange and somewhat disconcerting.

"She really seems to care about him," I said. "Is that so weird?"

"I guess not. But nurses are like that, aren't they?" she replied. "They care about people, even the bad ones."

"I got the impression she thinks he's a great guy, as it happens. I don't think she'd say he was bad."

Mom continued smoking and shook her head as if all this surprised her. I smiled at her and thought about taking a cigarette from the pack, but resisted.

"I was thinking we could go and meet her while you're here," I told her. "She lives a few doors down, with her grandmother. They're both friends of Rob's as far as I can make out. I think that's why she called us. As a friend rather than as a nurse."

"Why would we need to meet them?" Mom asked me.

"She just offered to help with some of the arrangements when the time comes, that's all," I explained. "Practical stuff, like talking to the guys at the funeral parlor, sorting out the money. She knows her way around this place better than I do and she's nice that way. Friendly, helpful, you know?"

She stubbed her cigarette out and shrugged. "Well, if that's what she wants to do then I won't stop her. Anyway, enough about Rob. How are you doing? How's Will?"

I didn't need to tell her. She saw it in my face immediately.

"Oh, Carla, what are we going to do with you?"

JONATHAN HUTTON, JULY 1972

Yesterday—at least, I think it was yesterday—anyway, whatever day it was, I didn't think about anything.

I didn't think about my mom, or my dad, or my sister, Amy. I didn't think about home, or my friends, or school. I didn't want to. I didn't want to think about how close they were. They were right there. Just down the street. How could it feel so far away?

He asks me about them sometimes.

"Are they worried, do you think? Are they looking for you?"

"Yes," I told him. And my voice was strong because I wanted him to know how sure I was of it.

So he hit me. Wrong answer.

"No one's looking for you, kid."

Kid. He asked me my name, but I didn't tell him. He keeps on asking me, but I can't say it. Because I don't want him to know my name. I don't want him to know me.

Then, this morning, the light in the stairs, his footsteps, some bread, a glass of milk.

"Here you go, Johnny," he said.

And I almost asked him, "How do you know my name?"

He smiled at me. "Johnny. That's your name, isn't it?"

I nodded. But still, I couldn't tell him. Still, I couldn't say it out loud. I couldn't give him that piece of me.

He went back upstairs and left me alone this time. Left the small light on at the top of the stairs too. The first time he's done that.

Maybe he forgot. He was too pleased to stand there above me and say my name out loud.

I guess he didn't understand it made me happy too.

Was it in the paper? On TV? My name, in the news. In the news because they were looking for me. Because they cared. And they'd find me. I knew it then. They were looking and they would find me.

"I'm here," I shouted. "I'm right here."

And I didn't care if he heard me.

I'm Jonathan Hutton, I thought. *And they're going to come and get me.*

CHAPTER SIX

Over dinner we didn't say much. Mom was too tired to talk, and I was worried about Gina's arrival, because Gina would have things to say, she always did. And she'd say them loudly. Where Rob was concerned, my sister was incapable of whispered politeness. As if to speak of him in a normal tone of voice was a sign of deference or something.

"So, you and Will," Mom asked me. "You want to talk about it?"

"Not really," I said. "These things happen."

"I thought you'd be sad, at least," she said. "Will's a good man, Carla."

"He is, I know that. But that doesn't mean we were right for one another."

She sighed and shook her head, and I knew what she was thinking: *Why do these things always happen to you, Carla?*

"So, what now?" she asked.

"I've got a bit of money. Enough to get by a while."

"A while?"

"A month, maybe two. If I can stay here, maybe even three."

"Stay here? What, you mean in Newcastle?"

In a way, it was better to talk about it now, just the two of us, before Gina got here. If we could get it sorted out first, then Gina would go along with what we'd already decided.

"Will stayed on in our old place," I explained. "So, you know, this is as good as anywhere else right now. No rent to pay, for starters."

"And work? Have you figured that out, when your '*month, maybe two*' is over?"

I hadn't. Or, maybe I had some vague idea, more a hope really, that I'd be able to get set up here, once I'd got my bearings.

"I'm a photographer, remember? I can work anywhere."

She didn't reply to that, but I knew what her silence meant. She thought I was deluded. That I'd need to come up with a better plan. She'd never considered photography to be a stable profession and had always made it clear she thought of it as more of a hobby.

"I'm going to sit out back," she said. And she picked up her wine glass, scraped her chair back and left the dirty dinner plates there on the table, making no attempt to tidy them away, didn't even glance at the pots and pans filling the sink.

It was her way of letting me know that if I was serious, if I really was planning on making this my home, then I might as well start immediately. She would consider herself a guest now, so all the mess, all the business of tidying up and sorting things out, was mine to deal with.

"So, you think I should head back to San Francisco, is that it?" I asked, as I took the plates to the sink.

"Hey, seems to me you've got it all figured out, so who am I to tell you what to do?"

I wanted to tell her she could always tell me what to do, it was what moms were for. But she was already heading out to the back yard, and I watched her walk across the lawn to the tree that stood at the far end. An apple tree, sturdy and old. A few days ago, Suzie told me it "gave a good yield come autumn" like that was supposed to mean something and it had taken me a moment to understand what she meant.

"Feel free to come and pick as much as you need," I told her. And Suzie had smiled that smile again and told me, "Rob always let me take what I needed. I think because he knew there was always a pie in it."

And again, I had been unable to react, because it made little sense. The sweet, corny undertone of apple-pie wholesomeness. We were talking about a different man, we had to be.

When I'd finished tidying the kitchen, I went out to the back porch with a new bottle of wine and Mom came and sat beside me. It was dusk already and the garden buzzed with the thick sound of insects. From somewhere the lemony smell of insect repellant filtered through and mixed with my mother's cigarette smoke. It was the kind of timeless, end-of-summer night that leaves you drowsy and empty-headed and feeling as if everything is okay in the world.

We sat and drank our wine in silence, just listening to the night, marveling at how quiet it was here, compared to San Francisco. But something about it all left me restless and unsettled. The ordinariness of it all, the sounds of the neighborhood that permeated the stillness, a radio someplace, someone laughing, a door slamming. This surface suburban pleasantness, a veil they drew over the more sinister truth.

"Johnny," I mumbled.

"What's that?" Mom said.

"Oh, nothing," I replied. And she looked at me, discerning the evasion in the tone of my voice. "It was just something Rob said to me the other day."

"I thought you said he was unconscious."

"He was. Well, more delirious. Like I said, he didn't seem to realize it was me. I think he was mumbling gibberish."

"Oh," she said. "You want to talk about it?"

"There's not much more to say, really," I lied, because I wasn't in the mood to take it further and ask her if she knew who Johnny was and if Rob had some connection with the poor kid. "I'm just thinking about tomorrow. About going to the hospice with Gina."

And she lifted her wine glass and took a large sip.

"Yeah, well, let's just enjoy the calm before the storm, shall we?"

I picked up my glass and chinked it against hers and drank down my wine.

The calm before the storm. Yes, that was exactly what it felt like.

CHAPTER SEVEN

Gina pulled up in front of the house at midday and stepped out looking unusually disheveled.

I watched her from the window as she parked in the driveway and hoisted her overnight bag over her shoulder.

The last time I had seen her was a few months ago at a surprise birthday party David had arranged to celebrate her thirty-ninth birthday. She'd looked radiant that day, far younger than her age and full of energy, as if nothing had ever troubled her enough to line her forehead or crease her eyes.

But the woman who walked up the driveway now looked older, and I needed a moment to absorb the changes and be ready with a smile and an embrace when I opened the door and welcomed her.

"Hey," Gina said, as she stepped inside. "Where the hell is this place? I think I spent, like, an hour driving through nothing but forest. It felt like I was in a goddamn David Lynch movie. Though this is an unexpectedly homely sort of neighborhood, isn't it? Not what I was expecting at all. I'd have thought Rob would be out in some log cabin in the woods, just him and the bears."

I laughed and pulled her towards me and kissed her on the cheek.

Gina smiled and then held me at arm's length to take a good look at me.

"You look good," she said. "I guess these northern climes suit you." And I laughed and elbowed her in the ribs. "Oh yeah, I feel so at home here."

"Hey, Gina," Mom called out from the kitchen. "Get yourself in here and quit with the small talk."

Gina winked at me as she walked past and pointed to the end of the hallway.

"I take it she's in the kitchen?" she asked, and I nodded. "Yup, where else?"

I was waiting for Gina to notice the photographs on the wall. Waiting for her to stop in her tracks and stare at them just as Mom had done. But Gina was oblivious. She just walked to the end of the hall and into the kitchen.

"Hey, smells good," she said. "What are you cooking?"

"Spaghetti with clams," Mom told her.

And I heard Gina let out a little whoop of joy at the prospect of her favorite homecooked lunch.

When I walked into the kitchen, Gina was already sitting at the table, her bag on the floor and her shoes kicked off and Mom was pouring her a glass of white wine. I pulled up a chair opposite and accepted a glass.

Wine in the afternoon. It felt a little too decadent, celebratory even, as if this little reunion was a happy event and not something triggered by an impending bereavement. But the coziness of the room, the delicious smell of the clams and the garlic as the food simmered in the pan, left me feeling unexpectedly happy and safe. It was a talent my mom had developed out of necessity over the years, this ability to create a nurturing atmosphere. All she needed was a kitchen and a big table to sit around. And I realized I was glad they had come. I needed them to change the energy in the house, to fill it with comfort and laughter and blow away all the melancholy and the unsettling atmosphere.

"So," Gina said as she sipped at her wine. "How's Dad?"

"Comfortable," I told her. And she looked at me, her head tilted to one side.

"Is that good or bad?" she asked.

"I don't know," I said. "Good, I guess, given the circumstances. I mean he was very woozy and delirious when I saw him, but he looked okay, you know, considering…"

Mom placed a bowl of spaghetti on the table and began to dish it out onto our plates. "She means, he's stable and pain-free," she told Gina.

Gina began to eat and shrugged. "Well, that's something, I suppose," she said between forkfuls of pasta.

For some reason her disdain annoyed me, even though I understood where she was coming from. "They're just trying to keep him comfortable, Gina," I told her. "No one deserves to be in pain if it can be prevented."

She set her fork down in her bowl and reached for her wine, taking another sip before answering.

"That's not what I mean, Carla. Difficult as it may be to believe, I don't actually want him to suffer."

"Sorry," I said. "I just… it sounded like…"

"What?" she said. "So you never thought the same thing then? Not even for a second?"

I had, and she caught the glimpse of shame in my eyes before I could turn away. She smiled at me and then nodded. "Listen, I'm just being honest, but don't worry, I had enough time on the flight up here to process all of this, so I promise I'll be in a better mood when we see him. I don't want my last moments with him to become a torment for me later, you know? I promise I'll play nice."

It was good to know she understood that this was our last chance to say goodbye on peaceful terms. But I already knew it wouldn't be easy. I had run from him, after all. Run from a dying man who could do me no harm, but a man I still feared, nonetheless. And I wondered if Mom and Gina understood what lay ahead of them, and hoped that, together, we could summon enough energy to face him without fear.

Mom poured us all more wine and leaned back in her chair, letting out a small sigh and loosening the top button of her pants. "You know," she said. "We might as well get it all out of our systems now before we go and see him. I don't want there to be any fuss at his bedside later."

Gina looked at her and frowned, as if she wasn't quite sure how to react. "I'm not looking for some last-minute reconciliation or anything, if that's what you mean," she told Mom.

"Why not?" Mom asked.

"What?!" Gina replied, her voice a little higher and tinged with surprise. "It's way too late for that, don't you think? I mean, that's not what we're here for, is it? I know it's not what I'm looking for in any case. I'm just here out of obligation, nothing more. I don't want anything from him, and I don't expect anything either. And besides, we're only here for a couple of days, so we might as well be realistic."

Mom shrugged and got up from the table and started to clear away the dishes. "I don't think I am being unrealistic," she said.

"Oh, Mom, please!" Gina cried. "You know who he is, and you know what he's done to us. I'm only here because you asked me to come. As far as I'm concerned, we owe Rob nothing. To be honest, we don't even owe him a goodbye."

Mom stood by the sink and didn't turn to face us as she spoke. "It's true, I do know who he is. And I'll never forget what he did to us, the mess he made of our lives. But this isn't about forgetting. It's just about saying goodbye, on our own terms. You'll thank me one day for making you do this, Gina. Trust me."

I thought about that for a moment. "Our own terms." Is that what this was? Because in many ways it didn't feel like it. We were all here because he had asked us to come, and I still wasn't sure what I wanted to get out of it. I was here because it was convenient, as much as anything else. My motives weren't wholly pure.

And I knew I couldn't promise Mom—when the moment came, when I could finally bring myself to talk to him—that I wouldn't use it to say all the things I had wanted to say to him over the years. To just let all that pent-up pain and poison ooze out. I wanted him to know what he had done, to know how it felt, the way the pain lingered. The way he took up space in our lives even when he wasn't around to hurt us anymore.

That was the reason I had walked away from his bedside the other day. When I heard him call my name, the sound of his voice, as faint and weak as it was, was still enough to provoke all those old feelings. The rage I thought had gone resurfaced uncontrollably, and I knew that if I hadn't been in a hospice, I would probably have let it all come out.

"Listen," I said. "Shall we just go and get it over with? Suzie is waiting for us."

"Who's Suzie?" Gina asked.

"His nurse, the one who called us," I told her. "She's nice. You'll like her."

And I stood up and started clearing away the remaining plates from the table.

"I'll just warn you now," Gina said. "If he is awake, and if he can talk to us, then I'm not sure how I'll react. I mean, I'll try to keep things civil, but…"

I exchanged glances with Mom to let her know that I would help her keep Gina calm, and she nodded to me and touched my arm as she walked past me on the way to her room to get ready.

"Seriously, just say what you have to say to him, Carla," Gina said. "Get it out of your system while you have the chance. It'll do you good."

*

Suzie met us at the reception, and I introduced her to my mom and sister.

"I'm so glad you all could be here," she told us. "It's a huge comfort for him."

Gina stared at her and I heard her mutter "Geez," and was glad that Suzie didn't catch it.

Instead she led us down the corridor to his room. "He's having a better day today," Suzie explained. "When he heard you were coming, he asked me to help him sit up in bed. I think just knowing you're all here has given him some energy."

I knew Suzie didn't mean anything by it, and that her enthusiasm was simply relief that we were all there to see Rob, but it was too much for Gina. Just as Suzie was about to open the door to Rob's room, Gina reached out and grabbed my arm and I felt her shaking. "I need a moment to compose myself, if that's okay?" she told Suzie. "Please, could you give me a minute?"

I could see the confusion on Suzie's face. She seemed bewildered and unsure what to do as she stood there with her hand on the door handle.

"Why don't you go in first?" I told her. "You can tell him we're here."

She nodded and I waited for her to go inside, then squeezed Gina's hand. Mom walked over and embraced us. For a few minutes, the three of us stood in the hallway in a huddle, comforting one another. To any passersby, we would look like the recently bereaved.

"Listen," Mom whispered. "Why don't you let me do all the talking? You don't need to say anything if you feel you can't."

Gina nodded and sniffed away a tear and it was only then that I realized she was crying.

"You okay?" I asked her.

She pulled out a handkerchief and blew her nose and smiled. "I guess I underestimated how this was going to make me feel. I thought I could tough it out, but, damn it, he still has the power to do this to me."

I kissed her on the cheek and told her we all felt that way, but we'd get through it together. We waited a couple of seconds for Gina to compose herself, then headed into the room.

It was a shock to see him sitting up in the bed. He looked so different to the man I had seen just a couple of days ago and Suzie noticed my confusion and came over to me and explained that he had asked to be given reduced pain medication so that he could be more alert when we came to visit him.

"He's in more pain than he'll admit," she whispered to me. "So try and go easy on him. I know he looks okay, but, trust me, he's in a lot of pain."

I nodded and we waited for her to leave the room before we each took a seat at his bedside.

We sat in silence for what was only a moment but felt like hours, no one knowing what to say, no one daring to start. It was Rob who finally managed to speak, his voice still weak, and raspy, as if he needed a drink of water.

"It's good to see you," he said, each word stretched out slowly as if he was speaking a foreign language he hadn't quite mastered. "I didn't think you would come."

Mom nodded. "Well, here we are…"

Rob smiled at her and held out his hand and I saw her hesitate before taking hold of it. Gina could not stop herself flinching when they entwined hands, this small intimacy too much for her to accept.

"It's okay," Rob said to her. "I'm not expecting anything. That you came is enough. To have my hand held, well…"

There was something different in his voice, beyond the ravages of sickness and age. Something softer, more reflective. As if he finally understood the importance of the things he said. It was an almost imperceptible change, but I saw Gina and Mom react with the same blinking disbelief as me. And again, I wondered if it was possible for someone to change after all. There was this other man within him. A man we didn't know. The man everyone in Newcastle seemed to know and love.

"How are you?" Gina asked him.

"Dying," he said, and we all saw the tiny wince as he tried to smile. "But apart from that, I'm doing great."

"That's good," Gina said, unsure how to react to his flippancy. Though when she looked at the lines sticking out from his veins, it was clear she was struggling to hide her distress.

"The doctors do what they can," he reassured her. "They manage the pain for me. That's about all they can do. But that's enough."

"Listen, we won't stay long," Mom said. "We don't want to tire you out."

He lifted his free hand and tried to make a dismissive gesture, and again his brow wrinkled, and his jaw clenched as he tried to contain a spasm.

"I'm glad you came," he managed to say, his voice almost a whisper as he spoke through clenched teeth. "All three of you. I never thought…" Then he closed his eyes and his face contorted again, his breath becoming uneasy, quick and short. Unable to contain the pain this time.

"Shit," Gina said. "Is he okay?"

"I'm fine," he said between breaths. "Honestly, it'll… pass… in a… minute."

I looked at Mom's hand and saw how tightly my dad was holding it, his fingers gripping hers as he struggled and waited for this wave of pain to subside. And I knew now that it was already too late. Too late to talk about the past, too late to seek some sort of peace. He was too weak and it would be cruel to demand anything of him, no matter how much I wanted to.

I drew closer to his bedside and took hold of his other hand and he opened his eyes and looked at me.

"Hey, Carla," he said. "Reckon you'll stick around this time?" he asked me. And Gina and Mom looked at me, a little confused.

"Huh?" Gina said.

"I think I scared her," Rob said. And he coughed and laughed. "Hell, all these tubes and machines, I'd have run too. You're not still scared of me, are you, Carla? After all these years?"

And as he squeezed my hand, I looked at him, and thought I saw it there, that old Rob, the man I used to know. A man who hadn't changed after all. Perhaps all of this, this tender deathbed scene, calling us all up here to be with him, was just a game to him after all. Rob trying to see how far he could push us, what he could make us do, how much control he had. Even now, half paralyzed with sickness and old age, he had that inexplicable meanness to him. One last chance to torment us.

"I was just upset seeing you like this. I wasn't prepared for it," I told him. And he nodded and stroked my hand with his thumb, squeezing it tighter as if what I'd said was almost too much for him to bear.

"Suzie says you're staying at the house," he said. And I smiled and nodded.

"That's good," he said. "That's good."

"Yeah, she's been really kind. Helped me get settled in."

"It's not much of a place," he said. "Not very homey, but it's comfortable enough," he said. "You all doing okay there?"

Gina smiled at him and stroked some hair away that had started to stick to his forehead. "It's fine, Dad," she said.

"I liked the photos in the hallway," Mom told him. "I wasn't expecting that."

He looked at her and held her gaze for a few seconds and I got the impression he was trying to fix the moment in his mind, to lay down a tender memory that he could hold on to in the coming days.

"I used to say hello to you all every morning on my way out," he said. "It was nice, you know?" And Mom nodded.

And it struck me then how easily he had shifted the direction of the conversation. *You're not still scared of me, are you, Carla? After all these years?* Barely a minute had passed since he asked me that, but he'd noticed my discomfort, sensed how tense it had made me, and had managed to divert the conversation to a different topic so naturally, I had almost failed to notice. He might look frail, but he still knew how to control a situation. I was still scared of him, I realized. And I thought again of that box, hidden away in the dark corner of the cupboard. Those secrets of his. He was unknowable still.

"Yeah," I said. "The house is full of surprises. I'm discovering all sorts of things."

And he sensed the slight sharpness in my tone and turned to face me, and I could see something there in his eyes, something close to panic. I'd struck a nerve. And I knew immediately what it was. It was the box. He hadn't meant for me to find it. Not while he was still alive at least. I could see it in his face, a terror almost in his eyes as it dawned on him what I meant.

And I saw that look in his eyes, and I needed to push it further. To scare him the way he scared me. So I leaned in close to him as if to brush a kiss on his cheek or utter some soothing words. "Who's Johnny?" I whispered. "You called me Johnny, do you remember? Did you mean Johnny Hutton? The kid in those notebooks? The ones in that box?"

I heard him gasp as I pulled away, the air choking in his windpipe as he coughed again, harder this time, his eyes white with panic and something else, something I had never seen in his eyes before: fear.

"What?... I... No... Carla, I..."

I let go of his hand and stood up and saw Mom looking at me, confused and uncertain as to what had just happened between us.

"What's going on? Carla?" Mom said. "What did you say to him?"

But before I could tell her, a shrill beeping filled the room. An alarm. One of the machines that connected to him and kept things under control. And as he struggled for breath, the room was filled with energy and action. Nurses appeared from nowhere and surrounded his bed, pushing us aside. "Will he be okay?" I heard Gina ask. And my father managed to reply, quietly, his words coming out one by one between breaths, speech clearly something he found difficult.

"I... am.. okay... Gina. Please... don't... worry."

Then the nurse turned to face us. "Please, you need to leave," she said.

Suzie was suddenly there, taking Mom by the arm and leading her from the room and turning to me and Gina. "Let them take care of this," she said. And we nodded and followed her.

I could hear Gina shouting at me as we stumbled out into the corridor. "What the fuck did you say to him, Carla?"

"Nothing," I told her. "It was nothing."

"Nothing?" she yelled at me. "Are you fucking kidding me? You almost gave him a heart attack. Carla, what did you say?"

And I could see Suzie staring at me, her gaze hard and focused and angry.

"I'm sorry," I told her. "I'm sorry if I upset him. I didn't mean to. I shouldn't have come. I'm sorry. I'm just not ready for this. Every time I think I am, I just..."

"Listen, perhaps it's better if you all go home for now," Suzie said.

"But will we be able to see him again?" Mom asked. "We were barely in there for ten minutes before—"

"I'm sure you'll be able to see him tomorrow," Suzie told her. Then she turned to me and took my arm and said, "But, Carla, seriously, you can't upset him like this. He can't take this kind of stress, and if I think you're going to put him at risk, in any way, then I won't let you be with him. I'm sorry, but it's my duty. I can't have something like this happen again."

"Don't worry," I heard Gina say. "We'll make sure of it."

*

"So," Gina said when we got home. "Are you going to explain what that was all about?"

"It's complicated," I said.

"Oh, damn it, Carla. Everything always is with you," Gina said. "I mean, you get us to come all the way up here so we can say goodbye to a man none of us love, and then, when we finally get in the room with him, you whisper something in his ear that is apparently so terrible, you almost kill him. What the hell is going on?"

I looked at her, aghast. "None of us love? That's taking it a bit far, isn't it?"

"Okay," Mom interrupted. "That's enough, Gina. It's been an emotional day for all of us and maybe we just need to have a glass of wine and talk things through."

"What's there to talk about?" Gina replied. "I have to head back home in a couple of days, and if we don't get to see Rob now because of this little stunt of Carla's, then I'm allowed to be mad about it. I could be home with David and the kids instead of having to deal with his shit."

"Okay, okay," Mom said. "I get it, but let's hear what Carla has to say first. And let me get some wine. I need a drink."

I sat down in the chair by the window and waited for Gina to settle on the sofa and for Mom to return from the kitchen. But when she came back, I suddenly realized I didn't know what I was supposed to say. Because now that I'd had time to think, it seemed ludicrous.

"Oh, Rob muttered this boy's name the other day and I thought he was just hallucinating or something. Then I found this box full of diaries and some old newspaper clippings about some boys who were murdered here, and I don't know why, but the things he wrote about them, it feels as if he knew them." It was an absurd idea now I thought about it. It *feels* as if he's connected to it all in some way. How the hell had I managed to jump to that conclusion?

And yet, something about it *did* bother me. An intuition that had only strengthened when I saw the look in Rob's eyes as I had pulled away after whispering Jonathan's name. I had seen something there, some recognition or fear, and I definitely wasn't imagining it.

"Okay, listen," I began after I had taken a large sip of wine. "I'm sorry I upset him, and maybe I've made a terrible mistake, but—"

"Carla, you need to start at the beginning." Mom said. "What did you say to Rob? And why the hell did you have to upset him like that now?"

I had no answer for that. I'd reacted in the spur of the moment and it was something I regretted.

"Wait here," I said. "I need to show you something, otherwise none of this is going to make any sense."

Mom lit a cigarette and Gina curled up on the sofa and sipped her wine. I heard them whispering as I climbed the stairs, Gina complaining that I was a mess and needed to get my shit together, and Mom telling her to hush in case I heard her.

"Oh, let her hear," Gina said. "She knows what I think."

Upstairs, I took the box from under the bed and brought it downstairs, then set it down on the table in front of them.

When I opened it up and laid out the contents, Gina asked me what it was and I was glad I heard a quiver of hesitation in her voice, as if just seeing those notebooks made her nervous.

I opened up one of the books full of newspaper clippings and explained what they were, and she stared at me with a look in her eyes that was a mixture of worry and disbelief.

"I don't understand, what has this got to do with Rob?" Mom said, as she picked up one of the notebooks and flicked through it.

"They're diaries he kept years ago, some of them are from when he lived here as a kid, and some are from when he was older, and already in San Francisco," I told her.

Gina had picked up one of the scrapbooks and skimmed the headlines of the yellowed newspapers and then looked up at me.

"It says some kids were killed. Here, in Newcastle? Seriously?"

"Yeah, three boys," I told her. "Two of them were found dead, but one of them was never discovered."

Gina put the book back on the table as if she could no longer bear to hold it. The news it contained, something dirty and contemptible.

"My kids keep stickers of ponies and puppies," Gina said. "What the hell is this morbid shit?"

"Hey, you know how kids can be," Mom said. "Ghoulish stuff fascinates them."

"Does it?" Gina said. "I would have thought most kids didn't keep a notebook about murder. You have to admit, that's a bit weird," and she shivered and reached for her wine again.

"I think it makes sense that Rob was a weird kid," I said.

"Whatever," Gina shrugged. "Anyway, what you said to him, was it about all of this?"

I picked up one of the diaries and opened it up at a page where Rob had written some notes and showed it to them.

I nodded. "He called me Johnny, the other day, when I went to see him. And I didn't know what he was going on about, until I read these. I mean, it has to be the same kid, don't you think?"

Gina sat back in the sofa and stared at me. "It could be, I suppose. But so what?"

"I don't know. I mean the way he writes about them and the way he reacted when I mentioned Johnny, it just felt a little creepy is all. A bit sinister, you know?"

"Oh, come on, Carla!" Gina cried. "It's a diary. A kid's diary. How can you see something sinister in that?" She took the diary from me and read the notes Rob had made, then threw it on the coffee table in front of her.

"I mean," she said. "Just because Will wrote that book years ago about those boys—"

"Huh?" I cried. "What the hell has that got to do with anything?"

"I just mean, you can sometimes be a little morbid when it comes to things like this. Honestly, it's like you only want to see the bad in people."

"What?" I cried. "Morbid? Gina—"

She picked up the notebook and handed it to Mom. "Seriously, read this and tell me *I'm* the one who's overreacting. This is batshit crazy, Carla, and you know it."

Mom looked through the notebook and shook her head.

"Gina's right," she said. "This is just the kind of thing a boy of his age would do. He was just playing detective or something. Or maybe he just wanted to keep a diary about what happened. I mean, this must have been a big deal back then. A small town like this with three missing boys, it would have made a big impression. There's nothing sinister about any of it. That's just..." She stopped short of agreeing with Gina that it was "batshit crazy," but I could see that was what she was thinking. Then she continued. "Seriously, sinister, is that really what you'd call this?"

It was a strange question, given what she had just read; notes Rob had written about the two boys who had been found. Maybe they weren't sinister, but they were definitely harrowing.

The way he pleaded for Adam Peterson and Danny McIntosh to be returned home, unharmed. *Danny cries for his mom, every day. Says he's sorry, every day. Asks her to come and find him, come and get him. Adam thinks about the hiking trip he had planned with his dad up around Tiger Summit. He talks to himself some nights, imagining the trip, planning for it, willing it to happen. He thinks, if you plan for the future, you can still make it happen. The* way he empathized with those boys, imagining their distress as if it were his own, was haunting. His words, his tone, those of a child who seemed to understand something he was not meant to understand, something he was too young to understand. And I didn't understand how Mom and Gina couldn't see it.

"I never understood why he hurt us," I said. "But maybe... I mean, sometimes the things you experience as a kid, bad things, traumatic things, they can turn you into the sort of adult who—"

"No, Carla. Stop it!" Mom said. "I don't know what the hell is wrong with you and maybe it's just the stress, what with Rob, and you and Will, but you need to get a grip."

"I'm not 'stressed,' Mom—"

"Carla," Gina said. "Don't do this. Please, don't. I'm not here looking for some reconciliation with him, I told you that already. And I am definitely not looking for some explanation or excuse for the years of suffering he caused us—"

"That's not what I'm saying at all, Gina," I said. "I just think there's something there. I just think... damn it, read that diary again and tell me you don't think he knew those poor kids—"

"And maybe he did. This is a small town, Carla. Everyone here probably knows one another. But so what?" Gina said.

"So, there's nothing to any of this, it's all in my imagination, is that it?"

"Yup, that's it," Gina nodded.

"But he wrote about them, he—"

"Carla," Mom interrupted. "He kept some notebooks when he was a kid. Collected a few newspaper clippings and wrote down some thoughts. Kids are like that. It was a mystery. Something exciting. That's all. There's no trauma there, if that's what you're looking for. There's nothing here that's going to explain Rob to you or help you understand him better. Damn it, I wish there was, but..."

"Okay," I sighed. "Can we just forget it? I mean, obviously you both think I made a mistake and got carried away."

"Just promise you'll drop this, Carla." Gina said. "Please? It's not healthy."

I was about to challenge her. "Not healthy." I didn't like what it implied. That I was prone to flights of fancy and let myself get carried away with unfounded suspicions. All I'd done was react to the notebooks I'd found. To their strangeness and their shocking contents. It was unfair of Gina to make this into some sort of judgment of my state of mind. It was better to say I'd let it go. That way I'd get her off my back at least.

"I promise, okay? Please, can we just forget it now?"

Mom must have noticed the frustration building in me, because she stood up, before Gina had a chance to say anything more to upset me. "Right," she said. "Let's eat, shall we? I brought some good wine up with me. I figured we'd need it."

Gina stood up and followed Mom into the kitchen. The discussion was clearly over.

"What sort of wine did you get?" I heard her ask.

"Pinot Grigio," Mom replied. "I chilled it this morning."

This was always how they were, I remembered. Any argument, any disagreement was always resolved with food or drink. Healing always started at the table. These simple things mattered to them, and nothing could deter them from preparing a meal and placing a bottle of wine in the fridge to chill. But it was nice to listen to them in the kitchen, and it reminded me that I had come here looking for a new start. And this was the first step towards it. Letting the small things matter again. Understanding their importance.

Though I wondered if I really could make this place my new home. Gina didn't know about my plans yet and I wasn't sure how I should go about explaining it. Because she would want to sell this house when Dad died, I was sure of it.

But without Will, I had no choice, at least for a few months. Just to get my feet on the ground, get myself sorted out.

"Here we go," Gina said as she came back into the living room and placed a tray on the table filled with plates of salami and sun-dried tomatoes, olives and cheese, and thick slices of crusty white bread. Behind her, Mom carried three wine glasses upside down, balancing the stems between her thumb and forefinger, and in the other she held the chilled bottle of wine, the label expensive looking, little flecks of gold glinting in the sunlight. No doubt she'd picked it up during a vineyard tour. That was the California Gina and my mom belonged to.

Mom set the glasses down on the table next to the tray of Gina's delicacies and poured three generous glasses for us.

"Don't worry," she said, when she saw me gape at them. "I've got two more bottles in the fridge. I figured this was going to be a day for wine. Or do you want something stronger?"

I laughed. I wasn't a drinker and she knew the wine would make me woozy after just the one glass. So I took a slice of bread and cut some cheese to eat with it.

"Thanks," I said, and then we chinked our glasses together, not quite a toast, but neither were we drowning our sorrows.

"Truce?" Gina asked me. And I nodded and sipped my wine.

"Anyway," Gina said once she'd taken some sips of wine. "What's all this about you staying on here?"

I looked at Mom and saw her smile and give a little shrug.

"I take it Mom told you about me and Will then?"

And Gina nodded but said nothing because she knew whatever she said, I would take it the wrong way.

"For what it's worth," Mom said. "Now that I've had time to think about it, I think it's a good idea. It'll give you time to figure out what you want, and a small town like this, well, it could be a good place to be to just let things settle. San Francisco isn't going anywhere. When you're ready to head home, we can sort things out then."

Gina stayed silent. But she stared at me, looking for some sort of certainty there. As if she wanted to ask me, "Are you sure this is what you want?" but she knew she had to keep quiet.

Clearly, she had talked it over with Mom at length. There was no way Gina would have agreed to something like this without some sort of discussion. It just wasn't my sister's style. Gina liked life to be organized and planned and predictable. She needed certainty.

"Thanks," I said. "I just need a few months is all. A bit of breathing space."

"Take as long as you need," Mom said. And I noticed that she looked to Gina as she said it. *As long as you need* was clearly not part of their agreement.

"So, what are you going to do then?" Gina asked me.

And I misunderstood the question.

"Well, this place needs a bit of a clearing out, I reckon. I need to make it feel like it's my own place, maybe go through some of his things and keep a few items we might want, photos, things like that—"

"No," Gina said. "I meant what are you going to do for money, for work?"

"Oh, right, I see."

Money was a thought I'd wanted to put out of my mind for as long as possible. But Gina fixed her critical gaze upon me and even Mom turned to look at me with the same question in her eyes, and so the solution appeared before I'd had time to really think it through.

"I was looking at the dining room, it has great light, south facing, it would make a great studio. And the basement could work as a darkroom setup, if I wanted to get back into analog stuff again."

"You want to set up a photo studio? Here? In Dad's crummy house?" Gina asked, her voice tinted with disbelief and what sounded like a touch of mockery.

"Sure, why not? I mean, the space is good, the location's pretty central, and I have most of my equipment with me to get set up digitally at least. And I don't think it would take much time, I think I can get things ready quickly. A lick of white paint, some blackout on the windows downstairs."

"Looks like you've thought it through," Mom said.

I hadn't, of course, and they knew it. The way I had sputtered out a reply to Gina, the nervous breathless churn of my words was always the giveaway—I was thinking on my feet and trying to get myself out from under any scrutiny.

But, for all that, I had felt a strange flicker of hope, as if the words themselves were forming something more solid. As if I could feel the reality of it coming into existence. *I could make it work,* I thought. *It wasn't a bad idea.*

"Listen," Gina said. "If you're serious about this then let me help you out. I can give you a few bucks to get things started."

"That's okay," I replied. "I can manage. It's just a bit of paint and I've got some cash stashed away."

"It's not a gift, Carla, it's a loan. I'd take it if I were you."

"Let her help you out, Carla," Mom said. "If you really want to make a go of this, then let us help you."

"Okay, okay," I agreed. "Donation accepted."

And Gina checked the wine bottle and saw it was empty and got up to fetch a new one from the kitchen.

"This calls for a celebration," she said. And she drank down the last of the wine in her glass. "I mean, if something good can come out of all this, then that's all we can ask for, eh?"

And maybe it was the wine, maybe it was the sheer weight and strangeness of the day, but the more I thought about it, the more it made sense. I could make a go of it; I was sure. A small studio doing family portraits, school photographs, maybe the odd calendar with local landscapes, greetings cards, that sort of thing. The local newspaper may even need a photographer. It was possible, wasn't it?

Gina was right. Why not? Why not let something good come from all of this. And I raised my glass and nodded to them.

"Here's to new starts."

And Mom clinked her glass against mine and tried her best to smile and seem enthusiastic. But I could see that her heart wasn't in it.

*

That night I lay in bed and thought about the argument with Gina and Mom. I'd promised them I would leave well enough alone. And, who knows, maybe I would have if I had been able to stop thinking about Jonathan Hutton. I couldn't figure out why Rob would have bothered to follow his story. He was twenty years old when Jonathan went missing and was already living in San Francisco. The diaries about Adam and Danny may have been a childish fascination, but a twenty-year-old man? The same couldn't be said about him.

Rob had used a red pen to highlight sections from the reports, statements from Jonathan's mom. Occasionally there would be a few words written there too. *Poor Alice, she doesn't deserve this. Tell Alice where her son is. Don't do this to her! Damn it, this has to stop!* I couldn't figure out who these comments were addressed to because it felt as though he was talking to himself, or someone he knew. The person who had taken Jonathan.

Alice could still be out there, I realized. Still hoping her son would be found and that she would have peace at last. I lay there thinking about her and wondering how it must feel to live with such a terrible loss hanging over you. Never knowing what had happened to your son. The longing you must feel to find him and say a proper farewell to him.

If Rob knew anything about this, if he could help bring Jonathan home, then I had no choice, did I? Whatever I had promised I had to ask him what he knew. Even if asking him caused him to suffer in some way, if he knew something, then he should say so while he had the chance.

No, I couldn't keep my promise. Because every time I thought about those notebooks, about those headlines and my dad's scribbled notes in the margins, a shiver went down my spine. Gina might think I was wrong about this, she might even think I was deluded to pursue it. But I couldn't quash the feelings I had, the instinctive sense that there was something to all of this. Something I needed to unravel.

And it would bring me closer to my dad, it would help me understand him better, I felt sure of it. He had never been a good father or a good husband. And though I knew now that his lack of love and attention was not down to a fault in any of us, a part of me had always thought it was. I had always wondered what I could have done to make him love me, us, more. If we'd only been better, maybe we'd still be together. It was a hopeless and crushing idea. I knew that.

But what if he'd been incapable of love? What if he inflicted all that pain because of something that had happened to him? Something that had stopped him from feeling? It wasn't that we didn't deserve his love and attention. It was simply that he had no love to give. His heart wasn't big enough.

And I knew what Gina's response to that would be. "Or maybe he just likes hurting people, Carla."

Growing up, it had always seemed that way. His rage, his unexpected lashing out at us. Here was a man who relished his power, who enjoyed dishing out blows and screaming obscenities.

And he had hurt us, in unimaginable ways. There was no escaping that bitter truth. And I couldn't understand why that didn't help Mom and Gina to at least consider the possibility that a man like this was also the kind of man who was capable of keeping a secret. A man who knew the whereabouts of a missing child, but refused to reveal it.

It was a horrible thought. And it may even be unfounded. But it was worth pursuing.

I'd do it for them as much as for us. I'd find out for those boys. For Danny McIntosh, and Adam Peterson, and poor, lost Jonathan Hutton.

JONATHAN HUTTON, JULY 1972

Is this what happened to Danny and Adam? Did he take them too? That was so long ago, but no one here has forgotten. I know their names. I know their stories. Everyone here does. How they disappeared and were found weeks later, in the forest, both of them dead. Their stories always scared me and I never wanted to think about them. I didn't want to know what happened to them. But maybe what happened was this? Maybe what happened, was him? And now I can't stop thinking about them.

Danny McIntosh was the first. I remember the first time I heard about him. It was five years after he had died, and the newspapers were full of his story again. We were at the breakfast table and my dad was reading the newspaper.

I was trying to read what was written there, the snippets of Danny's story. It was a Sunday afternoon, and he had been down at the lake, fishing with his best friend, Kevin Cooper. They went there most weekends, and were allowed to go on their own because they were twelve. I can't remember the details. All I know is he was found in the forest. All I know is that the word murder was used. All I know is they never found out who did it.

I remember wondering why they were allowed to go down to the lake on their own, so I asked my mom and she told me "twelve-year-old boys don't need supervision."

"But maybe they do," I'd told her. "I mean, Danny did, didn't he?" And she'd looked at me with this sad sort of look and said,

"That poor woman, she's going to think about this for the rest of her life."

My father looked up from his newspaper and said, "What's that? Who?"

"Danny McIntosh's mother," she replied, pointing to the paper. "She's always going to wonder if she should have let him go down to the lake. If she should have gone with him. She's always going to blame herself for this."

And my father had looked at her and swallowed and then replied in a low voice, the one he used when he wanted us to know we should listen carefully to what he had to say. "I don't think that's a topic to discuss in front of Johnny, do you?"

And my mom had sighed and watched as my dad folded the paper in half and placed it on the table. "I just think it's a sad business," she said. "And I can't stop thinking about it, even now. How must she feel —Martha McIntosh, I mean?"

"Do you think he was scared?" I asked my mom.

And my father had replied immediately, his voice louder and sharper this time.

"This was all a long time ago, Johnny. There's no need to worry about it now. Nothing like this can ever happen again, do you understand? So let that be the end of it."

I wanted to ask him how he could be so sure that nothing like this could ever happen again. Because I'd seen another name there in the paper too. Adam Peterson, after all. It had happened to him. It had happened again. But I didn't dare mention it. I knew better than to go against my father. If he said this was the end of it, then this was the end of it.

"Yes, sir," I said.

We never mentioned Danny McIntosh again. But at school the kids would talk about him. And Adam Peterson too. That was where I heard that name for the first time: serial killer.

I didn't know what it meant until I heard Melissa Atkinson explaining it to her friends at school. Someone who kills more than once, she explained to them, as they crowded around her in awed silence. She used another word too: psychopath. Which meant he would kill again, she said. And her voice was so certain, her conviction so clear that it gave me goosebumps and brought on nightmares which I didn't dare explain to my mother. Because these boys were not something I was supposed to talk about at home. Neither she nor my father wanted "that darkness" to be brought into the house. But that vision of him, the shape of him, the idea of him, it haunted me. Psychopath. I didn't need to have it explained to me. I could feel the full horror of it in every syllable.

And then, one morning, there he was, Adam Peterson staring back at us from a newspaper. Another anniversary. Another gruesome tale. Another frightening headline: "Who Killed My Son?"

And my mother had seen me crying when I took my satchel and headed to school. And she didn't need to ask me why.

"Why don't you walk home from school with Luke Osborne from now on, Johnny?" she told me. "It's safer that way, do you understand?"

And I nodded and said, "Yes, ma'am" because I did understand. We all did, every kid in town had that shadow hanging over them now. He wasn't only in our nightmares. He was real, and he was somewhere in our town. We knew we weren't safe. We knew that to be alone was to put yourself in danger. Because he was out there. Biding his time and watching.

Oh, and he waited such a long time. Such a long, long time. So long, we thought he was gone. Until, one day, he found what he was looking for. He found me.

CHAPTER EIGHT

They paid their final visit without me in the end.

"Let us say goodbye to him without any stress," Gina had said. "You'll have another chance later. Let Mom and me go alone."

I'd agreed, because the truth was, I wasn't ready to face Rob again so soon When they came back, the disappointment on Gina's face was hard to see. She'd hoped Rob would be awake, but he was unconscious the whole time, the impact of our previous visit had clearly lingered.

I felt bad about it. They deserved to say their farewells and I had taken the opportunity from them and they would never get it back. But there was nothing I could do now. It had happened and maybe this was simply the way it was supposed to be.

After they'd headed home to San Francisco, the house felt too big without them and Gina's parting words still hung in the air, no matter what I did to shake them off. "You know, it's a shame about Will. He was one of the good ones."

She hadn't intended to be mean, I knew that, but it stung all the same. Her tone of voice had been just a little too sharp, like a schoolteacher admonishing a first-grade child. That was what it had felt like—a scolding.

It had left me in a sour mood, and unable to focus on anything. I felt disoriented still from the last couple of days and unsure what I was supposed to do; how I was supposed to embark on this unplanned-for new beginning I seemed determined to arrange for myself.

I had spent the morning wandering around the house, looking in every room and trying to imagine how I could change it. But the work seemed too vast, and the energy required to transform it seemed too enormous, so I had closed each door behind me and then found myself sitting back at the kitchen table, the clock showing it was already past noon and half a day of my supposed new life was already wasted.

Outside, the sky was a Delft china blue and the sun was shining, so I opened the door and stepped out into the garden. *Maybe it would be better to sit here a while,* I thought, *and read a little, drink a coffee and just wait for the energy to return. I could try and get some sort of plan together. Make a list of things I had to do and get some things ordered.* But even that small task seemed beyond me.

From the far end of the garden I heard some bird chirping, its song unfamiliar. Even the birds here sang a different song to the ones in California. And the light, that shadowy aspect to it, even on a sunny day; the way the pine trees seemed to tint everything with a blue-gray hue and perfume the air with a sharp almost antiseptic tinge. I wondered how long it would take before the warm yellow glow of home called me back. Because deep down I knew I wasn't made for somewhere as dank and dark and wild as this.

And I heard the bird again, the rise and fall of its song, like laughter, as if it was mocking me almost. "You're right," it seemed to chirp. "You're not cut out for this place."

And I turned and stepped away from the trees then and tried to pull myself together.

"Geez! Get a grip, Carla, it's just a bird." The sound of my voice filling the garden and making me aware again of the emptiness around me.

Then I turned and walked back into the kitchen and set about making coffee and went looking for a pen and notepad while the machine spluttered to life and filled the air with a rich oily tang that already made me feel better.

I'd shoved my bag with all my miscellaneous stuff under the sofa the day before Gina and Mom had arrived, knowing that if they saw my things strewn around the floor, they'd comment on it. Neat and tidy, that was how they lived. I was always the odd one out, the one with dirty clothes thrown in a pile, with books and magazines discarded on tables and chairs, with dirty plates and cups by my bedside.

It was a habit that had irritated Will too. What was the word he had used again? Slovenly, yes, that was it. I remembered laughing when he said it because it made my habits sound dirty, animal even. The word, more than just a criticism. It was an insult.

He had looked at me and asked me why I was laughing, mistaking my amusement for something more rebellious, and I had not been able to explain it to him, why it was I found his criticism ridiculous.

"I just don't understand why you can't respect my opinion about it," he had explained. "I don't like living in a mess. It's important to me. Is it really so difficult to tidy your shit away?"

And that word had made me shudder: respect. That old, familiar demand I knew so well, a word I had heard on my father's lips so often.

"Show some respect!" I remembered Rob shouting at Mom. That word, reverberating down the years so that whenever I heard it, I always took a long look at whoever had said it, appraising them as I watched them, looking for the telltale signs of muscle tension and strained sinew, the slight flourish of the skin. Weighing them up on the basis of that one word and then deciding who they were. Good or bad. To be trusted or avoided. To be respected or ignored.

Will wasn't Rob, I knew that. But the memory had a force still, and it made me look at Will with a wary eye, as if I didn't quite recognize him, as if I wasn't sure what he was capable of.

"What?" he had asked when he saw me draw away from him. And I had shrugged and said it was nothing, just a little déjà vu.

But this is how people pull apart from one another. Moment by moment, with a lifetime of unspoken history wrapped up in every second. This was how we started to unravel.

As I pulled my bag from under the sofa, I caught sight of the box on the coffee table, where we had left it the night before and decided to take it into the garden with me.

And an image flashed before me, unexpectedly. Jonathan Hutton's school photo, like a false memory, as if he was someone I had known. His bright smile haunted me, his fate something I couldn't let go.

And I felt the curiosity rise to the surface again. Perhaps if I read a little more I could try and figure out why Jonathan had held the same fascination for Rob.

I took the box and my bag out to the garden and set them down on the small wrought-iron table, then went inside and poured myself a mug of coffee. There was still a plate of food in the fridge that Mom had made for me and I took it from the shelf and unwrapped the plastic wrap, the smell of oil and garlic greeting me like a warm hello. Olives, cheese, sun-dried tomatoes and thick slices of fatty salami. My mom's presence lingering there in every salty mouthful. And I could imagine, for a moment, my dad standing in this sparse gloomy kitchen and missing these small thoughtful touches, missing his wife, missing his family. These tastes were something he would have longed for. I was sure of it.

Back in the garden, I settled into one of the wicker chairs and drank my coffee and thought about fetching a glass of wine to wash down the food, but the sun on my cheek and the hit of the coffee had sharpened my focus and I didn't want to lose it. Because there was something in that box I needed to pay attention to. Something which required a clear head and alert senses.

When I had finished the plate of food, I wiped away the traces of oil from my fingers and then reached for the box, the silky sheen of it surprising me again. It was the only expensive item in the whole house and the way the sheen had been preserved, the way the box had clearly been looked after, made me wonder again why the contents were so deserving of such care and attention. Of such respect. That word again. The weight of it. Yet it seemed right to use it to describe this box. I could feel it; the traces of the respect Rob must have had as he polished the wood and checked on the contents.

I lifted the lid and let it fall back on its hinges, then took out the contents, piece by piece, and laid them out on the table in front of me, hoping I would see an order there that I could follow. But the notebooks were not numbered, and I noticed now that not all of the newspaper clippings had been cut from the paper with their dates. If there was any chronology here, then I was going to have to piece it together myself.

And I sighed and sat back in the chair, closed my eyes and enjoyed the warmth of the sun on my face for a while.

Then I came to a decision. I would start with the clippings. Read the story as it was reported at the time and leave the diaries for later. I wanted to form my own idea of what had happened, I wanted to read the facts as they were reported back then, and only then, once I understood what had happened, only then would I read Rob's diaries.

Because I wasn't sure I trusted him to tell the truth. Even in the pages of a book he thought no one would ever read, even within the confines of those secret pages, I knew it was still possible for lies to hide there. We were all capable of fooling ourselves. But my father had been an expert in it.

*

It was early evening by the time I finished reading, and the clippings had been rearranged into as good an order as I could manage. Each case set aside in its own small pile. Three of them. Three boys. Two found and one missing.

Danny McIntosh, aged twelve. Adam Peterson, also twelve. And Jonathan Hutton, the last and the youngest, just eleven. They had disappeared in that order. Three schoolkids with no real connection beyond the ways everyone always knew one another in a small town. They had attended the same school. Perhaps their parents were acquainted, but only casually. A nod of hello at church or at the grocery store, that sort of thing. The only thing connecting them was this town, Newcastle. Other than that, their disappearances seemed random events, and I tried to imagine the fear that must have gripped every parent in the town then as they confronted the terror that, one day, without warning, their child could disappear. Even in a place like this. A place that seemed safe, a place that seemed homey and good and far from everything that was wrong in the world.

It had taken me a while to notice the gap in the dates. It was only when I had arranged the piles that I saw a line in an article about the discovery of Adam Peterson's body. The Sunday killer, it read, and I had paused at that because it sounded so absurd and contrasted so sharply with the way they had later reported on Jonathan's disappearance. It was the type of lurid headline you would expect to see in some cheap garish tabloid, not a local newspaper. But it had grabbed my attention and I had taken up the clipping and read it. Danny and Adam had both disappeared on a Sunday, it appeared, and some journalist had tried to make a connection.

But when I checked the pile of clippings for Jonathan Hutton, the newspapers reported he had disappeared on a Wednesday, and the journalist's theory, that scurrilous idea that there was someone out there taking children on a Sunday, fell apart. Nothing more than a tabloid sensation after all.

It was only when I was tidying things away that I noticed the other difference that had been staring me in the face all along. Nine years. 1963 and 1972. I hadn't paid it much attention at first, too engrossed in the stories to notice the detail. But there it was—a nine-year gap between the first and the last disappearances.

Three kids in such a small town, though, three boys, more or less the same age. It made no sense that they had never found the killer. Someone here must have noticed something. Even in the short period I had been here, I understood the kind of place it was. Close. Observant. Aware. No, someone here knew, they had to.

And I thought of my father then. In 1963, he would have been about the same age as those boys. Eleven years old. How terrified were his parents? I wondered. Did they let him roam as he always had, down to the river to fish, out on his bike to meet his friends, sauntering home from school. No, they must have been on edge, vigilant. Terrified.

And Gina was right, this must be the reason for this strange and sad collection. A boy that age, confronted with such crimes, with such horror, would have been filled with that peculiar mix that children sometimes have, of fear and curiosity. Of wanting to know everything and wanting to avoid it all.

Oh, and he would have known them too. Danny and Adam. Two boys his own age. They may have been friends, even. And this was how Rob remembered them, this was how he kept their memories alive, by gathering the evidence and preserving it in a box, so that one day, perhaps, someone would find it and wonder what the story was.

Though Jonathan Hutton. By 1972 Rob had already moved to San Francisco. He would have known nothing about this boy. And yet, there he was, his story neatly documented alongside the others.

And it could only be because there was a connection. A connection my father understood. Jonathan belonged in that box with Danny and Adam. He belonged there because he shared their awful fate, but there was something else linking them too, I realized. They had been brought together by the same person.

Whoever had taken Danny and Adam had taken Jonathan too. And I shuddered as I thought about it.

What was it you knew, Dad? I thought. *What was it you knew?*

*

Adam Peterson, October 1964

I knew his face, from school. He was the kid no one really spoke to. The kid no one ever hung out with. There was something about him that made you feel uncomfortable. Something about him that just felt wrong.

I knew his mom had died a few years back. A car crash or something like that. Something awful anyway. You could see in his eyes how much he missed her, and I think that was why he never really looked at anyone. He didn't want to see us pitying him. Not that we did. He was too strange for that.

He'd wander about looking all sad and weird, but it didn't make you feel sorry enough for him to go over and say hello. The way he kept his eyes down, the way he kept away from everyone, it was obvious he wanted to be left alone. And so that's what we did. I didn't know a single kid who had ever spoken to him or gone to his house or was his friend. No one knew anything about him. He was the weird kid and that was all we needed to know.

Mom had scolded me once about it. I'd come home from school and said something about him. I can't remember what it was, something mean in any case, something about how he had been sitting by himself during the lunch break. Everyone ate in groups, but he was always alone. I think I made some comment that he was a weirdo and that I wished he and his dad would move houses and stop creeping everyone out. Anyway, Mom had told me not to be so cruel and to remember that his mom had been in an accident and that I should be kind and try to imagine how I would feel if it was me. I did actually do that. I tried to imagine being him. But all it did was make me feel glad I wasn't.

I should have remembered all this when I saw him. I should have wondered why he came over to talk to me. Because it was strange and unexpected. I should have noticed that. I should have paid attention. I should have said to myself, "Why's he talking to me all of a sudden?" Because he was never the kind of kid to just come up to you and start yakking.

But I guess I was curious. I guess I felt sorry for him and a little guilty that I had always looked at him like he was some sort of hopeless case. I think I just wanted to know what the hell he'd talk about.

And I think I remembered what my mom had said: "Imagine how you would feel." So I tried to do the right thing. I tried to be kind. But he was worse than a weirdo. He was more than just the kid who lost his mom, the kid we should feel sorry for. He didn't feel sorry for us. I know that now. He wanted to hurt us. He didn't care.

I'm going to tell my mom that when I get out of here. I'm going to tell her: "You were wrong. That kid, Rob Allen? He's bad. He's really, really bad."

CHAPTER NINE

The project of sorting out the house consumed me once I took a good look at the downstairs room and realized it really could be set up as a studio.

Originally, it must have served as some sort of dining room. It looked big enough to take a large dining table that could sit twelve comfortably, a past which seemed too grand for it now. Rob had apparently used it as some sort of storage space for furniture and miscellaneous things he had no use for. It was definitely spacious enough to set up a corner for lighting and backdrops and create a separate space for the editing equipment. And once I had cleared it of Rob's stuff, I had been surprised at the potential.

And with the money Gina was forwarding to me, I'd be able to make it look good. Professional and serious. *Yes,* I thought. *I could really make this work.*

I was sorting through some equipment when the doorbell rang, and I heard Suzie calling out to me.

"Hey, Carla, it's me!"

It was only then that I realized I'd spent the last few days alone. Not seeing anyone or even talking on the phone. Suzie had called me a few times and left voicemails, but I had not picked up her calls or listened to the messages, because I didn't want to face her after what had happened in the hospice. I figured she would want to know why I had not been back to see my dad. And would probably ask me what I'd said to him to make him so upset. But I didn't have a good enough explanation yet. At least, not one that wasn't a lie.

It was a relief when I opened the door and saw she was smiling.

"Hey," she said. "I just thought I'd come by and check that you were okay."

And, once again, her kindness disarmed me. "Yeah, I'm fine, thanks," I told her, and I beckoned for her to come inside, then led her into the front room.

"I was worried, when you didn't come by to visit Rob."

"I was planning to," I lied. "But I've been a bit busy with things here in the house." We walked down the hallway and when we reached the studio, I stopped to show her what I'd been doing. "I'm thinking of turning this room into a photographic studio. What do you think?"

Suzie looked round the room and then turned to face me and smiled a broad, beaming smile.

"Oh, so you're a photographer? I didn't know that."

And I nodded. *Why not?* I thought. This was an opportunity to start again, a chance to define myself any way I wanted, in a place where no one knew me. The last year, I had barely taken my camera out of its case. I had no enthusiasm for it but something about this room had triggered that desire again, as if I was seeing the world anew. It was corny to put it like that, but it was true. Something had changed and I wanted to embrace it and see where it took me.

"That's so cool," Suzie said. "So does this mean you're planning on staying?"

"I don't know yet. Maybe, if I can make this work," I said. "But it's a tough business, and projects aren't so easy to come by so, you know…"

"Wow," Suzie said, "I just assumed you would be heading back to San Francisco, you know, after what happened the other day with you and your dad."

I couldn't look her in the eye because now it looked like I was taking advantage of the situation. My dad, lying there alone in the hospice, while I was busy taking over his house. I could imagine how callous and mercenary it looked and I had no way to explain it.

"Listen, do you want a beer or something?" I asked her. "We can sit on the porch and talk."

She seemed so relieved when I offered and I realized that this was why she had come over. She wanted to talk to me.

We sat out on the front porch and drank a beer, and I was surprised at how easy I found it to hang out with her. For some reason, she put me at ease. That nervous habit I always had of chatting full speed whenever I was in the company of people I didn't really know, didn't overwhelm me when I was with her. But there was no point in spoiling it by trying to figure out why that was. Just let it happen, I figured.

"So, anyway," Suzie said eventually. "How are you holding up?"

"Yeah, not too bad," I replied. "Look, I know it must seem weird that I'm sorting out his house while he's lying there in the hospice, but honestly, having something to do makes it easier for me to cope."

"Hey, everyone copes in their own way and, to be honest, it's good to hear that you're planning on staying a while." She took a sip of beer and shifted in her seat, and I could see that she wanted to talk to me about what had happened the other day at the hospice with Rob. But she was unsure how to go about it.

"I'm sorry," I told her. "You know, about what happened at the hospice?"

"I know there are a lot of things that have happened between you all," she said. "And it's really not my place to get involved with any of that if you don't want me to. But he was really happy that your mom and sister decided to see him one last time. And despite what happened, I hope you'll come by to see him again. I know he wants you to. And that's why you came up here, wasn't it, to say goodbye to him?"

"Yeah," I said. "And I promise I'll be better behaved the next time. Last time, I just…"

"Hey, you don't owe me any explanations, okay? I just know he wants you to come and see him, and I know it will do him good. He needs you, Carla. I hope you know that?"

And I realized then what she meant. I could see it in her eyes, the unspoken worry. He had deteriorated and there was even less time now.

"How bad is he then?" I asked her.

"He's okay, but… Can I be honest?"

I nodded and waited for her to continue.

"It can go very fast sometimes. Someone can be stable for weeks and you can even convince yourself they might have a miraculous recovery. And then, in a matter of days, everything changes and all you can do is keep them comfortable and ease their passage."

"Is that where he is now then?" I said, and I immediately thought of Mom and Gina and whether I needed to call them back. Though I wasn't sure how easy it would be to convince them this time.

"Not yet, no. He's doing okay," Suzie said. "But I'd be lying if I said there'd been no deterioration, and I just thought I should tell you, because I don't want it to come as a shock, if he does decline fast."

"Right, I see."

"Also," and she paused to let me know that this was the real reason she was here and to make sure she had my attention and that I was listening.

I took a sip of my beer and then nodded to her. "Go on."

"He wanted me to pass on a message. He says there's something he wants to explain to you. I guess it's about what you said to him the other day."

I drank my beer down and let my head fall. I felt her squeeze my arm, a small gesture of sympathy and understanding that I appreciated and found touching.

"Okay," I said. "I'll try to come by soon." It wasn't a promise though. But I decided to keep that to myself. When I was ready to see Rob again, I would go. But not before then.

"Good," Suzie said. "I'm glad to hear that. And in the meantime, you can get set up here. A new life."

I tried to imagine me and Gina sitting together on the porch like this, chewing the fat and sharing a beer. Comforting one another. But it was impossible. That was not who we were; at least, not with each other.

With Mom it was possible—just—though even then, the atmosphere would not be as relaxed as this. Mom always needed to be doing something, to have an outlet for her emotions in some sort of activity. But that was okay. She had her reasons for never wanting to talk about things or overanalyze her life.

"Keeping on, that's how you get over things in life," she had always said. And there was some sense to it. It did no harm at least. Though there were times when I had wished I could have talked to her about things. And not just about the big stuff. The small, seemingly impossible things that happened sometimes, I would have liked to have been able to have turned to my mom for that. Advice, I supposed. That was what I wanted sometimes.

But now, here I was, pushing thirty-six and with a vague plan of what I wanted to do, and there was Suzie beside me, satisfying my need for comfort and assurance. Sipping her beer and acting like a new life was the best idea she'd ever heard. As if there was nothing to it. You just packed up and moved yourself someplace else and started over. Simple.

And maybe it was. Maybe that was all you had to do after all. Just do things. No thinking, no talking, just action.

"So, what do you think of this town then?" Suzie asked me. "You reckon you can make this place your home?"

"Only one way to find out, I guess."

"True," Suzie agreed. "It can be a strange place sometimes. But don't let that put you off. Deep down, everyone here is a good, well-meaning sort. They just take a while to warm to outsiders is all. But if you need anything, just ask. I know this place inside out. All its little quirks and secrets."

And I thought about that. The secrets this place held. I had a box full of them sitting inside. A little pile of yellowing papers that spoke of scandal and pain and something more than just a quirk.

"You know anything about those three boys?" I asked Suzie. More as a way to keep the conversation flowing than a genuine enquiry.

"What boys?" Suzie asked.

"Danny, I think one of them was called. And Jonathan. Yes, Jonathan Hutton."

And Suzie put her bottle of beer down on the porch beside her chair and leaned back into it, the wicker creaking as she adjusted her position.

"That was a long time ago," she said. "A very long time ago."

"Yeah, 1960s, '70s, or something like that," I said. And I noticed that Suzie didn't look at me and I felt the change that had occurred. The silence between us was awkward and filled with a feeling close to dread.

"Like I say, that's a lifetime ago. You'd be hard-pressed to find anyone around here who talks about it much."

"Your grandmother, maybe?"

And I wasn't expecting the swiftness of Suzie's response. The almost snake-like speed with which she attacked. A lung of sound and decisiveness.

"No," she said. Her voice almost like spit. "There's no need to talk to her about that."

And we looked at one another, our gazes fixed. Suzie's eyes glowing with a panic that glinted like ice in the flecks of her irises. While I sat there and blinked back, once, twice, as I tried to make sense of Suzie's sudden outburst.

"Listen, I'm sorry," Suzie said. "I didn't mean to snap at you like that. It's just, I haven't heard those names in years, and I wasn't expecting it. I mean, how did you know about that? It's years ago."

"I read about it online," I explained. "I didn't know where Newcastle was and when I googled it, all these news stories about those boys came up."

"Yeah, well," Suzie said. "It's not something anyone here needs reminding of."

"I can imagine. I mean, a small place like this, you'd never think something like that could happen here."

"Like I say. No one talks about it anymore."

And as she said it, I understood what was being said between the lines. This wasn't advice. It was a warning. Don't talk about it. Don't ask questions. Do not disturb. But I wondered why she seemed so agitated about it all. If it really wasn't something anyone here spoke about, then I didn't understand why it seemed to matter to her so much.

She stood up from the chair and took a last glug from her beer.

"Anyway," she said. "Thanks for the beer and the chat. I need to get going. Lots to do before I head to work."

I stood up and walked with her to the gate. "Hey, I'm sorry," I said, "you know, if I said something wrong or spoke out of turn. I didn't mean to."

"That's okay," she said. "You couldn't have known it still upsets people around here. Forget about it, yeah?"

I nodded. "Yeah, sure."

"Hey, and maybe we can go out some time. Get a beer or something to eat?"

"I'd like that," I told her. And she smiled at me and waved a goodbye as she headed down the street. But something about her voice had changed. There was less warmth there. A little more distance. As if she wasn't quite sure what she thought of me now.

She was acting as if everything was okay, but she wasn't the type of person who could hide their feelings well. What I'd said to her, about those boys, about the sad reputation this town had, it had upset her more than she cared to admit. And I had the feeling that if I mentioned it to her again, she would turn away from me. Her dismissal as swift as her welcome. And as I watched her walk away, I felt deflated. My first chance at building a friendship in this town, and I had apparently blown it already.

What the hell happened here? I wondered.

CHAPTER TEN

I was wrong about Suzie. I had crossed a line the other day, when I asked her about those boys, but she wasn't the kind of person who dwelled too long on something you said. Her call still surprised me though. Her kindness and thoughtfulness still something I wasn't used to.

"Hey," she said. "I've been thinking about your photography business."

I sighed, and was about to tell her that it was only an idea still. I had no business, just a vague sort of plan that had as much chance of failure as it did success. But Suzie seemed unfazed, my sigh barely registering.

"Listen," she said. "I hope you don't mind, but I have a friend, Mark Davenport. He's got a real estate business and I spoke to him yesterday because I remembered he was looking for someone to go out to the houses and take a few pictures for sales brochures and the website. That kind of thing. Anyway, I told him about you and he said you should give him a call. He's really busy apparently. So it could be something. If you're interested?"

"Oh, wow," I said. "Thanks so much."

"No problem," she said. "Here, let me give you his number. He's expecting your call. Today, if you have time."

I didn't know what to say. It was such an unexpected act of kindness and it had come at just the right time. I got a pen and a piece of paper and jotted down Mark's number and promised to call him straight away.

"I really appreciate this, Suzie," I told her.

"You'll be doing him a favor," she said. "And who knows, this could be the start of something, eh? I mean, one contract is all it takes to get started and for word to get round. So call him, okay?"

Usually, I would have sat around thinking about it. But I did as Suzie told me, and called Mark immediately. If this really was going to be a fresh start then I had to get on with it. No thinking. No delays. Just jump in and see where it took me.

When I called Mark, I expected him to ask me about my portfolio or pricing but he wasn't interested in any of that. "If Suzie recommends you, then that's all I need to know," he told me. And then he gave me an address and told me to meet him there.

Twenty minutes later I pulled up outside a rather run-down-looking house where Mark was waiting for me. I could see another woman there, walking around the front yard and taking notes. She was dressed in a peach-colored pantsuit with red patent leather shoes, a combination which made me think of Florida.

When I caught sight of myself in the car mirror, my hair tousled, my jeans and T-shirt too casual, everything unkempt and uncared for, I wanted to turn the car around and drive away. I definitely wasn't dressed for the world of real estate and I cursed myself that I hadn't thought to make myself presentable.

Mark smiled when he saw me and I registered his gaze, not disapproving, more amused. He walked towards me and held out his hand. "You must be Carla? I'm Mark Davenport." I nodded as he shook my hand, his grip vigorous and confident, but not overly macho. I liked him.

He was a lot younger than I expected. An energetic thirty-something with the physique of a runner or maybe a rock climber. He had that healthy and clear-eyed look about him, as if nothing ever troubled him. He slept well every night, confident that he had it all under control. Only a good deal of money could give you that kind of peace of mind, I figured. I couldn't remember the last time I had noticed a guy this way, and I wondered what it meant for me and Will.

"Sorry I didn't get spruced up," I told him. "I just rushed over after we spoke on the phone."

He laughed. "No, that's fine. I'm just impressed you could get here so fast."

I decided not to tell him that I had nothing else to do and smiled what I hoped was a confident smile, and tried not to focus on how sophisticated he seemed, the perfect embodiment of that elegant surname. I knew it was supposed to signify something. To let me know he came from some local prominent family. So I decided to let my out-of-town origins provide me with an advantage. *Just keep it casual*, I thought. That way I'd be able to control my nerves and stop myself from saying anything stupid. Because I badly needed this gig.

"Thanks for asking me to do this," I told him. "I'm new in town so it means a lot to get a project like this."

He was astute, I had to give him that. Picked up on my informality immediately and shifted effortlessly in synch with me. And I wondered if all real estate agents possessed this skill. Putting people at ease was no doubt the key to making a sale.

"Hey, no worries," he said. "Anyway, let me introduce you to Annabelle. She's going to be dressing the house so she's going to take you round the place. I have to get to another appointment. But it's nice to meet you. If you need anything just call the office and we'll sort things out."

He handed me a business card with an embossed logo, and I tucked it in my jeans pocket as Annabelle came over and introduced herself, then took my arm and led me towards the house.

"Honestly," she said. "I'm so glad you'll be here with me. I thought I was going to have to do the look over on my own and I really wasn't up for that."

I smiled at her and watched as she fumbled with the key in the lock.

"Why?" I asked her. "Is it dangerous or something?"

"Huh? Oh, not really," she said. "I do it all the time. It's just, well, you know, this house, what happened here, it's …"

I looked at her, not knowing what she meant.

"Oh, I see," she smiled, "I guess Mark didn't tell you about this place then?"

"No, he just told me to get here as fast as I could. Why, what's wrong with it?"

"Oh, nothing. It's just me getting spooked." She laughed as the key turned in the lock and the door swung open. "I can get a little superstitious and this place belonged to the Petersons. Their son was murdered, can you believe that? And I always feel a tragedy like that hangs around in the air, don't you?"

Peterson. Peterson. It took me a couple of seconds to make the connection. Adam Peterson. One of the boys that went missing. But that couldn't be right. It would be one hell of a coincidence.

"Adam Peterson?" I asked Annabelle. "Are you sure?"

And she turned to look at me, her face a little pale, her pupils dilated. "That's right. How do you know about him?"

Her stance had altered ever so slightly, her legs a tiny bit wider apart, her feet firmer on the ground as if she had taken her heels off and was standing in her bare feet. That defensiveness again, the same reaction I'd seen in Suzie when I mentioned those murdered boys. So I decided to lie, and use my dad to put her at ease.

"My dad's from around here," I told her. "Rob Allen? He mentioned those murders once or twice when I was growing up and it stuck in my mind because it sounded so awful, you know?"

And she softened immediately, "Oh, I didn't know you were Rob's daughter. How's he doing?"

"Not too great, actually. They moved him into a hospice a couple of weeks ago."

"Oh, I'm so sorry. I hadn't heard."

"That's okay. They're taking good care of him, so you know… all we can do now is wait."

She shuffled her feet and straightened the jacket of her suit even though it didn't need adjusting. Murdered boys and dying fathers were clearly not the kind of things she liked to talk about.

"Well, shall we take a look around and see what needs doing?" she asked me. "I don't think they touched this place in over thirty years. It's going to need a lot of work to get it ready."

And I suddenly realized I didn't know what I was supposed to do. I'd brought along my equipment but now I understood that this was just some sort of preliminary visit to see what needed to be done in preparation for the photoshoot for the sales brochure.

"What do you want me to do?" I asked Annabelle.

"Huh? I don't know. Don't you need to check the lighting or something?"

I shrugged, "I guess so," even though there was no point in planning any shots given that she was probably going to go and change everything.

"Actually, maybe you could get me some shots of the rooms so I can use them later to get an idea of the layout and the dimensions," she said. Then she hurried off down the hallway and left me standing there, facing the staircase. I still wasn't sure why I needed to be there, because she could probably take the photos herself if that was all she needed. But a job was a job, so I figured I might as well take a look around.

It was only then that I saw the house was still furnished and recalled Mark had mentioned the owner had recently died and there was no family to clear it out. I wondered if I'd have come if I'd know it was Adam Peterson's house.

I could hear Annabelle walking around and decided to head upstairs. I didn't want to be with her when I first took a look around because I was scared she would notice how nervous I was, and would be suspicious again.

At the top of the stairs I turned left down the hallway and saw the door to one of the bedrooms was open, so I headed there. The floor was covered with a worn carpet, with some strange headache-inducing pattern of yellow-and-blue swirls that belonged in the 1960s. On the walls, the wallpaper was torn in places and had faded to a very pale blue. There were pictures in wooden frames, the whole length of the wall, that on close inspection turned out to be children's paintings. Naïve brightly colored houses, imaginary animals of some sort, part lion part dragon, fantastic landscapes with snow-capped mountains and turreted castles. On the frames, someone had made the effort to add small brass plates with a title and a name and a date. I read them and couldn't stop myself from letting out a shocked "Oh!"

"Are you okay?" Annabelle called up to me.

"Sure," I replied. "I just banged my toe on something." And I heard her laugh. "Okay, well, you be careful up there."

But my heart was racing as I stared at the little brass plates and read the inscriptions.

"Imaginary creature"—Adam, aged six.
"Home sweet home"—Adam, aged four.
"The Ice Queen's Castle"—Adam, aged ten.

I stumbled into the bedroom and sat down on the bed and tried to control my breathing. It seemed wrong that those intimate, personal items had been left behind in the house and would probably end up at the waste disposal. Those last pieces of Adam, so lovingly curated and preserved, presumably by his mom. It made me shudder with sadness, because I had caught an unexpected glimpse of the boy he was. His innocence and imagination. His brightness and color. He was a source of delight and the object of much love and affection. The boy behind the newspaper headlines, real and alive.

It was only when I looked up, hoping to get some relief, that I realized where I was. The room was decorated with all kinds of baseball paraphernalia. Posters of old-time major league stars, some of whom I recognized—Yogi Berra, Joe DiMaggio, Jim Landis. And scattered among them were prize ribbons and photos of a kid in junior league. I knew it was him, this small boy, standing at home base, bat in hand, squinting into the sunlight, and biting his lower lip in concentration. But I couldn't get any closer. I didn't dare look at him. That he had died the way he had was unbearable, unimaginable.

And I wondered then how often his mom had sat on this bed and stared at that wall, her son there, full of life and energy and hope. How did it feel to lose so much, to have all that taken from you so cruelly? But the fact that she had left this room as it was, as a shrine to her son's memory, to the fact he had been alive, was an indication of just how much she must have suffered.

"Geez, I thought the rest of the house was out of date, but this is something else. What is it, a time capsule?"

I didn't realize Annabelle was there and her entrance made me jump up.

"Oh, sorry!" She laughed. "I didn't mean to scare you."

Then she stopped and stared at me. "Hey, are you crying?" she asked me. I couldn't say anything and just nodded and wiped my cheeks.

"Why, is something wrong?" she said. I gestured around the room, at the posters and the photos and the other childhood mementos.

"I guess this was Adam's bedroom," I managed to say. And I watched as she walked around looking at everything, picking up a trophy and staring at the photos on the wall.

"Wow," she eventually said. "Yeah, it must have been." She picked up a book, some boys' adventure tale and examined the cover before placing it back on the bedside table. "This is pretty spooky."

It wasn't the word I would have used, but I knew what she meant, because it had freaked me out.

"Yeah," I said. "I wasn't prepared for it. That poor kid."

"Listen," she said. "Why don't we get out of here. I'm going to tell Mark that we need to get this place cleared out first before we can start working on it. All of this stuff," and she gestured around the room. "It has to go. It's too depressing."

She was right, there was no way I could see any more of this house now. And I wasn't sure I would want to come back even when it had been emptied, because it was true—what she had said earlier—there was something left behind here, some remnant of emotion. You could feel it in the air. The grief, the loss, the hopeless agony of it all. For some reason, it felt as though the room had been kept intact, not so much as a shrine, but because his parents needed to be sure their son had really been there, that he had existed and his short, brief life had not been something they had imagined. They needed this hard proof. Because their memories were not enough.

And it was this that had made me cry. The way the things in the room allowed you to not only see what had been lost but to feel it too. Being there turned the Petersons into something more than a newspaper headline, more than a note in a diary. They stopped being strangers and became real to me. And it touched me more than I expected it to.

"Come on, let's go," Annabelle said. And she headed out of the room.

And I don't know why I did it. I guess it was the idea that some of this needed to be preserved, that it was wrong to leave it here knowing it would be thrown away. Adam mattered, and as short as his life was, it wasn't right that every trace of him should be eliminated. His parents had preserved all this for a good reason and I felt their wish should be respected in some small way.

On the table beside his bed, I spotted a baseball mitt that had been left there. And I took it off the table and slipped it into my camera bag, then headed out the room and downstairs to find Annabelle.

"You okay?" she asked me, and I nodded.

"Just a little shaken. That was hard to take in."

She was already locking the door and chatting away to me, the weirdness of what had just happened in Adam's room already forgotten now that she was back outside.

"Yeah, sorry about that. It was kinda creepy huh?" She put the keys in her purse and with that gesture it was all apparently over. "Hey, Mark says you're planning on sticking around up here. You like Newcastle then?" she asked me.

"Yeah," I said. "It's nice to be someplace quiet and friendlier than a big city, you know?"

She smiled at me. "It must feel so different here though. But hey, Seattle is close by if things here get too much for you."

"I'll bear it in mind," I said. "Though I've felt very welcome here so far. Sure, it's different but I think Rob being my dad has helped break the ice a lot."

"Oh, for sure. Your father was... damn, I'm sorry, *is,* he *is* a great guy."

She blushed a little and cringed and I smiled and told her it was okay, which was her cue to change the subject again.

"So, you're living at Rob's over on 135th Avenue?" she asked me. "Great area. You like it?"

"Yeah, I like it a lot."

"It's a fabulous location. Really popular with families and commuters into Seattle."

"Probably worth a ton of cash then, I guess."

And she laughed. "Why, you looking to sell?"

"No. Not yet at least. I guess it depends how well I get myself set up here."

"Ah, right, yes. Listen, please don't think every day will be like this. Mark is usually so organized, I can't think why he didn't get that place cleared first. But I promise, this is a great job and Mark is a great guy to work with."

I nodded, but her realtor enthusiasm about this place made me shiver. The truth was, I knew this town preferred not to talk about those boys at all, at least not to outsiders like me.

People like Annabelle and Mark looked around and saw "fabulous" neighborhoods filled with opportunity and potential. But all I saw were those yellowing newspaper articles and the innocent faces of Danny, Adam, and Jonathan. All I understood was that this town was capable of kindness and deception, and I still wasn't sure if I could trust it.

And I thought again of that box of my dad's and those strange mementos he had gathered. I had a memento of my own now. Adam's baseball mitt hidden in my bag. A piece of this town's history I had saved because I needed to be sure it wouldn't be glossed over. That I had a piece of him, some sort of proof that what had happened to him was real and couldn't be forgotten.

Maybe it was something I shared with my dad, I wondered. Maybe we both needed to preserve the truth of what had happened here. And now I wanted to read more of what he had written there in those diaries. I'd taken that mitt on the spur of the moment, a spontaneous act driven by the overwhelming emotion I'd felt sitting there in Adam's room.

But Rob had been more diligent when he had decided to keep those newspaper clippings and write those diaries. And more than ever, I wanted to know why he felt so connected to all of this. Why it was that even now, decades later, the mere mention of those boys' names had been enough to make him anxious.

Those boys meant something to him and the more I thought about that, the more I needed to know why.

*

It was early evening when I sat down with the box. There was a host of stuff I should be doing, but the idea had taken hold now—one of my "distracting obsessions," as Gina would put it—and I didn't want to let it go. I figured I would start at the beginning and work my way through, so that evening, I sat at the kitchen table and spread out the books about Danny McIntosh. The others, I left. One at a time, that was all I could cope with. Their stories were too grim to deal with simultaneously.

I opened a notebook I'd bought at the store the other day. One of three. A different color for each boy. I chose the dark red for Danny and thought it was a random decision until I remembered a detail from one of the news reports. He'd worn a red T-shirt under his overalls, and I shivered a little at the thought of it, then shook myself straight.

"God, Carla," I said. "Stop imagining ghosts and start thinking."

Because I had to get the story straight in my own head and in my own words. Step by step, everything that happened from the day he went missing to the day he was found. I would list the key events and then try and see if there was something there, a pattern, a clue, something that had been missed. I was good at that sort of thing. At picking up on the details, my photographer's sense of looking closely at things and discovering the essence of a thing.

The newspaper articles were easy to line up and I quickly had a rough timeline for what had happened to Danny.

He'd gone fishing with his friend Kevin Cooper, and they'd stayed by the river all day, frying some fish for lunch on a small fire they'd built on the riverbank. They did this most Sundays and that day had been no different than any other. No one approached them and Kevin didn't remember seeing anyone watching them. They were alone. Just fishing.

At four o'clock they'd packed up and headed home. The next day was a school day so they had to be home before dinner to take a bath and do on their homework. It was all so ordinary. Then at six o'clock, Mrs McIntosh had called Kevin's mother on the phone asking if her son was with them. They waited a little longer for him to come home, but by seven o'clock their annoyance had turned to panic, and they had called the police.

That evening, a group of men had gone down to the river and called out to him, but there was no reply. All night they had searched for him, walking through the neighborhood and calling his name. Those suburban streets echoing to the sound of his name. "Danny! Danny!"

And I thought of the children asleep in their beds that night. Did they hear the men calling that name in their dreams? Did they wake the next morning with the sound of it still ringing in their ears like a warning of sorts: this is what happens when you don't go straight home?

A whole week they searched for him. A whole week he was missing. Dogs were sent out along the riverbank and through the forest. People went door to door asking, "Have you seen him?" But nobody had. In a town this size everyone knew each other so such enquiries were not necessary. Anyone who had seen Danny McIntosh that day, or any time after, would have known who he was, and would have come forward long ago. But they needed to keep asking. They needed to keep searching. Because to stay quiet, to do nothing, was impossible. It would feel as if they had given up on him. On a twelve-year-old boy. So they kept on going. Until there was no need to.

He was found, twenty miles north lying in a small gulley, deep in the pines. His body left exposed to the elements. No attempt had been made to bury him. He was meant to be discovered.

He was still wearing his T-shirt and overalls. A small detail that shocked me when I read it, though I couldn't think why.

There was no mention of his injuries or the cause of death. Not in the newspapers at least. Which meant I would have to try and find the medical examiner's report. Though how I was supposed to go about getting hold of historical information like that, I wasn't entirely sure.

And I leaned back in my chair then and thought about what I was doing. Sitting there in my father's kitchen making notes about a death that had occurred so long ago the records probably no longer existed. Thinking I could solve the missing piece of the puzzle. Maybe it was a stupid idea. I didn't have the skills to do something like this, and curiosity alone was no substitute.

I looked at the notes I had scribbled on the page. Find Kevin Cooper. Get a hold of the autopsy report.

Who was I kidding? It was ridiculous, when I thought about it.

I snapped the notebook shut and then headed to bed. I had a life that needed sorting out and real, everyday problems that couldn't be ignored while I fooled around with something that was none of my business.

But Danny McIntosh wouldn't let me sleep. All night he was there in my dreams. Walking home with his fishing rod slung over his shoulder. Walking straight towards me and looking me right in the eye as he told me: "Keep going. Please keep going."

CHAPTER ELEVEN

Will called on the landline and it took me a few seconds to grapple with the realization that he had called Rob's home phone number.

"Hey," he said. "It's me."

"Will?" And I deliberately emphasized the question so that he understood I wanted to know how he got this number.

"Sorry for calling you like this," he said. And he hesitated, waiting for me to say something, but I remained silent. "Your mom gave me your number," he continued. "She said you wouldn't mind."

"Oh. She forgot to mention that."

"Carla, you changed your cell phone number, what the hell else was I supposed to do?"

"Oh, I don't know. Take that as some sort of indication that I didn't want to be contacted maybe?"

"Shit, I just wanted to call you to say I heard about your dad. But I guess I made a mistake."

He was about to hang up on me and I surprised myself by catching him before he could do it.

"Okay, okay… wait, I'm sorry. I'm just a little on edge still, what with seeing my dad again and then finding myself up here without really knowing what I plan to do."

I'd already said too much, but it was out before I had the chance to check myself and I already regretted it. Will didn't need to know that I had no idea what I was doing. He didn't need to know that I was feeling pretty lost now that the reality had set in. And he definitely didn't need to know where I was. The more I thought about that, the angrier I felt, because my mom had no right to give him my number. She should have called first and asked if it was okay. A small courtesy, but it was one that mattered. Though I knew what her response would be to that.

"Oh, but he's such a nice guy, Carla. I like Will. He's one of the good ones."

And it was true, Will was a good guy, but my mom clearly thought that gave her permission to act, because her daughter was incapable of making good decisions.

"I just wish you'd told me that was where you were headed," Will said. "And also, maybe why. I mean, your dad, if I'd have known…"

What? I wondered. *If you'd have known, then what? Would you have tried harder to keep us together? Would you have insisted on coming up with me to lend me some support? Would you have stood by me, no questions asked, no criticism, no obligations?*

But for some reason, I didn't want him to know how sure I was that I had made the right decision, that something had lifted since I left San Francisco. Some sad weight I hadn't noticed was there until it was gone.

"You okay?" Will asked.

"Yeah, I'm fine. I just don't know what to say."

"You don't have to tell me anything, Carla. I was just calling to check how you were doing."

"Like I say, I'm fine."

"Carla?"

"Yeah?"

"If it's not fine, will you call someone? I don't mean me. I just mean…"

This was what Mom meant when she said Will was one of the good ones. And it wasn't as if I wasn't aware of it. I knew he was. I knew what he had said just then was sincere. He wasn't some phony guy. And yet…

"Everyone here has been very kind to me, they're helping me out. I'll be fine."

There was a slight snark in my voice I didn't attempt to hide. I was laying down boundaries. Telling him—don't come any closer. And don't go gossiping with my mom either. I don't know why I couldn't just accept his care was genuine, why it was I didn't think I was worth it. *Because that was what it was, wasn't it?* I thought. That was why I was up here on my own and trying to not look over my shoulder and see what I had left behind. Just another mess. But so what? After all, I was the messy kind, wasn't I?

"I'm glad to hear it," he said. "No one should be alone under these circumstances."

"It doesn't feel like that," I told him. The words falling out again before I had time to contain them.

"Sorry, what? What do you mean?"

And now I had a choice. Talk to him because I clearly needed to right now; or hold back again just as I always did.

He's so far away now, I thought. *The distance could make things easier. So just talk to him.*

"Rob is a complicated man and it's hard to summon up affection for someone you haven't seen in almost fifteen years, even when they're lying on their deathbed."

He paused for a couple of seconds before he spoke, the cold, harshness of my words sinking in. I regretted them almost as soon as I said it. Because it wasn't completely true. I did have some sympathy for my dad, but it was only enough to sit at his bedside, no more than that.

"He's still your dad though. You went up there to see him, to help. And I can only assume it's because you needed to."

It was disconcerting, the way he could do this. See to the heart of what was troubling me and then express it in so few words. He knew me, and I couldn't deny it. Some people went their whole lives looking for someone who understood them this intimately. Longing for it even. And there I was, running away from it.

"It just seemed like the decent thing to do. He'd have been alone if I hadn't come up here. That's not something I wanted hanging over me. We have enough pain to process because of Rob, I don't need to add a layer of guilt as well."

"Why did you never tell me about any of this?"

"Why does everyone think it's always so necessary to talk about this stuff? Some of us don't need to."

I didn't mean to sound so defensive, but the emotions were too strong for me to keep a hold on, and I hoped that he would do what he always did when I became dismissive, that he'd try to explain to me the importance of talking things through. He was a firm believer in that. You talked about your past because that was how you controlled the present, that was how you determined the future. But sometimes it could feel like an interrogation. The journalist in him taking over and prying too deep, crossing boundaries. So I braced myself, waiting for him to push things further.

But all he said was, "Okay, I just thought, you know…"

"We needed him out of our lives, Will. It wasn't only me. My mom, Gina, they'll tell you the same. Sometimes, some people are best forgotten."

"I'm glad though," he said. "That you went up there. It's the right thing to do. To be kind."

Kind. Was that the word I would have used? It didn't feel kind. Dutiful, perhaps, but not kind. But, when I looked at it that way, I felt the rush of sadness wash over me again, as powerful as it had been the afternoon I had sat by Rob's bed and whispered in his ear.

And I couldn't talk anymore now. He had struck too deep. Again.

"Listen," I said. And I didn't try to disguise the quiver in my voice, the fact that I was on the verge of tears. Because he knew I was hurting. He chose his words carefully and knew the impact they had. *Kind.* That was a punch to the gut. "I need to hang up now, okay?"

"Sure," he said. And then, "Can I call you again? Just to, you know…"

"Okay," I replied. My heart overruling my brain. A piece of me, at least, knew what was good for me.

*

I needed to get the conversation with Will out of my head. There was so much I had to get sorted and arranged, and the visit to Adam Peterson's house was still affecting me. I'd felt paralyzed and incapable of concentrating on anything.

I looked around the studio room, at the chaos of it all—the tins of paint and brushes waiting for me to get started with the decorating, the boxes stacked in the corner waiting to be unpacked, the sheeting that needed to be rolled out over the wooden floor to protect it from paint splashes, and all I could do was sigh and turn away from it all. Work I'd hoped would keep me busy and take my mind off things but which now felt like a burden.

I needed to get outside for a while and decided to take a wander around the neighborhood, just until my head had cleared, and I could think straight. Hopefully, after a walk, the nervous tension which was cramping my stomach would settle.

It was a bright afternoon, but already a little cooler than when I arrived a few weeks ago, fall making its presence felt as August limped closer to September. But despite the sunshine, the streets were strangely quiet. Just a few people out in their gardens or driving by. There was an old-fashioned Sunday afternoon feel to it all despite it being a weekday.

Suburbia, I realized. I wasn't used to it, and the unfamiliarity of the afternoon silence made me uneasy. It was like that childhood dream I used to have, the one where I woke up one day to find I was the only person left in the world. Everyone had disappeared without explanation. I'd call out to them and get no reply. Just the echo of my voice in the emptiness. For a couple of years it had terrified me and left me with night sweats and waking in a panic.

And these streets, they looked unsettlingly familiar, as if they had been pulled from my dream. The houses set back from the road, their well-manicured lawns and mature broad-leafed trees providing an insulating distance between the inhabitants and the outside world. As if the people who lived there did not want anyone to know their business. Or their secrets. Things could happen beyond those lawns, everything shaded and hidden in the shadow of those sturdy trees.

I knew nothing about small towns. I was a city girl at heart. I knew the hustle and bustle of anonymous crowds, the ever-present background thrum of traffic, the neon glow of twenty-four-hour grocery stores and the midnight voices of people on the streets. What I didn't know was whatever it was I had felt out on my walk. There was a strange emptiness to the streets. The houses, the gardens, the curbsides all felt desolate without people around. No crowds, no faces, no noise. Just an eerie void and the sort of disquiet that makes you look over your shoulder because you're sure someone is following you. But when you turn to look, no one is there.

And for the first time since I arrived, I could imagine it. The figure lurking there, watching everything, waiting until the opportunity presented itself. A young boy, alone on the street, there for the taking.

It was as if I could see him walking towards me. Danny McIntosh heading home that spring day in 1963, his fishing rod propped against his shoulder, a hessian bag filled with fish, his blue overalls muddied and dirtied after a day by the river. All those details I had read about in the newspaper flooded me now. Danny a sad mirage, a ghost boy who walked the streets where he used to live, still trying, after all these years, to make his way safely home.

I looked around at the houses and wondered if one of them was his, his parents living there still, old now, but waiting for him, even though they knew he was dead. They had buried him after all. But there must be moments, I imagined, when the hope took over. When it sparked a little madness inside, so that you opened the door to welcome him home. Danny, living on in this imagined realm. The realm of grief I had now also found myself occupying as I waited for Rob to die.

At a four-way junction, I stopped, unsure which way to go, that image of Danny momentarily slowing me down. I wasn't the superstitious kind, but for a second I was sure that if I looked around, looked up at one of the windows, I would see him standing there, face pressed against the glass, watching me.

And maybe he was, I thought. Maybe he knew that I had read those newspaper articles and had seen my father's notebooks. Maybe Danny McIntosh knew that I was in possession of something important—the missing piece of the story that everyone still needed to hear.

What happened to them? The unanswered question that had lost none of its power.

What was it Suzie had said? "No one talks about that anymore."

I respected that. It was understandable that people would prefer to let the memories fade. A pain as strong as that is not one you can bear too long.

But what of Danny McIntosh and Adam Peterson and poor, lost Jonathan Hutton? What of them? They didn't deserve to be forgotten. They didn't deserve to be lost. They deserved the truth. Some sort of justice. And what if I could get to it? What if I could provide it?

Is that the reason I'm here? I thought. *Is that the reason I decided to stay? Am I here to help you, Danny, Adam, Jonathan? Well, okay then. Okay.*

But I would need to be discreet if I planned to delve into this. Take things slowly and stay aware of all the long-buried emotions. Because I could unleash decades of hurt if I wasn't careful.

What Suzie had said was something I needed to bear in mind at all times. It wasn't just that no one wanted to talk about tragedies that happened here. It was also true that they would not want to talk about them with an outsider.

I may be Rob's daughter, but that would only get me so far. I had been welcomed, but that wasn't an invitation to walk inside and settle down. Acceptance was something you earned in a place like this. And you earned it over years; years in which you were watched and assessed and judged. Years in which you didn't rock the boat.

It meant I would have to go it alone. There was no one here I could turn to and Mom and Gina had made their thoughts on the matter clear. Then I thought of Will. If anyone would know what to do it would be him. And he would help me, I knew he would. I just wasn't sure if I wanted his help yet. For now, all I needed was a plan. And, in the meantime, Rob would have to wait. First I needed to sort myself out and then figure out what I was really dealing with. All I could do was hope he would hang on a while longer.

CHAPTER TWELVE

I decided to go over to see Suzie and thank her for introducing me to Mark. I wanted to tell her that the house I visited belonged to the Petersons and hoped I might be able to talk to her again about the boys without it seeming like an intrusion this time. I would just be asking questions because my visit to that house had left me shaken and made me curious. It would be natural.

I wasn't expecting Suzie's grandmother to open the door. She was a small woman, slightly stooped with age, and hair bright and silver as a birch tree. Her eyes were clear and astute.

"Oh," I said. "I'm sorry, I was looking for Suzie."

She was wary when she saw a stranger standing on her front porch.

"Suzie's not home at the moment," she told me. "She works Monday to Wednesday at the hospice."

"Oh, of course. I think she mentioned that. Sorry, I forgot."

She looked at me, assessing me, before asking, "Can I help you with anything?"

"She did me a favor and I wanted to thank her."

"You're Carla, aren't you?" she asked me. "Rob's youngest?"

"Yes, that's right," I said.

"I'm Cece, Suzie's grandmother."

"I'm sorry if I disturbed you," I said. And I was ready to turn and leave, but she opened the door a little wider and looked at me more closely. "You look a lot like him. Same eyes. How's he doing?"

"Not so good," I said, and I felt an unexpected surge of emotion wash over me.

"I'm sorry to hear that. Look, why don't you come inside and have a cup of coffee? You look like you could do with some company."

I wanted to decline and say I had to be on my way because I had so much to do, but her smile was so warm and her eyes so kind, that I found myself saying, "Sure, that would be great," as I followed her into the kitchen.

It was strange to walk through her house. The layout was exactly the same as Rob's place, but Cece's home had undergone some major upgrades. It was surprisingly modern and bright. The home of a young person rather than the white-haired septuagenarian that walked ahead of me down the hallway.

The one similarity, though, were the family portraits lining the walls. She had decorated both walls almost from floor to ceiling, and I glanced at the smiling faces and caught a glimpse of a teenage Suzie staring back at me, her smile awkward and lopsided.

"Rob did the same thing," I told her as we entered the kitchen.

"What's that?" she replied.

"The photos in the hall. My dad hung photos of all of us there too."

And she nodded and indicated a stool where I could sit, and said, "Yes, well, I know he missed you all. Having you there in the hallway was a way of keeping you near, I suppose. That's the comfort I take from it at least. We all need to see our loved one's faces from time to time, don't we?"

I smiled and nodded and mumbled, "Yeah." I wasn't going to admit to her that I'd gone years without missing my father's face. But Cece's sharp eyes missed nothing and when we sat at the table with our coffees, she took control of the conversation before I had time to explain why I had come over.

"Rob is a good man," she said. "I know you all have had problems in the past, and I'm not trying to diminish any of that. But he is a good man."

Her voice was steady, her words slow and precise. She fixed me with those penetrating ice-blue eyes, so intelligent and undiminished by old age, and I got the impression she knew instinctively that I had come here not just to say goodbye but also to try and understand my dad a little better.

But I wanted her to understand my truth as well. I wanted her to see that the Rob I knew was not the man this town had known and loved. That father, that husband was not a good man. *Do you see it, Cece?* I thought. *Can you see what he did to me?*

"People have many faces," I told her. "And I'm sure for many people here my dad is a good man. But, like you say, things happened between us, and…"

She reached over the table and tapped my hand, a small act of tenderness that surprised me. Her unexpected touch making me freeze as if human contact was something I was unfamiliar with.

"You know," Cece said. "I'm not one for giving advice or telling people how to live. But you have a chance here, not to change what happened or even make things better. But you have a chance to say goodbye. To at least not be left with that regret. And you should take it."

"Did Suzie tell you then? About the way I messed up at his bedside the other day?"

"No, she didn't, as it happens."

"I think I might have misspoken about something with her too and I wanted to come by and tell her that I hadn't meant to upset her."

"Oh, I'm sure you didn't. It takes a lot to upset Suzie."

"It's just being new around here. I know this is Rob's hometown, but he didn't really talk much about his childhood and the things that happened here. I didn't mean to open up old wounds. That really wasn't my intention. I just—"

And I watched as she set down her coffee cup and clasped her hands together, almost as if she was in prayer.

"I see," she said. "In that case, I can only assume you spoke to her about Jonathan."

"I didn't know," I said. "I'd just been reading about them. I didn't mean to cause offense."

"Don't worry," she said. "It was all a long time ago. Before Suzie was born even. But she gets upset whenever it's mentioned."

She sighed, and I waited for her to continue, but for some reason she seemed to become engrossed in her own thoughts, as if the memories of what had happened all those years ago had taken control of her.

"I just didn't understand why she would be so upset about it," I told her.

And Cece stared at me for a moment, a small frown of confusion knitting her brow.

"Oh, I see," she said. "So she didn't explain."

I shook my head and was about to say, "No, she didn't," but she was already on her feet and walking back out to the hallway.

"Here, come here a minute and let me show you something."

I followed her out to the hallway and watched as she stopped before the wall of pictures and then focused on one, pointing to it and nodding to me to come and take a look.

"This is a photo of my son," she said. "He was ten years old when they took this photo. It's the last one anyone ever took of him."

I walked towards her and stopped in front of the photograph and was met with a set of bright blue eyes. The smile familiar to me. The image already seared in my mind.

"His name was Jonathan," she said. "Jonathan Phillip Hutton."

"Wait, so you're Alice Hutton? You're Jonathan's mom?"

And she nodded, and I heard her say, "Everyone calls me Cece," and keep on talking, but her words were lost in a buzz of adrenaline that filled my head. Flashes of Suzie's face from a few days ago rushed at me, and I understood now what it was I had seen there in Suzie's eyes—her grandmother's pain passed down through the generations without diminishment. A genetic code of pain and love.

"Anyway," Cece said. "Now you understand why Suzie was so upset."

"I'm sorry. I don't really know what to say."

"That's okay. Life goes on, as they say."

It stunned me to hear Cece say that. A mother who'd lost her son. A son who had never been returned to her. How did life go on? I wanted to ask her. How do you live beyond that?

And perhaps Cece saw those questions there in my face because she answered, "I had a daughter to take care of. Suzie's mother, Amy. You keep going for the ones you still have."

And I nodded even though I didn't understand.

"Can I ask you something?" Cece asked me.

"Of course."

"You said Rob never really talked about this place. But he told you about Jonathan? About what happened to those boys. To Danny and to Adam. Why did he tell you about that, do you think? There are so many things he could have told you about this town, why focus on the worst of it?"

And I had to decide. Make a split-second decision. The truth or a lie. But I wasn't ready to tell anyone about my father's notebooks. Not until I had read them all properly. Not before I knew what was in them.

So a lie then. A small one. Just to buy some time.

"I guess it made a big impression on him. I don't know why he told me about it. Awful things leave their mark though, I suppose."

I could feel Cece staring at me, watching me. Scrutinizing every flicker of emotion on my face. Looking for the telltale signs that I was lying. And when she found them there, she sighed a little, and then said, "Well, anyway, now you know."

I looked at that photo hanging on the wall. At the lost boy, the lost son. And I thought of my dad, of that "good man." A man who might know more than he admitted. A man who might be able to put Cece out of her pain and suffering.

And I knew then, for sure. If he had kept a secret like this from a woman as kind as Cece, a woman he knew, a woman who thought of him as a friend, as a "good man," then everything I knew about him was true.

He was bad. Rotten to the core. And if he had decided years ago never to help her, then I could make it right. I could help her. I had to.

CHAPTER THIRTEEN

There would be no turning back, I knew that. I would learn things I may prefer not to know and there were moments when I thought I should let it go, because what was the point in delving into something that had happened so long ago? There was probably no way to ever uncover the truth about what happened.

But then I would take out Adam Peterson's baseball mitt and remember the way his parents had preserved his bedroom, or I'd recall Cece's face as she had looked at the photograph of her son. She had claimed "life goes on" but I had seen it there in her eyes, the veil of grief that shrouded the brightness when she looked at Jonathan.

And it made me wonder why Rob had never spoken about such a defining moment in the lives of everyone who had lived in Newcastle at that time. It wasn't because he had been trying to protect us from some horrific truth. He had never been the type of father to shield his children from the horrors of the world. The news channel had always played in the living room and he had never flinched from letting us see the bloody and grim reports of wars and deaths and economic upheaval.

"This is what the world is like," he had told me. "You'd best accept it." His face impassive and calm, as if he needed me to believe there was nothing anyone could do to change things. The world could never become a better place. "This is just how it is."

That was what he taught me, that was the sum total of his fatherly advice. And I had taken heed of it, I'd accepted that the world was a chaotic, uncontrollable place because that was what he told me. Though there were plenty of times when I felt the hope rising, rebellious and contrary, a little voice inside me telling me Rob was wrong.

Until now, I had never thought about the reason he had come to think this way. It was just who he was, one of those morose sorts of people. But his silence about those boys hinted at something deeper than cynicism and made me wonder if the violence I had witnessed as a child was connected in some way to what had happened to Danny and Adam and Jonathan. A deep-rooted response to their deaths that he had inflicted upon us, without us ever understanding why.

But Cece was right, while he was still alive, I had a chance to confront him about it. To ask him what he knew.

*

It was Thursday, so I knew Suzie wouldn't be at the hospice when I went over. I would be able to sit with my dad in peace, and if he was awake, I would be able to say what I wanted to him.

When I arrived, the receptionist seemed surprised to see me.

"I thought you had returned to San Francisco," she said. And when I explained that I had decided to stay on in Newcastle "until the end," I saw her expression soften. I was the good daughter again, come to help her father through his last journey.

She took me into the room and explained that he had been asleep most of the time, the last couple of days. When I asked her if he would be aware I was there, she shook her head.

"I'm sorry," she said. "I don't think so. His medication's very strong, and… I mean, he has some lucid moments and I could call you when he's doing well, if you're close by and can come over quickly?"

"Could you?"

She nodded.

"Is there any chance I can maybe just sit with him today?" I asked her.

She nodded, and I thought maybe I should take a chance and ask her.

"The last time I was here, the doctor said Rob had asked for less medication, because he wanted to talk to me. Would it be possible, do you think, to maybe…"

Her firmness surprised me, as did the speed of her response. "Oh no," she said. "That really wouldn't be a good idea. He's in a lot of pain and to reduce the medication now, from a care point of view, I don't think that would be something we could consent to."

"I see. But if he consented himself?…"

"Well, that would be different, but at the moment he's not in any state to be able to do that."

"Okay," I said. "I just thought I'd ask, you know…"

She nodded and then gestured for me to follow her down the corridor to his room. We walked in silence and when she opened the door and I stepped inside, she didn't say anything. Just closed the door quietly behind me.

I went to his bedside and sat in the chair beside him and tried to see if there were any noticeable changes, but he looked the same as the last time I had seen him. Strangely calm and at peace, his breath rising and falling in gentle waves. If it wasn't for the lines leading from his veins to the machines at his bedside, it was possible you could imagine he was simply sleeping.

It seemed impossible anything would permeate that pharmaceutical haze, but it was worth a try, so I opened my bag and took out the notebook I had brought with me. The diary he had written about Danny McIntosh.

"Hey, Dad," I said, as I opened the pages. "I thought I'd read to you for a while. Would you like that?"

And there was a flicker of something there behind his eyelids. An awareness. And when his lips opened slightly and his cheeks quivered, I was sure of it. He could hear me. "I just need to know, Dad. What happened to them? To those boys? Where's Jonathan? I know you know them. I know you remember them. Do you remember? Let me help you."

And I started to read to him from the diary he had written all those years ago.

*

Sunday, April 24, 1963

Kevin Cooper says they'll never find him. And I think he's right. He says they're looking in all the wrong places. Trawling the river and checking in barns and outbuildings. But no one smart is going to take a boy and then keep him there. Some place so obvious. That's what Kevin thinks. And he's right about that. Danny McIntosh is missing, and they'll never find him. At least, not where they're looking for him.

He'll be scared, I reckon. Really scared. It's Wednesday today and he was taken on Sunday. That's three days now, almost. That's a long time when you're scared.

In the paper, they put his story on the front page and I cried when I saw it and Papa got mad.

"What are you crying for?" he yelled at me. So I showed him the paper and he snatched it from my hand and said, "you shouldn't be reading things like this in the newspaper, if you don't have the stomach for it."

It was stupid to let him see me cry like that. But what else could I do? It's only normal to cry. Because Danny McIntosh is scared, and so am I.

At school they made us pray for him. Pastor Thompson came by and we all sat in the hall while he spoke. He asked God to bring Danny safely home. And he lifted his head when he asked that. I watched him. He looked up to heaven like he was talking straight with God. Like God was right there in front of him, listening.

And I thought, maybe the pastor has the power. Maybe he can make it happen. So I bowed my head and I asked him too, just to be sure he heard. I asked God. Please, listen to the pastor. Please, bring him safely home. Don't let him die.

Sunday April 28, 1963

God didn't listen. They found Danny in the woods. Miles from home. He was dead. Now, not even God can bring him back. Pastor Thompson said he was at peace and in God's hands. But he cried as he said it, as if he wasn't sure. Like the rest of us, he knows Danny should still be with us. He knows heaven is no place for a kid. But he's better off in God's hands. I know that for sure.

*

The rest of the notebook was empty, and I stopped reading and sat and watched my dad, looking for any traces of recognition here on his face. But there was no sign that he had heard me.

"What happened, Dad?" I said. "You know more than this, don't you? You can help Cece, can't you? Help her find Jonathan. Help her find her son. You can put an end to this."

Nothing. His face was as passive as it had been when I first entered the room. The brief signs of life I thought I had seen were little more than the usual twitches and muscle spasms that always shifted on a face. Tiny movements I only noticed because I had been scrutinizing him so closely. Hoping for signs of awareness that weren't there.

I flicked through the notebook again, to be sure, because the story couldn't end there. I was desperate to know more and frustrated that he had suddenly stopped writing all those years ago. But there was no mistake, the pages were empty.

And I thought of my dad. An eleven-year-old boy trying to make sense of something terrifying, something horrific. Scribbling notes in pencil until he no longer could. Perhaps it was simply that the story had reached its natural conclusion. Danny had been found, so there was nothing more to write down. But for some reason, I felt he was holding back.

Even then, I thought. *Even as a kid, he still held things back. Even in a notebook not destined for anyone else to read, my father still withheld the truth.*

"Damn it, Dad!" I said, just as the door opened and the nurse walked in.

"Is everything okay here?" she said, and approached the bed and looked at the readings on the machines, checking to see that my dad was okay, that I hadn't disturbed him again.

"I'm sorry," I said to her. "I was just reading to him," and I held up the notebook so she could see I was telling the truth and she smiled when she saw it. "I hoped so much that he could hear me was all," I told her. "But seeing him like this, knowing he can't hear me, I just…"

I felt bad for trying to fool her this way, especially when she walked over to me, placed a hand on my shoulder and said, "I can imagine. It is a very hard thing to go through, but I know that he would be so happy to know you were here with him. And who knows what he can hear or understand? I mean, even if he just recognizes your voice, that will be a comfort."

I nodded and took hold of Rob's hand and concentrated on looking at him so that I didn't have to meet her eye. I had to play the concerned daughter if I was going to be allowed back again. And I had to be allowed back because I had to keep talking to him. I had to find a way to make him tell me the truth. To do the right thing, for once in his life.

CHAPTER FOURTEEN

I had just finished eating dinner when the doorbell rang. Suzie. She looked tense, the porch light casting a glare above her head that made her look worried and drawn.

I knew she would come over at some point. She was bound to be angry about my conversation with Cece, and I'd hoped I'd have an explanation ready by the time she arrived, but seeing her standing on the porch, I realized I was unprepared.

"Hey," I said. And Suzie smiled at me and asked if she could come in.

"Sure, of course," I said. And I stepped aside and let Suzie pass me, then closed the door. She headed to the living room, the house as familiar to her as her own, and I followed her and tried to think of something to say.

It was Cece who had initiated the conversation, wasn't it? I couldn't remember. But I was sure that Cece had volunteered the information about Jonathan. I had not pushed her into anything. I had not pried. It was just the way the conversation had turned. And I was sorry about it. If it had upset Cece, then I was sorry. That was all I could say.

I motioned for Suzie to take a seat and then I sat in the chair opposite her, regretting it immediately, because it felt as if we were on opposing sides. It felt as though I was about to undergo some sort of interrogation. Maybe I was.

"My grandmother told me you came by," Suzie began.

"Listen," I interrupted. "I'm really sorry. I didn't go over there to ask her about that. It just came up somehow, and then she told me about her son, and..."

"It's okay," Suzie said. "She explained it to me. In fact, she set me straight after I told her I'd told you never to talk about it."

"She did?"

"She thinks there was no point in making a big secret about it."

"Still, I'm sorry. If I'd known Jonathan was her son, I would never—"

"It's okay. How could you have known?"

"The papers called her Alice Hutton, so I never made the connection."

Suzie stared at me, a small crease of confusion tightening in her brow as she tried to process what I had said.

"What papers?" she asked.

It had slipped out without thinking, my need to apologize had made me jittery and for a second I didn't know what to say.

"I was tidying up the other day and I came across some old newspapers. My dad must have kept them, for some reason. I flicked through them because I was curious, and one of them had an article about Jonathan."

"Oh, I see. That's a strange sort of thing to keep."

"Yeah, that's what I thought."

"Then again he's probably not the only one to have kept things like that. It turned this town upside down and people here don't forget something like that."

"I can imagine."

She tilted her head and focused her gaze upon me, and I could feel the question coming before she even asked it.

"Is that what you spoke to him about in the hospice? When he had that attack?"

I nodded. There was no point in denying it.

"Listen," she said. "If you want to know anything about it then ask me. I can probably tell you anything you want to know. There's no need to upset your dad about it."

"I don't want to know anything really," I lied. "I was just wondering why he had kept those papers. I probably shouldn't have asked him about it though. I realize that now. I just thought, at first, he was connected with it all somehow and that was why he had kept a record of it."

"It's a small town, Carla. People know one another. Everyone here was affected by what happened, in some way. He would have been at school with those other boys, I can't remember their names—"

"Danny McIntosh and Adam Peterson," I said.

And she stared at me again and took a deep breath. "Wow, you seem to know a lot about all of this."

"Not really. Just what I read in those articles."

"Anyway," she continued. "The point is, I think it might be better if you didn't mention it to him again. During an attack like that, he suffers. He can't breathe. His heart rate shot up to really dangerous levels. So please, if you want to keep visiting him and have any meaningful time with him, then keep him calm and don't upset him."

She would hear from her colleagues that I'd been to visit Rob, so I figured I would be better telling her first. "I went to see him earlier today, actually," I told her.

"Oh," she said, and she smiled. "Well, that's good. I'm glad you decided to try again."

"I didn't mean to upset him the other day. I didn't realize he would react so badly. I just read to him for a while this time. He was asleep, but I think he could hear me, or knew I was there at least."

"I'm sure he did. We see that a lot. Patients relax a little when they hear a familiar voice."

"Still, I'm sorry if I upset him and your grandmother too. It really wasn't my intention."

"I know, and honestly, it's fine. I think she likes you. You remind her of Rob."

"You say that as though it's a good thing," I said, and she looked at me and laughed.

"It is! Anyway, I was wondering if you wanted to go out this evening. Maybe get a beer or something to eat?"

"Sure, I'd like that."

"Cool. Though don't get your hopes up. This place is no San Francisco."

And I laughed and told Suzie I was glad about that. "San Francisco's not always the place to be."

*

The bar was small and more modern than I imagined it would be. Whoever had designed it was apparently influenced by minimalist Scandinavian chic. The walls were painted a muted sage green that turned a sea gray in corners where the light was more subdued. One wall had been filled with photographs but there was no theme, as far as I could tell. Black-and-white portraits mingled with colorful panoramic shots of mountain ridges and close-up shots of flower petals and the bark of trees. I wasn't sure if I liked the overall mood. It was trying too hard, I thought.

Overhead, the lighting consisted of clusters of bare lightbulbs, all different sizes and suspended from cords of different lengths. The effect was a little dizzying and made me wonder how I would feel once I had drunk a few beers.

Around the room, the tables had been placed at random, as if the customers were constantly moving the furniture around to suit the size of their party. Each table was surrounded by chairs of natural wood with wool and cotton seating elements, all in those same muted, natural colors—sage green, wheat yellow, marshmallow pink. It looked more like a hip coffee house or bookstore and I had to laugh as I took it all in. I was surprised that Suzie would choose a place like this.

"What is it?" Suzie asked me.

"Oh, nothing," I replied. "It's just a bit too hip here for someone like me, I think."

Suzie laughed and took a seat in a small two-seater sofa, then took her jacket off and placed it beside her, leaving me to find a chair opposite her again. It made me feel that she was always defining her personal space. Laying down boundaries so it was clear just how close you were allowed to get. Friendly, but not overly so. And I wasn't sure if it was just the way Suzie was, or if she only acted this way when she was around me. A stranger, from out of town, who needed to be kept at a distance until more was known about her.

But I wanted Suzie to know me. Every time we spoke, I got the sense that here was someone I could talk to. Here was someone I could trust.

"Seattle is just over the water," Suzie was saying. "I guess some of their fancy ideas must have made their way across the sound."

And I nodded and laughed, not sure yet if Suzie's comment was a criticism or a joke. If the city was a place to be mocked or admired. When the waitress came over, I let Suzie order some locally brewed beers and a plate of snacks. "It's cheese, mostly," Suzie informed me. "But it works really well with the beer."

"We have places like this too, downtown," I said. "But I never went to them much."

"No? Why not? You're what, thirty-two, thirty-three? The same age as me? What do you think you should be doing then? Staying at home baking cookies?"

"I'm thirty-six, and I think that's what my sister imagined for me," I said. And Suzie gave me an appraising look and then smiled.

The waitress came with our drinks and the food and laid it out on the table between us, then asked if we wanted anything else. Suzie shook her head and thanked her, then picked up her glass and one of the beer bottles, poured it, and took a sip before sitting back in her chair with a satisfied sigh.

"You don't think your sister would like this place then?" she said.

I shook my head and poured myself a beer, then sipped it and enjoyed the sweet hop-filled tang as it hit my throat.

"Yeah, she would. We just see the world a little differently," I explained. "Gina's more conservative than I am. She likes home and family and that sort of thing."

"Yeah, well, it is important," Suzie said, and she leaned forward and took a piece of cheese. "I mean, family is all you ever really have, isn't it?"

"Is it?"

"Oh, sorry," Suzie said. "I didn't mean anything by that. I guess I was talking about myself, more than anything."

"No, it's okay. I mean, you're right. I know if you asked Gina, she'd say it's the most important thing for her and I can understand her reasons for putting family first."

"Sounds ominous."

"Oh, it's not meant to be. It's more, we had a tough sort of childhood and it leaves its scars, you know? My dad wasn't an easy man to live with, and when my mom left him, even though we all knew it was the right thing to do, it was hard for her. A forty-something woman with two kids to bring up. It's not easy. Gina wants to do everything she can to make sure none of that happens to her and her kids."

"No one can ever know what's going to happen in life though," Suzie said.

"No, I know. But David, her husband, he's a good guy. He gets it, you know, what's important to Gina and why."

"Lucky Gina."

"Yeah."

"What about you then?" Suzie asked me.

"Me? Not so lucky."

Suzie called the waitress over and ordered more beers. "You want to try a different one or the same again?" she asked.

"I'm easy. You decide."

I watched as Suzie placed the order. Something different this time. And different snacks to go with it. Crackers or something, I wasn't quite sure. And it struck me then that this place might be expensive, and I didn't have the cash to go throwing around on drinks and snacks in some swanky bar.

"I better make this the last one," I said. And I saw Suzie deflate a little.

"I've just got a lot of things to sort out over the next few days," I told her. "With the studio and everything."

"Hey, tonight's on me, okay? I think you need to let your hair down. It's been a tough few weeks for you. So let's enjoy ourselves, what do you say?"

It was so nice to be with someone who noticed these things and cared enough to do something about it. And so we stayed, the beer flowing easily and plentifully along with the chat. The night passing in a blur of easy laughter and clinking glasses.

*

The next morning, I woke with a parched throat and a thumping headache. I must have come home and rolled straight into bed, because I was still wearing my T-shirt and the curtains had not been drawn. When I let my head fall on the pillow, I saw it was smeared with mascara and there was a musty taste in my mouth, some stomach-churning mix of garlic and sweet beer. And I remembered then. Suzie and a host of swaying, glowing lightbulbs.

I lay back in bed and looked out the window at the tree that was fluttering in the breeze. The sky was not quite bright yet and when I turned the clock to face me, I was surprised that it was only six fifteen in the morning.

I should close my eyes and try and fall back to sleep, otherwise the day ahead was going to be intolerable. I had too much to do to be skulking around with a head like cotton wool. And a vague recollection of a plan filtered through my pounding head. Something about meeting Suzie over at her place to design some flyers I could then get printed at a shop in town.

God, I thought. *Why the hell did I agree to stay out, drinking?*

I buried my head in the pillow and tried to fall back to sleep, but my conversation with Suzie kept coming back to me. I remembered telling her why we had lost contact with Rob and the way she had stared at me, a tiny frown forming on her forehead as she listened, as if she was struggling to believe me. Because the man I described to her, was not the man she knew.

Every now and then, she would stop me and say, "Sorry, run that past me again. He did what?" as I listed the injuries my mom had suffered. The broken arm, the lost tooth, the ever-present bruises.

I lost track of the amount of times Suzie had told me how nice Rob was. How he had helped them with so many things. Little repair jobs that needed attending to around the house, heavy work in the garden, that sort of thing. And then it had been my turn to sit and frown and shake my head in disbelief.

And I'd asked Suzie the question that kept coming back to me. "Do you think people can change?" And Suzie had nodded and said that she did, and that in Rob's case it had to be true, because she swore to God that he was one of the kindest people she knew.

And I believed her. I could see it in her eyes, the way she was clearly torn by the idea that Rob could ever have hurt someone.

"He's genuine, Carla. I mean it. It's no act. He is a good man. Ask anyone around here, they'll all say the same thing."

"Then why did he hurt us?" I asked Suzie. "Because those things happened, Suzie, they really did."

"Oh, who knows. Things happen to people. That's what I believe, in any case. No one's born bad."

"Yeah? So you think something happened to my father to make him so violent?"

"I don't know. Maybe. That's often how it is, no?"

"You know what I think?" I said. "I think the guy you all know isn't the real Rob at all. He just learned to be nice because he had to."

"Nah, that's not possible," Suzie said.

"Why? Some people are bad."

"Carla, that's like saying it's in their blood or something. Like it's some sort of character trait that's passed down. A genetic blip you can never get rid of. I mean, can you imagine that?"

We had sipped our beers and mulled it over. But I didn't know what to say. It was too complex a subject for a Friday night in a bar. I didn't know my own father's family. My family. All I knew was that Rob's mom had died when he was a kid, and his dad was the kind of distant, authoritarian figure people run away from as soon as they get the chance. Rob never talked about him and became angry if you even asked him about his father. It was all off limits.

"I mean, think about it," Suzie said, the topic seeming to have caught her imagination. "That'd mean that you'd have it in you too. Like a sort of stain. I mean, that's just ridiculous, don't you reckon?"

"Okay, then what about the guy who took Jonathan?" I asked her. The beer drawing out the question before my brain had time to engage. "I mean, that's the sort of thing that makes me think it's possible, you know?"

And Suzie had sat in silence for a second and absorbed it and then said. "Well, okay, maybe him. Maybe he was born bad. A man who can do such a thing. To three little kids. He has to be an evil sort of person don't you think?"

"Huh? So you think it was the same guy? For all three of them?"

"Oh, shit, Carla. I don't know. Maybe, why not. Cece always thought so."

"Really?"

"Yeah. She always said it was impossible that there could be two people out there, who'd be able to do a thing like that, not in a town as small as this."

"What I don't get is that they never caught him."

"You mean, how can a town this size hide a man like that for so long?"

"Exactly."

Suzie shrugged. "People have strange loyalties, I guess. Cece always thought that someone here must have known who took Jonathan, but they kept it quiet for some reason. And I think she's right."

I'd gone to bed thinking about that. The idea that someone had kept that secret for nine years. Had watched first Danny go, then Adam, and had said nothing. Done nothing. And then, when Jonathan was taken, they had still remained silent. Just watched it happen again.

And I could feel the way that thought had left me restless throughout the night, the damp sweat of it there in the cotton of my T-shirt. And a little stray thought of Suzie's pounding in my head.

"He was someone's husband. That's what gets me. He was probably someone's husband, someone's father. Someone knew him. When I think about that…"

And I threw back the sheets and rushed to the bathroom, making it to the toilet just in time, the vomit and the bile retching uncontrollably from my stomach and into the bowl.

Someone knew him. It made me sick to think of that.

CHAPTER FIFTEEN

What the hell are you doing? I must have thought that a hundred times as I wound my way through the forest, the road ahead as sleek and black as a winter lake. I had not anticipated the isolation. Only a few miles from town and yet the density of the forest and the deep darkness was disconcerting. That a wilderness could exist so close by made me uneasy. I preferred it when nature, and every danger it contained, was far away.

But I could no longer resist the urge to see where they had found Danny McIntosh. I knew it was irrational to believe the forest could hold any trace of something that had happened so long ago, but as I pulled into the trailhead that led to the spot where Danny had been found, I was overcome again by the sense that a place like this could hold some sort of ephemeral residue. As if the trees remembered everything and everyone.

I looked up at the pines and sought out the light of the sky high above the treetops and realized I should call someone. Let them know where I was and what I was doing, just in case.

In case what? I thought. There was no one here. No one hiding there waiting for me. The man who had committed those crimes was long dead.

But there were animals too, I imagined. Animals I knew nothing about. Cougars. Bears. Moose. *Did they have those here?* I thought so, but I wasn't sure. *So close to people, to towns and cities, did wild animals dare to venture so close? Or did they know better than to stray too close to us?* We were the ones who posed a greater danger, I reckoned. All I could do was hope they were elsewhere. Up on higher ground perhaps, or farther away from the presence of humans.

I should check though, I thought. *It was stupid to walk into a forest with no sense of what was in there and no way of protecting myself.*

But if I called Suzie then I would have to explain. I would have to tell her why I was here. The notebooks, the newspaper clippings, the unsettling sense that my father knew something about all of this. There was no way I could call and tell her what I was looking for.

And what is it you're looking for then, Carla? I thought.

A boy long dead? Something hanging there still, in the pine needles, in the air, that's been waiting all these years, just for you to walk in and discover it?

And a fear I hadn't anticipated overcame me. I could still turn around. Just get back in the car and drive home, leave the trees to their secrets.

But no, some instinct had brought me here and I had to listen to it. So I pulled my camera off the backseat and strapped the bag over my shoulder.

The plan, if you could call it that, was to photograph the area and then print a set of photos back in the studio. I'd go to the place they'd found Adam and photograph that too. And then? I had a vision of the photos arranged on a wall or all laid out on the floor. I'd leave them there so I could take my time. Study them and get a feel for the place. For whatever it was I was sure I would find there.

And I looked again, into that damp, unfamiliar darkness, tasted the sharp tang of pine needles on my tongue. It was like a warning, of sorts, the smell of it. The forest letting me know that this was not a place I knew well enough; it was not a place I should enter.

It scared me enough to make me get out my phone and scroll down to find Will's name. If I called him, he would have my new cell phone number, but what else could I do? I sent him a text.

I've gone on a photo expedition. Just off the Red Town Trailhead in the Wildland Park. I'll message when I'm done. But, I wanted someone to know I'm here, you know, just in case.

A minute later I heard the phone ping. A message from Will.

Sorry, what? Carla, what the hell are you doing?

But I ignored it. If I answered, I would pause again and that would be it. I would never go in. And I had to. I would have no peace until I found out what had happened to those boys.

*

Somehow I missed the trailhead, but I could just make out a rough pathway through trees, a gap that wound its way between the pines and that was strewn with yellowed needles, their color like a beacon. The ground felt soft underfoot, as if the whole forest floor had been carpeted with moss, and every sound was absorbed. This was a place to disappear into. Where even the sounds faded to nothing. Occasionally a twig would snap as I stepped on it, and I would stop, instinctively, the way an animal would if it sensed it was being followed. Then the silence would envelop me once more, and I would have to move on because the stillness was too unsettling.

It took me a while to hear the sounds that were there. Distant birdsong, plaintive and haunting and unrecognizable. A cawing of some sort, but not like a crow. Some bird of prey, perhaps? It was moving away from me, I realized, its call becoming fainter. *Even the birds don't want to be here*, I thought.

Overhead, the pines shivered in a slight breeze, the sound in the branches strangely reminiscent of the sea, like the froth of a wave on a shore, and I looked up at the dense needle canopy and watched closely but could see no movement.

Up ahead the path undulated and then appeared to drop away. I looked at my watch to check how long I'd been walking. Only an hour. But it felt longer. The dim light and the lack of bearings seemed to have the effect of slowing time down. I thought I'd walked farther and longer. Yet there it was, no mistaking it, that dip there in the distance, it could only be the gulley that led down to the creek.

I walked on and felt my pace quicken as I hastened towards it. Though I was still not sure what I was planning to do when I got there. I simply stumbled on, over rotten tree stumps and moss-covered mounds, until the trees thinned out and the light filtered through, bright enough to startle me for an instant, the shafts of the sunlight radiating from above in beautiful columns of gold.

I had to stop myself from imagining something strange and transcendental—from believing that the sunlight was leading me towards something. But in a place like this, it was difficult to prevent my imagination running wild.

Okay, just calm down, I thought. *There's nothing here but trees and moss and sunlight. It's just a forest.*

But as I approached the gulley I felt the fear stiffen in my muscles. Because this was more than a forest, more than a dip in the earth, I knew that. It was also a grave. Perhaps the last view of the world Danny McIntosh had experienced.

I had imagined it ever since I read about it in the newspaper. In my mind, it was a fearful, terrible place, a vast hole into which things fell and never reappeared. A place where suffering occurred not only to boys like Danny, but to other creatures too. Deer and rodents and wildcats. In my imagination, they had all fallen into oblivion here.

But as I drew closer, I saw that it was nothing more than a deep hollow in the earth. A long, overgrown channel like a drainage ditch. It looked like it had been dug, rather than created by nature and the elements. When I looked around I saw it stretched into the distance in both directions and I wondered if a small brook or stream had once flowed here. A water course that had dried out at some point when the source became clogged and blocked with the moss and plants that seemed to grow here in unfettered abundance despite the darkness.

At the edge, I stood above it and stared into the hollow and thought about the man who had brought Danny here. He must have been familiar with the place and known how easy it was to access this site from the road, but also, how hidden it was, despite the proximity. When I turned to look back from where I'd come, all I saw were endless rows of trees stretching up to the sky and into the distance, the darkness thickening where the forest grew denser and older. You walked into a place like this and became invisible, hidden, lost.

There was no way of knowing if I was at the exact spot Danny had been found, but I thought back to the newspaper article and to a strange, sad little note my father had written in his notebook at the time. *Such a gloomy glade, such a lonely place to be left behind.*

And I could feel it. The same loneliness, the same sad defeat. If it wasn't here, then it was close. And for the first time since I had walked into the forest the fear left me and was replaced by a deep and overwhelming sadness, the emotion sudden and uncontrollable.

Poor Danny. This was not a place to die. The beauty of it was too melancholy, too oppressive, too close to the earth, and whatever lay under that soil. Some sort of hell, that was what I thought.

For a twelve-year-old boy it must have been terrifying to have been brought to this dark isolation. *He would have known*, I thought. *He would have understood that this was how it ended. This place was not a place for the living.*

And who did he think of at that moment, I wondered, *as he looked at the trees and smelled the earthy moistness of the moss and leaf litter?*

Did he think of his mother and cry out to her? Did he hope, in some small chamber of his heart, that his father would find him, protect him, and carry him home?

Or was he already dead?

The thought stunned me, because as soon as it entered my head, I knew it was true. The certainty was overpowering. Danny had been brought here to be discarded. Thrown away like some unwanted junk. No longer a boy, just a problem to be gotten rid of.

I knew it was an unfounded thought. My imagination taking over and convincing me of something which had no basis in fact. But it had taken root, long before I came here, I realized. I knew before I walked into this place that this was how it had happened. Danny, bundled up into a sheet and carried here at night or in the camouflaging gray of early morning.

I knew, because I'd been told about it by my father. In his own words written in his notebook, their meaning uncertain and undefined, until now. But here, in the place where Danny had been laid down in the dirt, I understood what he meant when he had written those words.

It's so cold there in the dark, under the trees. No one can hear you. No one can see you. The cars drive by and they don't know you're there. It's a good place to hide. Somewhere no one goes looking. Because it's dangerous. Everyone knows it. And the bears follow their noses.

I read that as something he had imagined. A frightened child empathizing with a boy his own age. The notes on the page a sign of how hopeless he felt and how sad. There had been something touching about it and when I read it I felt myself take a step closer to my father, to that young boy he once was. I had wanted to embrace him and comfort him and let him know I understood his fear and his confusion. In the horror he imagined, I saw the very human sadness in the face of inexplicable trauma. My father was imagining Danny's fate in such intricate detail because he felt it, at some deep level, and needed to get it down on the page as a way of processing it and coping with it.

But now, a question had arisen that made me wonder if what he had written was not the product of a sympathetic mind, but something unimaginably awful. He had not needed to imagine what happened to Danny, because the notebook was not a fiction. It was a clear reporting of the facts. Facts written and recorded by a witness. Or a participant.

I slipped my camera bag from my shoulder and unzipped it, taking out the camera and turning it on, adjusting the settings to the light and snapping a few shots to test the different apertures and shutter speeds. When I was happy with the exposure I started taking shots of the location. Walking along the gulley, looking up at the canopy of trees, catching the blue of the distant sky as it shone through. I photographed the moss in close up, the tiny flowers that bloomed among it, which I had failed to notice at first. I took shots of the tree bark, cracked like a thickened skin that had developed in the face of the unrelenting elements.

I tried to capture as much of the place as I could so that I could take the images home with me and print them out, then set them side by side as I re-read the description of this place that my father had written all those years ago.

I needed to be sure that what I was looking at was the same place he described, the same place he had been. This dark and lonely hollow where Danny McIntosh had been left to rot away to nothing.

And what if it is the same place? I thought. *What if your father did come here years ago, with Danny? What are you going to do then, Carla? Huh? What the hell are you going to do then?*

*

Danny McIntosh, April 1963

That kid. I'd seen him at school. Robert, I think his name is. He's in the year below me, I think, but I'd never really spoken to him until today.

He was there on the road, watching me as I tried to get the fish back into the bag. I don't know what I did. I tripped on a crack in the road or something, I guess. Fell flat on the ground and busted my knee and saw the fish fall out of the bag and scatter all over the place. I was picking them up and trying not to stand on my bloodied leg, when he walked over to me and asked if I was okay. If I needed help.

And I told him my leg was busted but if he could help me get the fish back in the bag then I'd really appreciate it. And he gathered up the fish and then hitched the bag over his shoulder and asked me if I had far to go. Couple of miles or so, I told him. And he looked at my leg and shook his head and said I should come with him and get it seen to. His mom could help clean it up and then his dad could drive me home if I wanted. I told him it was okay. It was too much fussing and I'd come this far so there was no need to make any trouble. He gave the bag to me when I asked for it and then watched me as I started off back down the road.

Every step hurt. My knee flaring and burning and when I looked down I saw a hole had ripped through the cotton of my pants and the blood was visible. Little grains of stone and dirt lodged there under the skin. It needed cleaning, I could see that. It was the kind of bloody mess my mom was always worrying about. Germs terrified her. There were things in the soil that could kill you. She always said that. Every tumble I took, every scrape, every knock, she was always right there with hot water and some stinging lotion that stained my skin brown and made me wince—the cleaning always worse that the fall itself. A gash like this would send my mom into a frenzy.

I heard him walking behind me, his feet shuffling on the gravel as if he was trying to keep his distance but wanted me to know he was still there. So I turned to face him and asked him what he was doing. Just going home, he said. Then he came up beside me and walked with me, looking at my leg every now and then and saying nothing, even though I knew what he was thinking. That it was dumb to keep walking. That I should take up his offer and have his mom take a look at it. Clean me up. Let his dad get me home.

"You catch much?" he asked me. And I told him he'd pretty much seen it all when he gathered it up and put it back in the bag. "Not a bad haul," he said. And I nodded. Then we walked ten minutes or so in silence, because I didn't want to talk, I just wanted to keep moving and not think about my knee. I guess he was quiet because he was shy or something. But that was okay.

When he stopped I kept shuffling on, and he called out to me and said he was close to his house and asked me again if I was sure I didn't want any help.

"You're walking slower, if you ask me," he said.

I hadn't asked him. But I knew he was right. The pain in my knee was growing and I could feel it swelling and stretching the fabric of my pants so that it felt tighter and tighter.

And I thought, *what the heck*. I might as well go and get my leg fixed up and then wait for his dad to take me home. I was close now, so maybe I wouldn't even need the ride. I could walk back if his mom fixed me up properly. So I said to him, okay, if he was sure his mom wouldn't mind then I'd go with him. And he nodded and looked a little worried. Something in his eyes, like he'd been the one to hurt me or something and not the ground and the gravel.

Maybe it was a warning. But I didn't see it that way. Why would I? I just wanted his help and to be on my way and that was what he was offering me.

His mom wasn't home though, and the place was dark. All the lights out even though it was getting close to early evening. "The corners of the rooms need lighting." That was what my mom always said when she flicked the switches and saw my dad frowning at her. He thought it was a waste of energy to light a room before it was dark out. But when I saw this place, all those dark corners, I knew my mom was right.

When I turned around, Robert was gone, and I called out to him, but he didn't reply. And when I went to go and find him, the door was locked. And that was when I remembered. Robert, he was that kid whose mom had died.

*

Back in the car, I checked my cell phone and saw I had three unread messages from Will and four missed calls.

He'd be mad at me now. Sending that message and then leaving him to panic and worry for close to two hours. I'd have to call him quickly, just to settle his nerves. Let him know I was okay but that I was driving home and needed to focus on the road, so I'd have to call him back later when I made it home.

"Carla!" he yelled when he picked up. "What the fuck is going on? Where are you? I've been calling every number I have for you for almost two hours now."

"I'm okay," I reassured him. "I just realized I needed to let someone know where I was, just in case something happened."

"Carla, I checked that roadside point you gave me. It's in the middle of fucking nowhere. What the hell were you thinking going out there alone like that?"

"I just wanted to get some shots of the forest, for a project I have an idea for. You should see this place, it's spectacular, so…"

"Oh, Carla, come on. Don't give me some spiel."

"I'm not. Honestly, I'm not. Anyway, when I got there it was a little wilder than I realized so I thought I better have a backup. I was nervous, that's all. I'm not used to places like this. Geez, I was just trying to do the right thing."

"What? Sending a text and then falling silent for two hours. You call that doing the right thing?"

He was about to hang up, I could hear it in the pitch of his voice; it always rose a couple of octaves when he got angry.

"I'm sorry," I said. "You're right. It was stupid and inconsiderate. I'm really sorry."

There was silence at the other end of the line, and I heard him breathing. Long and slow. He was composing himself, because he knew if he spoke immediately he would say something he regretted. When he finally spoke, his voice was lower and quieter.

"Are you going to tell me what this is all about then?" he asked. "I mean, it must be important if you felt you could give up your cell phone number."

"It's complicated," I told him, ignoring his snarky comment.

And I heard him sigh, as if he was tired of hearing me say this.

"Listen, I'm driving, and I'm frightened something is going to jump out on the road in front of me, a damn moose or something. I'll call you when I get home, okay?"

"You'd better."

"Will, I promise, okay?"

"Fine. And, Carla?"

"Yeah?"

"Think about what you do, you know? To the people who care."

"Will, I wasn't about to get eaten by a mountain lion in there or anything."

"You see. That's what I mean. Why do you need to be so flippant?"

"Okay, sorry. Again. I'll call you as soon as I get back, okay?"

"When'll that be?"

"Half an hour, something like that."

"Okay, half an hour."

Then he hung up, just to be sure I didn't back out of it. Which was a problem, because it meant I only had about ten miles or so to think about what I was going to tell him.

"Hey, I think my dad was involved in a series of murders back in the sixties and I might need your help trying to find out what happened."

It was an absurd thought. An impossible request. And yet. That was the gist of it. That was what I thought. I needed Will, whether I liked it or not. He was the only person who would listen to me.

When I got home I saw the answering machine blinking in the darkness, alerting me to more of Will's messages.

I dropped my bags in the hallway and walked over to the machine, flicking through each message in turn and deleting them immediately, not even bothering to listen to what Will had to say. But when the last message was erased I was struck by an unexpected regret. My nonchalance in the face of his concern was not my most appealing trait, I'd had to admit. After all, what was he doing? Just showing concern. Caring about me. Worrying about me. Why could I never just accept that? Why did I always push it away as nothing more than neuroticism on his part?

I headed to the kitchen to make some coffee and a sandwich. I needed to refuel before I called him. Spending half the day in the forest had exhausted me, not just physically but emotionally. I'd run in there all gung-ho and careless, thinking it was just another excursion. Treating it as a photography trip, nothing more. It was impressive the way I could convince myself to do irresponsible things sometimes.

In the fridge I was relieved to see that I still had enough to rustle up a decent chicken sandwich, but tomorrow I really was going to have to go to the store. I sat at the table to eat and make a shopping list, taking my time writing each item, as if the construction of such a basic thing required such dedicated concentration. Putting off calling Will because I still didn't know how to explain.

When the phone rang in the hallway, it was a relief. Will's patience had run out and now I was saved from confronting the dilemma.

"Hey, I was just about to call you," I lied.

"That was more than half an hour, so I thought I'd better take the initiative."

"Sorry, I just needed to get some food inside me and some coffee. I was out there too long."

I pulled up the little wooden chair my dad had set beside the telephone table, and set my mug of coffee down, then waited for Will to say something.

"So," he said. "Are you going to tell me why you were running around in the pines all afternoon, or do you want me to guess?"

I took a sip of coffee and decided all I could do was explain it as best I could and hope that he didn't think I'd lost my mind up here in the strange and unfamiliar air of the Pacific Northwest.

"Listen," I said. "Before I start I just want to give you the option to change your mind. Because it's all pretty weird and fucked up and I may even have the whole thing wrong and be imagining things that simply didn't happen because I'm desperate to find answers, to figure out who my father was and why he was the way he was, and maybe all of this is some sort of deluded quest that I should just give up on now because—"

"Shit, Carla," Will interrupted. "Slow down, will you? I have no idea what you're talking about."

I let my head fall back against the wall and sat there for a moment in the gloomy half-light and saw that the day was already falling into evening and I hadn't even noticed.

"Carla," I heard Will say. "Are you okay?"

"This is going to sound really weird, but is there any chance you could maybe come up here? I could really do with your help."

And he said yes too quickly. I was aware of that. Aware too what it meant. That I had inadvertently raised his hopes. But the thing was, I thought I felt a little pang burst through my chest after I put the phone down.

He was on his way, and it didn't worry me. If anything, I felt something close to longing.

CHAPTER SIXTEEN

I don't know what I was expecting. Some sort of revelation, I guess. But I'd been staring at the photos pinned to the board for almost an hour and it was becoming clear that all I had was a loose collection of images of pine trees and the forest floor.

If Danny McIntosh was in there, then he was hiding from me, his long-silenced voice incapable of telling me anything.

Shit, I thought. *What the hell did you think you were going to find? This is batshit crazy, Gina was right.*

But I kept the photos pinned to the board and decided to carry on with the project, even if it was a useless thing to do.

On the drive home I'd stopped for gas and noticed a map in the station shop when I went to pay. It was pretty large scale, but it detailed the national park and the hiking routes and drives in and around the Seattle area, so I bought it, thinking I could use it to find my way around if I decided to keep going with my search. But when I got home and unfolded it, for some reason it reminded me of those maps you see in TV shows, where the lead detective gathers his team in the investigation room and shows them a board of relevant information. The map always has places of interest highlighted, and photos are pinned around it showing what had happened where, and lines of red string stretch from point to point, in an attempt to try and determine unseen connections. Pattern recognition a key skill when it comes to hunting down criminals.

And it gave me an idea. I could pin it to the wall, beside the photo board and then do the same thing as the detectives in those

TV shows. I'd mark out where the boys had been found, overlay my photos, pin up the notes from the newspapers and the notebooks and then see if it revealed anything.

I took a pin from a box I'd bought at the stationery store, and stuck it in the map, at the spot where Danny had been found. I had no photo of him. For whatever reason, the newspapers had never printed one. I guessed his family had asked them not to. Or maybe they just assumed that in a small town, there was no need to print a photo of a boy everyone knew?

It was a shame though, because I would have liked to have seen his face. To be able to see the boy beyond the headline. The boy he was before he became a victim. All I had were the descriptions from the paper: four foot ten, dark hair, brown eyes, medium build, twelve years old. It wasn't much to go on and it made him seem like a ghost. Without a photo, he could almost be an imaginary boy. A character from a book or a film. And I needed him to feel more real than that. I wanted to be able to see who I was doing this for.

I'd have to ask Will if he could try and find a photo for me. There must be one in an archive somewhere. Perhaps a school yearbook, or some police file that had gone out at the time, in other states perhaps. I'd already decided that I was going to ask him to get the details of how they had died. Autopsy reports perhaps, or a coroner's report. Something like that. I had no idea how to go about looking for those kinds of things, and even the idea of having to make enquiries filled me with anxiety. But Will was used to it. He must have investigated and reported on tens, if not hundreds, of deaths for the *Chronicle*. He'd have no problem asking questions and tracking the information down.

But first I'd have to ask him. First, I'd have to explain why I wanted such gruesome details.

He'd know, of course, the way he always did, that it wasn't just some mission to discover the truth that I was on. It wasn't a mystery I needed to solve for those boys alone. There was something else going on, something I still didn't feel comfortable admitting to myself. But I would have to confront it, if I was to be able to look Will in the eye and answer his questions honestly and confidently.

I looked over at the box that sat on the desk, the golden whorls of the walnut wood glistening in the afternoon sunlight. Each little spark and flicker of light beckoning to me. Saying, "Open me, open me."

I'd been putting it off. Those notebooks. My father's childish handwriting. The strangeness of the notes he made. I knew he had to have a reason. Something more than morbid curiosity.

And now I had to discover what it was.

*

You did it again. I thought you wouldn't. But you did. You did it again. Why? Why are you always so bad?

I had read those lines weeks ago but hadn't understood what they meant and I'd pushed it to the back of my mind where my subconscious had taken over. My brain quietly processing the significance and working through it to try and make some sense of it all. I wasn't prepared when they suddenly struck me without warning.

The tone of it. So personal. Beseeching whoever he was addressing. Begging them. Because he thought they could hear him. Because he thought they would understand him. It was strange, almost as if he thought he could speak directly to the killer. *As if he knew them*, I thought.

And a shiver ran down my spine when I thought of that. He knew them. The more I thought about that, the truer it became. Though it made no sense. Rob was just a kid when Adam was killed. How could he know a killer? How could he come into contact with someone so vile and dangerous?

And then a memory collapsed upon me. My father in the kitchen, busy with something, while I stood in the doorway watching him. I had a question, but I dared not approach him because he was muttering to himself and walking around the room like a tiger in a zoo that had been caged for too long. He was agitated and I knew better than to approach him in this state. I should have turned and walked away immediately, but I was transfixed and intrigued, because he seemed to be in a trance and completely unaware of my presence as I loitered in the doorway. So I leaned in and tried to catch what he was saying.

Oh, you shouldn't have done that. You know you shouldn't have done that. It was so bad. So fucking bad. You're bad, Rob Allen. You truly are. You're bad.

And I thought of my mom. Her bruises. Her cries. Her sad face and her quiet voice. He was talking about her. About the things he did to her. The hurt he caused. The pain. And for a second, I was happy to watch him, happy to listen. I thought I was watching him suffer for what he had done. He was pacing that room, filled with regret. He felt shame, and that could only be a good thing. Because shame was a step towards becoming kinder, that was what I believed. First you had to understand that what you had done was wrong, and only then could you go about seeking forgiveness for it.

And I wanted to walk towards him and put my hand on his shoulder and tell him that it would all be okay. That we would help him. That we would forgive him. But when I took a step closer and crossed the threshold into the room, I broke whatever spell it was he was under and he turned to face me and blinked for a second as if he needed to familiarize himself with his surroundings and with my face. I watched as he gathered himself together and became bigger before my eyes. His shoulders expanding and his neck bulging, as if there was someone else there, within the shuffling, muttering man I had seen just moments before. Or perhaps he was simply reverting to his true self.

"What do you want, Carla?" he asked me. But there was no concern in his voice. He wasn't looking to help me out. The tone was threatening, and I took a step back and swallowed as I felt the panic hit me and the tears begin to prick my eyes.

"Just a glass of water," I told him.

He walked over to the cupboard and took out a glass, then went over to the sink and filled it. Not letting the water run cold.

"Here," he said. And he held out the glass to me and waited for me to walk over to him and take it.

When I took the glass from him I took care to say thank you clearly and then drank down the lukewarm water as quickly as I could.

I was walking over to the sink to wash the glass when he spoke.

"How long were you standing there?" he asked me.

And I froze. Because I couldn't tell him I had been listening to him. I couldn't let him know that I had heard every word he said. And I tried to speak, but no words came out. My tongue felt thick and useless, as if I had been stung by a bee.

"I asked you a question, Carla. Now you turn and face me and give me an answer."

And when I didn't move, when I didn't speak, he came at me and the force of the punch in the small of my back sent me reeling, the glass shattering on the kitchen floor.

"Answer me when I ask you a question," he shouted. And I felt my neck twist in a sharp angle as he pulled on my hair and turned me towards him, his face close to mine, his eyes glaring directly into mine.

"You're a bad man, Rob Allen," I said. "You really are a bad, bad man."

And I braced myself for the assault. Closed my eyes and prepared to fold in on myself. To curl into a fetal ball and protect myself from the blows.

But they didn't come. I felt him release me as if all the energy had suddenly gone out of him. Then he stumbled backwards towards the kitchen table, where he slumped in a chair and let his head fall in his hands. I stood there, immobile, not knowing what to do and watched as the shaking took hold of him. Silent at first, just a slow, steady shiver that grew and grew until it seemed as if his whole body was convulsing. And then, when it seemed as if he would shatter from the spasms, a wail filled the air. Something raw and animal. A wail that was filled with pain.

"Dad!" I cried out to him. "Dad, I didn't mean it. I'm sorry. I'm sorry. Please, stop crying. I promise you I didn't mean it."

A voice behind me making me jump.

"What the hell is going on?"

Mom ran into the kitchen and stopped when she saw Dad sitting there, shaking and crying. My words still hanging in the air, so she turned to look at me, confused.

"What did you do to him, Carla?" she asked me. "What did you do to your father?"

And then he stood up suddenly and looked at us as he left the room.

"She's right," he said. "I'm a bad, bad man."

Then he walked down the hallway and out of the house and left me standing there in the kitchen, Mom looking at me and waiting for an explanation, but I had none to give her.

And now those words returned to haunt me. *I'm a bad, bad man*. Like a truth that could not be silenced. I hadn't understood what he meant that day, but if what I suspected was true, then he wasn't just bad. He was closer to evil.

*

I couldn't sleep that night and after hours of tossing and turning I gave up and went downstairs to the living room and lay on the sofa, a cup of herbal tea beside me on the coffee table. I had made it in the vain hope it would help me sleep. But there was no chance of that happening.

My subconscious had gone into overdrive, filled with images of the forest and my father's words. The boy and the man had used the same word: *bad*. And the more I thought about it, the more unsettled I became. It was the way he had written those words when he was a kid that upset me. They possessed the same voice, the same energy, that he had shown years later, when I watched him talking to himself in the kitchen. He was admonishing himself on both occasions. The boy and the man filled with the same shame and guilt.

But if I thought I understood why he was filled with such anger as an adult, I was unable to figure out why he felt that way about himself when he was a child. *Did eleven-year-old kids think they were bad?* I wondered.

I had thought his diaries were simply the thoughts of a young boy reacting to overwhelming news and attempting to assert some sort of control over things. And if that memory had not resurfaced, that's how I would have understood it. But there was something about the tone, the way the words reverberated through the years that made me realize he wasn't talking to some unknown, unseen killer. He was talking to himself.

But why? I thought. *Why would a kid think he was so bad he had to write it down in a notebook? Almost as if he was making it official in some way. The words on the page an indelible truth, something he could look back at and read. He could see those words there on the page and understand there was no denying it. He was bad. It said so right there in black and white. It was like a confession, almost.*

I stared out of the window at the empty street. It was so quiet and still, the houses dark and everyone sleeping their untroubled sleep. The streetlights were dim and glowed with a cold blue light that gave the street an eerie tint, like an infrared photograph. And it made me feel lonely, lying there in the dark with no one to talk to about the thoughts that were troubling me.

If someone had been there with me I'd have asked them why Rob had needed to document his self-loathing alongside his thoughts about two murdered boys.

It was that mixing together of the two things that troubled me. Why conflate their deaths with your own self-doubt and anger? It made no sense.

Unless they're related, I thought.

And I wanted to curl up into the corner of the sofa and shut my eyes tight, as that thought took hold. Because it couldn't be true, could it? That my father was involved in all of this? An eleven-year-old boy? It was impossible.

But his voice filtered through again. Those words he had muttered to himself that day when he thought he was alone.

You're bad, Rob Allen.

And I knew then. There was no doubt about it. He may have been a kid, but he was a part of it. Those poor boys. He knew exactly what had happened to them.

*

I woke on the sofa, cold and with an ache in every bone in my body, and went upstairs to grab the dressing gown I'd bought a couple of weeks ago, the first one I'd ever owned. It was shocking how cold the mornings could be here and there were moments in the last few days when I'd longed to be back in California. The air felt different there, even on a foggy morning. Here the chill seemed to seep into every pore.

In the kitchen I set a pot of coffee going and tried to clear my head. Because if what I thought was true, then I didn't think I should continue. Not only with trying to find out what had happened to those boys, but with all of it. This new life I was supposed to be building, in my father's hometown. In my father's house. In this place where I now believed my father had played a role in the deaths of at least two, possibly three boys.

I didn't want to be here, if that were true. It was too awful.

But the fact that I didn't pack my bags and head south immediately was a sign of how strong the pull of that story was. Danny, Adam, Jonathan. For some reason I still couldn't let it go.

So, go and see him again, Carla. If that's really what you believe, then go and ask him.

*

The nurse was relieved when she saw me.

"Oh, perfect timing," she said. "He's awake and I think he's doing a little better today."

"Better?"

"Well, I mean, he's awake. Oh, he's going to be so glad to see you."

I wondered about that. If she knew what I wanted to say to him, then perhaps she wouldn't let me anywhere near his room. But I just smiled and told her I was glad I'd chosen the right moment to come and visit.

When I walked inside he was lying in bed, but he turned to face me. There was a tube in his nose delivering oxygen which hadn't been there the last time, and his skin had a decidedly sallow tinge to it.

"Carla," he said. And I bent over his bed and kissed his forehead and wiped his hair from his eyes. He felt clammy and smelled sour. The smell of sickness I realized. And for a split second I thought I'd better not go through with what I planned. Just stay for a while and chat and comfort him.

"I'll leave you guys to talk," the nurse said. "Or do you have another book to read to him?"

I didn't know what she was talking about at first and it took me a second to remember. "Oh, no, not today," I replied.

"That's a shame," Rob said, his voice barely audible. "I enjoyed the little story you told me the last time."

I looked at him unsure what to say and he held my gaze and said nothing while we waited for the nurse to leave. I could barely breathe as I took in the implications of what he had just said.

When she had gone, I asked him. "So, you were awake when I read that diary to you?"

He nodded and his head flopped back in the pillow as if even that small gesture was too much for him.

"What do you want, Carla?" he asked me.

"You pretended to be asleep, while I read to you? My God—"

"I wanted to hear what you had to say."

"Oh, really? Good, because I have more to say. I have so many questions, Dad—"

"Please, don't. I can't take it. You don't understand. Those notebooks. They're not important, Carla. It was just something I wrote when I was a kid—"

"It's okay, you don't need to talk, you only need to listen."

"No, Carla. I don't need to listen. Leave me alone. I don't want to remember. Not now. I've never wanted to remember it. Please. You should have waited until I was gone before starting all this."

And I realized then what he meant. He had wanted me to find that box, after all. But he hadn't reckoned with me finding it so soon. While he was still alive and aware.

"You need to tell me, Dad," I said. "You need to tell me what you know. What happened to those boys. I know enough now, there's no reason to keep it all a secret."

"Please, Carla," he said, and his eyes were creased in a frown as he pleaded with me. "Please just leave me in peace."

But the more he insisted I drop it, the more I wanted him to tell me the truth. So I pushed on.

"I went to the forest," I told him. "To the spot where they found Danny. It's exactly as you described it. I could almost feel him there. It's like he haunts that place still. A young kid, left to rot there like that. When I think about him—"

"You mustn't go there, Carla. Don't go there, the forest, the lake. It's dangerous."

"Is it? Tell me about it. What do you know, Dad? What did you do there? To Danny, to Adam? To Jonathan Hutton? Because he's up there somewhere, isn't he? Where you left him?"

He lifted his hand and I saw him fumble with a line and press a button, then close his eyes and take deep breaths.

"Dad, talk to me. Dad."

It was Suzie who rushed into the room. "Carla?" she said when she saw me there.

She walked over to the bed and looked at my dad and the readings on the machines, but he wasn't struggling and the readings seemed to satisfy her. I was about to tell her that I was just chatting to him, hoping she would simply nod and walk away, when Rob spoke.

"Tell her to leave, Suzie," he said. "I made a mistake. She's not welcome here. Tell her to leave. And don't let her come back."

"What is it you're trying to hide? Just talk to me. Please, tell me what happened. You're dying, so what does it matter to you? Tell me, please, just tell me."

"Suzie, please…" he whispered.

Suzie looked at me, unsure what to do, and I dropped my head, then stood up, resigned now to the inevitable. He hadn't told me anything, but perhaps he didn't need to. His reaction, his determination to say nothing, to send me away even, was all I needed to know.

"I'm sorry," I said to her. "I'll get out of his way if that's what he wants."

As I walked past her out of the room, she took hold of my arm. "You promised you wouldn't upset him. You told me you wouldn't talk to him about this. Damn it, Carla. Why?"

"Just forget it, Suzie, okay? Forget it." I pulled myself from her grasp and headed out the door. She would never let me see him again. I'd been stupid and now I was on my own. And as I walked away I could feel her gaze on the back of my neck. She was making sure I left. And she'd make doubly sure I never came back.

You're an idiot, Carla Allen, I thought. *A complete and utter idiot.*

CHAPTER SEVENTEEN

It was strange to see Will again. We'd been apart a month now, though it felt longer, because so much had happened in that short time. Enough to make me feel different. I was not quite the woman he had watched walk out the door.

He noticed it immediately. I watched him step out of the rental car and walk the length of the path up to the front porch and I could see it in his gaze, the way he was trying so hard to smile and look relaxed, but couldn't hide the slight wariness in his eyes, as if he needed to appraise me and figure out what it was that had changed.

"Hey, how you doing?" he asked, as he took the four steps up to the porch to greet me. And to my surprise, I moved towards his embrace and allowed him to hug me and plant a kiss on my cheek, which I returned. Then I took a small step back and smiled at him.

"I'm good. You know, considering. Anyway, come on inside," I said.

He walked ahead of me down the hallway and I noticed he didn't have any luggage with him.

"Do you not have a bag?" I asked.

He looked at me, slightly confused, and then nodded as he understood.

"Yeah, it's in the back of the car. I booked a hotel room in town. I figured, well, you know, now that we're not together…?"

And I felt myself blush involuntarily. *Fuck*, I thought. *He didn't even consider staying here with me.* And it made me wonder why I had assumed he would. He was right, after all. We were no longer a couple. I wasn't even sure if we were friends still. Though he had come up here when I asked him to. He had responded to my request for help without even questioning my reasons. But to be together again under the same roof? That was clearly too much, too soon, and I should have realized.

"Sorry," I told him. "I just thought, seeing as I have so much space, that I could help you out, save you some money on that at least."

"Right," he said, and he looked around the hallway and down towards the living room and the studio. "It does look pretty spacious."

"It's my dad's place. He grew up here."

He nodded and smiled and said, "If you prefer that I stay here then it's no problem. I didn't realize you were alone up here. I mean, this place is huge. I can't imagine you rattling around here on your own at night. Doesn't it freak you out?"

"Sometimes," I admitted. Though I didn't want to tell him how many nights I had walked through the whole house, closing all the doors and drawing all the blinds, and switching on all the lights. Trying to shut myself into one room some nights, when I felt too alone there. Too vulnerable. Unsure if what I was scared of was outside trying to get in, or already here, hiding in the shadows in some room, and lying in wait for me.

"You should get a dog, if you're thinking of staying here," he said. And I nodded and waited for him to realize that maybe what I really needed, perhaps even what I really wanted, was for him to offer me some protection.

But if he noticed, he pretended not to, and simply smiled at me and pointed down the hallway. "So, this way?"

"Yep," I said. "The kitchen's all the way at the end. We can have a late lunch, if you like? I made chicken soup."

"Ooooh!" he said. And I had to smile, because I still liked the way he appreciated a simple thing like that.

"Anyway," I said, my back to him as I walked away, just in case his reaction was not one I wanted to see. "If you do want to stay here then it's cool by me. I made up a room upstairs, so, you know…"

"Thanks," he replied. "I'll call the hotel after lunch and cancel. I should only lose the money for today, I think."

I walked to the stove and started ladling soup into bowls and made sure he didn't see me smile. I didn't want him to think that I needed him here for any other reason than the one I had asked him to come here for.

We took our time over lunch. Stretching it out with a glass of white wine and some crusty bread and cheese. It was as if we both needed the time to adjust to one another's company again. The conversation was slow and relaxed. I told him about the town and the neighbors, about the opportunity of work with the real estate agent and the plans I had to hopefully develop the photography business. He seemed surprised that I had managed to make a good start here, and pleased that I had gone back to the "one thing that made me happy" as he called it.

"I never really understood why you gave it up," he said.

I didn't know how to explain it. Why it was, a little over a year ago, I had packed my gear away and taken an office job. Money was the explanation I'd given him back then, and it was true, there was a financial aspect to it. But there was also the inspiration, or the lack of it. And a piece of me had blamed him for that. It was unfair of me, I know. But that was how it felt, as if our relationship had started to drain me of any creative impulse. I never told him that, because I knew he would call bullshit on me, and he'd be right.

Still, the truth was that on my own, my creative energy had returned. And he could see it.

"I really am happy you decided to do this," he said. "The business I mean."

"Yeah, well, let's see how it goes. I mean, hopefully I can make a living from here. I couldn't, in San Francisco."

"I reckon in a small town, if you have the right connections, it should be possible."

"It's funny," I told him. "I knew no one here when I arrived, but because of Rob I've managed to get things lined up. People here really seem to admire him."

"Oh," he said. And he fell silent as he tried to absorb this news. He'd never met my father, but he knew, from what he'd heard from me, my mom, or Gina, that Rob had made our lives unbearable.

"Yeah," I said to him. "That's been pretty much my reaction too."

"Do you know why?" he asked me.

"No. I guess he must have changed over the years. Either that or being back home in the town where he grew up calmed him down."

"Huh? So you think the scenery changed his temperament or something?"

I laughed, although maybe there was something to that. There were days when even I felt calmer here than I had felt in years. When it didn't unsettle me. There was also something soothing about the mountains and the forest.

"I don't know about that," I said. "I just mean that maybe you remember the little kid you used to be before you turned into the adult version. Maybe he just needed to be that kid again because that was how everyone here remembered him."

"Hmmm, I think you're reading too much into it," he said. "Sorry."

"No, that's okay. I might be. Why, how would you explain it?"

"Maybe it's just as simple as someone getting old and needing people. You have to be a better person when you need other people to help you out. Maybe after years alone, he just realized that all that macho shit was going to start causing him pain."

"Yeah, I guess."

"You'd still like to know who he was though, wouldn't you?"

It wasn't a question I felt comfortable answering, though I didn't need to, not to Will. He could see my reaction, he remembered all the conversations we had had in the past about my father, the many nights I'd been a little drunk and morose and had unburdened myself to him. He knew, more than anyone, the need I had always possessed to know my father.

We fell silent for a moment while I gathered my courage and he waited for me to start, knowing that all of this, the lunch, the small talk, was simply the prelude to the more difficult conversation we needed to have—the reason I had asked him to come all the way up here.

"So, are you going to tell me what this is all about?" he asked me.

And I nodded and let my head fall back as I sighed and stared at the ceiling.

"Just begin at the beginning," he told me.

"Promise me you won't think I'm crazy?" I said.

And he laughed. "Why the hell would I think that?"

"Because what I'm about to show you, what I'm about to tell you, plenty of people would think it was crazy. My mom and Gina said as much. And, who knows, maybe they're right."

"You'd never have asked me to come up here if that was the case," he said. "Whatever it is, I think you know you're not imagining it. So come on, Carla. Why don't you tell me what's going on?"

*

I left Will alone in the studio to pore over the notebooks and the newspaper clippings.

"I want you to read them yourself before I say anything. We can talk afterwards, and you can tell me what you think."

He nodded and looked at the box and asked me what it was he was supposed to be looking for.

"You're the journalist," I told him. "Look at it with a journalist's eye. I just want to know what you would conclude after reading them. And also, how you would go about looking into it, if you were going to investigate further."

"Investigate?" he asked me. "Carla, what are you talking about?"

"Just read it, and you'll see."

He picked up the box and opened it and took out the items one by one.

"Start with the brown notebooks first," I told him. "The ones with the newspaper clippings. Then read the others."

"In any particular order?" he asked me.

"No, it doesn't matter. They sort of repeat themselves anyway. But I still want to know what you think."

"Okay," he said.

"You want me to get you anything? Some chips, a beer? Something like that?"

He smiled and looked again at the pile of reading he had in front of him.

"Better make that a couple of beers, I reckon."

I left him to it and went to the kitchen to fetch the beer and chips for him and made a small plate of cheese and salami too. I figured he'd be there a while. When I set the tray on the desk in front of him, he looked up at me and I could see from the concerned frown on his face that he already wanted to ask me about the news item he'd just read, about Danny McIntosh, but I smiled and shook my head and said, "Ask me later, okay?"

He took a slice of salami and popped it in his mouth and said, "Listen, if you don't mind me saying so, I'm finding it a bit weird. Newspaper clippings about a child abduction back in the 1960s? What am I looking for?"

"Just keep on reading," I told him. Then I left the room and closed the door behind me.

It was early evening, and the weather was mild and inviting. I reckoned he would need a good couple of hours to get through it all, so I decided to take a walk around the neighborhood while he read. It would do me good to clear my head for a while. Just empty out and then come back home ready to explain to him what I thought was going on and what I wanted to do about it.

Most of all I wanted to pull myself together because seeing Will again had confused me a little. I hadn't expected to feel so relieved to have him here, and I wanted him to stay, I realized. Just for a few days at least. I needed him here. The trouble was, I was worried that as soon as he heard what I wanted to do, he would take off. Call me crazy and say he wanted nothing to do with it. And then I'd be back to square one, trying to solve a problem I was incapable of solving.

I wouldn't blame him if he refused to help me. But I hoped he would at least hear me out.

The streets, as usual, were pretty quiet. Just a few people out walking their dogs and the odd car pulling up into a driveway, their drivers home from work, looking tired and distracted, their every move automatic as if a day of thinking had stripped them of their ability to engage beyond simply putting one foot in front of the other, turning the key in the slot and slipping quietly inside. No cheery "I'm home!", no kids rushing to the door to greet them. Just a weariness that seemed to fit with the times.

I imagined the scene decades ago, back when Danny and Adam would have been living here. A place of homely cheeriness that no doubt only ever existed on television screens or in people's imaginations. But it persisted. Even half a century later, I could imagine it easily, how they would have run up those same garden paths and in through the front door, shouting "Mom!" and hearing her call back to them from the kitchen. It was a world away now, but it had existed once, I was sure of it.

Or maybe this was just a longing within me. It was what I wanted for myself. The childhood I wished Gina and I had had. The family life I wished my mom had had.

But there was a reason we had never lived this way and the more I thought about it the more I understood that it had never been possible. Rob would never have been able to live a life like that because it was a life he had never known himself. He had no example to follow. No mother there in the kitchen welcoming him home from school. No siblings to share the days with. It was just him and his father, a man he never spoke about. A man who had never existed for us. The grandfather who never was. I had always thought Rob never spoke about his own childhood because it was simply too sad, too empty. But now I had another idea. And I needed to talk to Will about it. I needed someone who had never known Rob, to hear what I had to say and tell me if it seemed possible, if it was an explanation for all the damage my father had caused.

I needed someone to answer my question: "Do you think it's possible my father was a killer?"

*

When I arrived home, Will was standing by the photo board I had made after my walk in the forest.

"Hey," he said when I walked into the room. "What's this?"

I walked over to him and stood beside him and pointed to the gulley.

"It's the forest where they found Danny McIntosh," I told him. "Or rather, it's more or less where they found him. I can't know exactly where it was, obviously."

He looked at the photos, then turned to me. "Is this where you were, yesterday?" he asked.

I nodded. "I wanted to get a sense of what that place was like. After I read my father's notes I wanted to see if he was talking about the same place."

"Okay, wait a minute. Your father's notes? What do you mean?"

"Those books I gave you, the diaries? They're his."

He had to absorb this for a second and I could see he was trying to figure it out, trying to calculate from the dates how old my father must have been when he wrote them.

"Are you sure? I mean, he would have been just a kid himself back then."

"It's his handwriting. A childish version of it, but it's definitely his. And I took them with me to the hospice and showed them to him, asked if they were his. They are."

He shook his head slightly as if he wasn't quite sure how to process this.

"But why would he write about something like this? I mean, when you read them it almost sounds as if…" He couldn't quite bring himself to finish the sentence. But I knew what he was thinking and I was relieved.

"I don't think I can bring myself to believe it either, but the more I think about it, the more it looks like the only plausible explanation."

"Listen," he said. "Can we sit down and talk about this? I need to think it through."

"Okay, but let me go get a drink first. You want some wine?"

He nodded and I went to the kitchen and took out a bottle of wine from the fridge and poured two glasses, then joined him in the living room.

"So," he said. "What do you think this is all about?"

I handed him his wine and took a sip from my glass. "I wanted you to tell me what you think first."

"I know you did, but why?"

"Because if you come to the same conclusion as me then I'll know I'm not mad."

"And if I think differently?"

I'd thought about this during my walk and had prepared an answer.

"Then I'd hope you'd hear me out and let me tell you what I want to do."

"Sounds like you've decided already what the plan is. So why bother with my opinion?"

"Because it's not just your opinion I want. I need your help too."

"Shit, Carla, are you serious?"

And I knew for sure then that he thought the same as me.

"So, I'm not crazy, am I?" I told him.

"Okay," he said. "Firstly, I don't think you can be so sure that your dad was involved in this. I know you had issues with him, but please, Carla, don't tell me you actually think that a kid, even if they did turn out to be an asshole as an adult, would somehow be involved in the abduction and murder of other kids. I mean, that's absurd. You know that, right?"

"Huh? I would have thought if anyone knew that was possible it would be you."

"Yeah, okay, but—"

"So you don't think they sound like a sort of eyewitness account?"

"Well, maybe, but..."

"No, please, hear me out."

"Okay, fair enough."

"I don't want to think those things about my father, you must know that. And I don't want to believe it either, even though every instinct in my body is telling me otherwise..."

"Instinct isn't evidence, Carla."

"Exactly. That's why I need you to hear me out. Because if there's any way I can prove it, or disprove it, then I have to."

"Why? This all happened fifty years ago. Why do you need to get involved in it all?"

"Because he's my father," I said. "And because I met the mother of one of those boys. She's really old now, but time makes no difference with something like this. Jonathan was her son, and she thinks about him every day. She misses him every day. And, I don't know, maybe I can help her? Maybe I can put her mind at rest."

"Jonathan? Isn't he the boy they never found?"

"Yes. Will, she never got to say goodbye to him. She never got to bury her son. Think about that. How awful it must be to know that he's out there."

"Wait a minute, is this what this is all about? Is this what you want me to do? You want me to help you find Jonathan Hutton?"

And I nodded and held his gaze. And he didn't look away. He looked at me and took a deep breath and said, "Fuck, Carla. That's some crazy shit you're getting yourself tied up in."

"So you'll help me then?" I asked.

And he sighed again, picked up his drink and took a large sip, then placed the glass back on the table.

"God knows why I'm saying this, but, yes, okay, I'll help you."

CHAPTER EIGHTEEN

"We're going to have to talk to the parents," Will said.

I thought it was a terrible idea. As soon as he suggested it I had my reservations because I considered it an unwarranted intrusion into private grief. The parents had suffered enough already without a journalist turning up decades later and asking to talk to them about their dead and missing sons.

"We don't need to involve them in any of this," I told Will. "There must be some other way of figuring this out."

"How?" he asked me.

"I don't know," I told him. "Just something else. I don't want to upset anyone."

"Listen," he said. "You asked me to come up here because you wanted my help. Because you didn't know how to go about this, and you weren't sure if you even wanted to go digging around. I'm a journalist, Carla. It's what I do."

"I know. It's just, is there something else we can do first?"

"Not really," he said. "I mean, we can wait for the coroner's reports to come through, but that could take a couple of weeks."

"You already asked for the coroner's reports?" I asked him.

"There was no cause of death listed in the newspaper reports. So I called in a favor."

"Okay, but why? I mean, it's not going to be helpful, is it? If we know how they died?"

"It will if the cause of death involved the kind of force a child could never have been capable of," he replied.

"Oh, I see."

"Carla, this is what you asked me to do. You want proof your father was somehow involved in this—"

"Or proof that he wasn't," I said.

"One way or another, you want evidence, in as far as that can exist after all this time. And that means I need to dig around."

"But if the reports show their injuries could only have been caused by an adult, then where does that leave me?"

"Carla, even if the evidence shows that a child could have done it, that still doesn't mean it was your father."

"And if it shows it could only have been an adult, that still doesn't mean my father wasn't involved in some way."

"True, but it would mean the probability he was involved is pretty slim, and, after all this time, that's probably as good as it's going to get, in terms of certainty. You're going to have to accept that you may never know for sure."

He was right, of course, but I couldn't help but feel frustrated by that idea. That the truth could be hidden forever if you simply waited long enough. Crimes like these, they deserved to be punished. Those poor boys deserved to have some sort of justice.

And the idea that whoever had done it may go unpunished left me despondent. If Rob was somehow responsible for this, in any way, then it meant he had lived his whole life knowing what he had done, had never shown any doubt or remorse. He had even come home, back to the town where these terrible things had happened, and he had lived alongside those parents, as their friend, as their neighbor, and had never revealed himself to them.

There was something so cold about that, so callous and heartless and wrong. *Was that the kind of man he was?*

But the answer to that was simple.

Yes. The man I knew was this way. The father I knew was a man who could live free of consequences. I had seen it as a child.

I had seen what he had done to his children, his wife, and the ease with which he had done it.

"Are you okay?" Will asked me.

"I was just thinking about my dad."

"You really think he could be involved in all of this, don't you?"

"I know it's just instinct at the moment. I know there's as much reason to doubt it as there is to believe it. But that's the point. The fact that the doubt exists, when there should be none, really, should there? I should never be able to even imagine something like this."

"So you'll let me look into it the way I think is best?"

"Okay. I suppose I have no choice."

"No, you do. If you've changed your mind and want to stop now that you know what investigating this will entail, then that's fine. You can absolutely do that. You know that, right?"

"Yeah."

"So…?"

"So, go talk to the McIntoshes."

"And I need to talk to Jonathan's mother too."

"No," I said, and I held his gaze and felt my jaw clench. "Please, leave Cece alone for now. Just until we see what comes up with the others."

"Do you mind if I ask why?"

"Because she's Rob's friend."

And I saw him blink as he absorbed this simple fact and figured out what I meant about it.

"I'd like to be sure first, that's all. I don't want to cause any unnecessary hurt."

"Okay, I'll be discreet," he said. "But she may find out anyway, so be aware of that."

"How?"

"If I talk to the other parents then she's bound to hear about it. It's a small town. Word will get around."

"Not necessarily," I said. "If we're discreet."

"Carla, think about it. These people, they're bound together by something unimaginable. And fifty years can't break a connection like that. Trust me, they'll talk to one another."

"Shit, then I don't know—"

"Hey," he said. And he came and sat beside me and wrapped his arm around my shoulder and pulled me close, like a parent consoling a disappointed child. "Trust me, okay? I won't do any harm."

And what else can I do, I thought. *I need to know. I need to put that doubt to rest.*

But it would cause a lot of harm. It would cause a lot of pain. How could it not? But I couldn't stop it now. Even if I wanted to.

*

Danny McIntosh's mother was a sprightly and alert woman now in her late eighties.

Will had suggested I introduce myself to her first and explain why he would like to talk to her about her son.

He had spent the previous day scouring the newspaper articles and writing up questions and lines of enquiry alongside a "reasoned argument" we could use to approach the families and ask them to talk to him. It was strange to listen to him plan things so meticulously, as if the emotions of such a thing were something he could put aside. But he had learned how to be this way, I supposed. He knew that this was the only way to ensure you didn't become overwhelmed.

Five years ago, he had written a book based on a true crime he had covered for the *Chronicle*. The case involved a group of teenagers who had formed a vigilante gang in an attempt to seek justice for one of their sisters. The girl claimed she had been abused by one of her teachers and, enraged, the boys had abducted him one evening and taken him to a remote location where they had tortured him for days.

A torture that killed him in the end. The case had been gruesome in every detail, but the last revelation had been particularly
horrific. The boys, it turned out, had taken the wrong teacher.
They had tortured and killed the wrong man. A married man
in his early thirties, with a young son and wife. I remember, at
the time, that it was this fact which lingered in people's minds.
Everyone imagining the shock and confusion of that poor man as
he was taken and brutalized without knowing why. As if this was
the most shocking thing about the whole case. As if the violence
would have been morally justifiable if they had taken the right
man. But I had always thought that what they had done was
despicable and wrong. Because whichever way you looked at it,
they had killed a man.

The case had drained Will of all his energy. His cynicism growing
by the day as he pieced the story together, his disappointment in
his fellow men something that became etched on his face as he
wrote. Every chapter of that book became a line on his forehead,
a crease around his eyes, a glum depression around his mouth.
It had been unbearable to watch him descend into that darkness
and I had tried so often to lift him out of it but was never able to.

So many times we'd sat facing one another in a restaurant or a
café and I'd stop talking when I realized he wasn't listening to me.
He had gone into a trance again, a strange zone he needed to enter
where he was closed off from the world. And it was a place where I
couldn't reach him, a place of refuge. I'd see his eyes glaze over with
a tiredness and a weariness and I knew it was better to head home.

And now I was asking him to enter that world again. That dark
and violent place that left you feeling detached from all humanity.
But he was the only person I knew who was capable of confronting
something like this. The only person who had the skills to delve
into it and discover the truth.

That he hadn't flinched when I asked him to help me, when
he understood the real reason I had asked him to come up here,

and had still said yes, was only something I fully grasped as I stood on the doorstep of the McIntoshes' home and stared into Danny's mother's eyes.

I was about to tell her that Will was researching a new book about unsolved murders and that he would like to interview her if possible. It was the plausible lie Will had come up with as a way to gain trust, but it felt unconscionable now that I was standing in front of her, and I felt the shame flow through my veins as I garbled my muttered introduction.

"I'm a little hard of hearing, so you need to speak up." Her first words to me.

"Hi," I repeated. "My name is Carla Allen. I was wondering if I could talk to you for a moment?"

She looked at me, her brown eyes almost amber, like a fox's, and just as wily. I could feel her evaluating me, trying to figure out if I was someone she could trust.

"I moved into the neighborhood recently," I told her. "So I could be with my father, Rob Allen."

"Oh, so you're Rob Allen's daughter?" she asked me. "I heard you were in town."

And she looked at me again, took a small step closer so she could get a better look, then said, "Ah yes, I can see it."

I smiled and thanked her and then waited. But she still wasn't sure. The door wasn't open yet.

"How is your father?" she asked me.

"I'm afraid he's very ill. He's in the Cascadia Hospice now, so…"

"Oh, I didn't know that. I'm so sorry. Did you come here just to tell me this?"

"No," I told her.

"Oh, then what can I do for you?"

"It's a bit personal," I said.

She took a step back then and clasped her hands together in a defensive position as if she knew what was coming.

"Go on," she said.

"Well, it's about my dad," I told her. And I could see her shoulders relax when I said it. The anticipated question not coming after all.

"Oh," she said. "I thought maybe you wanted to talk to me about…" And she paused, not quite able to bring herself to say his name in front of a stranger. Her son was too precious still, someone she wanted to protect and honor. "Then you'd better come in." And she stood aside and opened the door a little wider so I could step inside.

I followed her into the front room, and she beckoned to a seat in a large uncomfortable-looking leather armchair that had seen better days. When I sat down I sank a little into it as the springs gave way, and watched as she sat in a sofa opposite me.

I waited for her to begin but she sat there and looked at me in silence and simply waited.

"I don't know how well you know my dad," I began.

"Oh, not that well. I'd see him around town, and he went to the same school as my son."

"Right," I said. "I see."

"If you want me to tell you anything about your father then I'm not really the best person to ask."

I hesitated and smiled at her and when she stared back at me, her gaze left me feeling small, like a naughty child that's been pulled into the principal's office waiting to be disciplined.

I couldn't look her in the eye, I wasn't steely enough, and I turned away from her and looked around the room, noticing the slight shabbiness of it all, the worn, tired aspect of it.

The wallpaper was a pale pink damask with a faded pattern of fleurs-de-lis embossed into it. It looked almost like silk, like the sort of wallpaper you could imagine coming across in some beautiful French chateau. It made me sad to look at it because in that instant, I could imagine the room as it had been when it was first decorated, the expensive wallpaper glistening in the afternoon light, its pale pink tones lending a delicate, tranquil color to the room. But there was something melancholy about it now, as if it had been left to fade because the person who had papered the room needed to maintain some unspoken attachment to it. The paper itself containing an optimism that had long gone, the hope and aspiration of it all as faded as those silken fleurs-de-lis.

"Are you okay?" she asked me.

"I just don't know how to start. I thought I'd be able to explain it, but now that I'm here I can't seem to find the words."

"How about I get us some coffee?" she said.

She didn't wait for my answer and I watched as she rose from the chair and then walked slowly out of the room to her kitchen.

I listened to her moving around and took a look at the room while I waited. It was all so neat and tidy, a little spartan even. Everything you needed, but nothing more. It was strange, in a way, because it reminded me of my father's house. It had the same functional emptiness to it. But I hadn't expected it from a woman. From a wife and a mother.

I looked around for the usual embellishments, some feminine touches that would match the decorative wallpaper, but there were none. No photographs in frames, no porcelain figurines, or souvenirs from travels. It took me a moment before I understood why I found it so disconcerting: no memories. I could look for Danny in this room, I could look for signs of the past, but aside from the well-worn furniture and the faded curtains and wallpaper, there was nothing. No hint that there had been a family life here once. And I wondered then if it was the right thing to ask her about this past she seemed to wish to forget.

I was thinking of getting up and heading to the kitchen to tell her I had changed my mind, when she appeared in the doorway with two mugs of coffee.

She set one down on the table beside me and then went back to the sofa opposite me, setting her own coffee on the larger table in front of her. She didn't say anything, and she didn't look at me the whole time she did it, and again, I found myself becoming tense in her presence. She must have been a formidable woman when she was younger. The traces of that energy were still there in her movements and in her gaze. But it was when she spoke that the full force of her personality shone through.

She shifted in her seat to get comfortable, then coughed.

"So," she said, "Cece Hutton called me the other day and mentioned you. She said you'd spoken to her about her son, Jonathan."

I held my breath and tried not to gasp, felt my hands become clammy with sweat as I tried to figure out what this meant. She was probably going to tell me to leave without giving me the chance to talk to her at all.

"I may be old," she continued. "But I haven't lost my wits."

She leaned back in the sofa and turned to face the window, then continued.

"I spent a whole year sitting here once. A whole year just staring out of that window waiting for my son to come home."

I didn't say a word. I could hear my own breath rising and falling in time with her own. Then she exhaled and faced me and said, "It's Danny you really came here to talk to me about, isn't it?"

I nodded and shifted in my seat, torn between wanting to stay and talk to her, and wanting to flee.

"I can't think of any reason why you would want to talk to me about him. So, before you tell me what this is all about, let me speak first."

"Oh, of course," I said. "I don't want to be a nuisance or anything like that."

"Don't you think it's a little late for that now?" she said. And then she fluttered her wrist to dismiss me before I could answer.

"I'm going to start at the end," she said. "Because it's the end that matters most."

She paused to stare at me, that clear-eyed gaze leaving me disoriented again, then gave me a moment to gather myself together before she continued, and I couldn't help but wonder when she had learned to be so clinically calm. So aware of the emotions of the person in front of her. But she must have spent a lifetime watching people, I realized. Looking at the faces of the people around her for traces of something. Traces of him. Her lost son. She could interpret every flicker on a person's face, I imagined.

"My son was twelve years old when he died. But I assume you know that, so I won't dwell on the facts. What I will tell you about are the emotions. The consequences for the people that are left behind. What it does to them to lose someone they love. Especially when they lose a child.

"The details of a killing don't lie in the cause of death, in the police investigations, in the hunt for the perpetrator, that sort of thing. None of that matters in the end, if you give it enough time. Uncertainty and powerlessness. That's what it all boils down to. You have no control over things. Your son can't be brought back to life. Your life can't be altered in any way. There's only that one fact filling it. You will always be the mother of the murdered boy. And that's how you come to see yourself as well. That's who you *become*. A victim too. You don't want to, but that's what happens."

She stopped and took a sip of her coffee and then let the silence hang for a second or two just in case I wanted to say something. But what could I say? I didn't know what she was talking about. The things she had experienced were beyond my understanding. To lose a child. To have your child taken from you and murdered, there was no way I could understand the unfathomable amount of pain that must have caused her. This was one experience you had to live through to be able to understand it.

"What I mean," she continued, "is that I still stare out of that window every day. Just for a few minutes now, though in the beginning I could spend the whole day that way. It's where I look for him. But don't misunderstand me, I'm not harboring some strange delusion, I know he's not coming home. It's just how I choose to remember him. Pressing his face against the glass and tapping on the window to let me know he was home. Every day, he did that. And I can see him there, still. It's like an imprint. And it comforts me. Though whether it should or not, I have no idea. No doubt there are some who'll say it's unhealthy, especially after all this time. But the heart knows what it needs and if I've learned anything, then it's this. You know where to look for the things you need when the time comes. And that window, that's my solace."

She paused again and let her coffee sit on the table, kept her eyes on me. It was my turn to speak.

"Maybe it's better if I leave," I said. "I don't want to disturb your peace—"

"Oh, it's not peace. Don't be taken in by how calm I am. That's just the surface. Peace isn't something I know. Just the quiet sometimes. That's all I have. That's all there is."

"I'm sorry," I said. "I don't know what to say."

"No? Why did you come here then? For the same reason you went to see Cece?"

"Oh, no, that was an accident, I had no idea she—"

"Look, as soon as I opened the door I knew why you were here. And I thought about closing the door, but I decided not to. I let you in because I could see you had something to tell me, something you're afraid to tell me. And whatever it is, I know it can't be good. But trust me, I can absorb anything. I've had enough pain and grief to last me a lifetime. But I want you to know that if you change your mind and walk away now, then you'll leave me wondering what it was you wanted to tell me. And then I'll spend my days wondering if perhaps you knew something useful, something that would answer that unanswered question. Because you know they never found whoever it was that killed those boys—my Danny, young Adam, and Jonathan. And if you know something—and I assume that's why you're here—then I think you have an obligation to tell me."

I tried to remain calm and focus on what Will had told me just before I left to visit her. "Whatever you do, don't tell her why you're really there. Try to hold back and see what she's prepared to tell you. Let her lead the discussion, okay? And remember, you're an outsider, so she'll be wary of you. This is just to gain her trust and see if we can talk to her again later."

But Danny's mom was stronger than I had anticipated and I knew that if I told her even a little of what I suspected, she would demand I show her proof. And that was something I didn't have. Not yet. I had come here looking for answers from her, and I still hoped she could help me. *So a lie*, I thought. *Just a small one. Just for now. What harm would it do?*

"I don't have anything to tell you exactly, and I'm sorry if I misled you in any way," I said, and she stared at me, unblinking. Like a statue almost. Impenetrable and disconcerting. This was how our conversation was going to be punctuated, I realized. With disarming questions, unbearable silences, and fixed stares. She was clearly the kind of woman who appreciated straight talking.

I paused and hoped she would ask me a question, so that I could win a little time to figure out what I was going to tell her. But she didn't react, save to nod again, as if she was giving me a signal to proceed.

"I didn't really know my father," I continued. "My mom left him and after that, we rarely spoke to him. All I knew was that he had moved back to his hometown, into his childhood home, and that he seemed happy without us."

She smiled at that and nodded. "Some men would be better staying away from women, if you ask me. And fathering kids, well… No offense, I'm sure you're glad to be here, despite everything."

And I laughed at that even though it left me dazed. "Sure, I mean, of course I…"

"No need to think too deep about it, it was just a passing remark," she said.

"Right… thanks… eh…"

"Anyway, you were telling me why you're here. Or do you not know anymore?" she said.

"I do, I…" I took a deep breath and hoped she wouldn't catch the lie, that she would think my hesitation was simply nerves.

"My father said something the other day," I began. "When I was visiting him at the hospice. I really don't know what he meant, or why he said it. But I promised him I'd come and talk to you, so here I am."

"Is that so?" she said. "And what was it he said then?"

"Right, well, I was at his bedside and he kept mentioning someone called Danny. I didn't know who he was talking about. I thought maybe he was a little delirious, you know because of the medication? Anyway, he kept repeating Danny's name, and I didn't know what he wanted me to do, but he was so adamant. I mean, he's dying and he can't really talk for long periods, sometimes he's not even awake. But… sorry, I know this isn't making any sense. I guess, if I'm honest, I was hoping maybe you could explain why he insisted I 'talk to Danny's mom.' He kept repeating it, like it was really important to him. But, I can't tell you any more than that. That's it. That's why I'm here."

I was sure she didn't believe me. Her gaze was so unflinching I wanted to get up from the chair and run, even though that would confirm to her that the story I'd just told her was nothing but a lie. But instead she let her head drop, and folded her hands in her lap as if she was meditating and rocked back and forth ever so slightly.

"What makes you think it *wasn't* simply the effects of the medication?" she asked me, without looking up.

"Sorry? What do you mean?"

And she fixed that amber-eyed gaze upon me again. "I can't think of any reason why your father would say such a thing. It makes as much sense to me as it does to you."

"But don't you think it's a strange thing for him to have said?" I asked her.

"A little," she said. Then she shifted in her chair and leaned towards me. "I'm more interested in why *you* think he asked you to come here and talk to me."

"I don't know. I really don't. I assumed it was because Danny was a friend of his. The way he spoke to me, he seemed upset, as if Danny was very important to him. Are you sure they weren't friends?"

She looked at me, surprised that I was questioning her. That I had suggested that perhaps she had been wrong about her son.

"My son's murder was a sad moment in our town's history," she said. "And Adam's murder too, and Jonathan's disappearance. For a lot of people here, the loss felt personal. Almost everyone here at that time would have known those boys in some small way, and they were missed by everyone, no doubt, your father included."

"So you think that's all it was then, that it was just the medication and the memories combining and confusing him?"

"I'm no doctor, but it strikes me as the most plausible explanation, don't you think?"

"I suppose so. I'm sorry if I've upset you. I just thought there was a reason for him telling me to come here, that's all, and I… oh, I don't know… it just seemed like he wanted to talk to me about it. Or even to you. It felt like he missed Danny for some reason. That he *needed* to talk about him. I'm sorry, I'm really not doing a good job of explaining this, am I?"

"Danny was a year older than your father, but most kids back then were part of the same clubs and teams. Baseball, football, that sort of thing. I think they would have mingled often. Not good friends, not close friends, nothing like that, but Danny certainly knew Rob as a child, and I know Adam did too. Is that enough for your father to start remembering them on his deathbed? I don't know. Perhaps it is. Maybe Rob looked up to those older boys and couldn't imagine this happening to them? Boys have their own ways of reacting to things like this. Back then, no one really spoke the way we do now, about the emotional impact of things. We simply carried on. Anyone wanting to think things through—what is it they say now? 'Closure,' is that the word? Anyway, back then no one really thought that way, no one spoke that way. And like I say, I'm no doctor, but maybe, when you're sick and dying, your memory plays tricks on you."

"Really?" I asked her. "Something that happened so long ago? I can't imagine he would need to talk it through after all this time. I mean, my dad's not really the kind of man that looks for 'closure.'"

She smiled at me and licked her lips and cleared her throat.

"We all have things that have happened to us in our lives that touch us and affect us in many, many ways. 'Closure' is just a term, and it's not one I particularly like, if I'm honest. But it would be wrong to assume that Rob isn't as human as the rest of us."

I felt myself blush, a mix of embarrassment and anger. What she had said was true and I had perhaps been quick to judge my dad, but it felt unfair, because she didn't know what had happened between us. And she looked at me, and saw the color there in my cheeks, but she ignored it.

"I remember your father when he was a boy," she said. "He had no mother to comfort him so if he was affected by what happened here then he had no one to talk to, no one to turn to. His father, Sam, well, he wasn't the sort of man who was known for outward expression of his emotions. I don't know if that's what you need me to tell you?"

"He never spoke about my grandparents," I told her.

"Like I say, if his mother had been there at the time, if she'd still been alive, then maybe he'd have turned to her. Who knows? But anyway, we've strayed a little. You didn't come here to chew the fat about your father's childhood and your grandfather's emotional distance. Or, perhaps you did?"

"No," I said. "At least it wasn't my main intention. Like I said, I know so little about them, so hearing what they were like, even small things, is strange. It feels like I'm talking about strangers rather than my own family."

"You know, it strikes me that you really need to have a long talk with your father, while you still can. I don't know what it is that has come between you, and I'm not suggesting you tell me about it, but, if you want to know why he's on his deathbed thinking about Danny, then you should ask him, don't you think? I can't really help you to sort these things out."

I nodded and thought of the notebooks and the growing certainty that my father had an intimate knowledge of all of this. That he was closer to events than anyone imagined. He wasn't some boy sitting at home following the news and gathering the reports together. He was more involved than that. The emotions in his notebooks testified to that.

But instinct isn't evidence. Will was right about that and I knew it. And it was one thing to talk to Will about my suspicions. But it was something else to share them with someone I didn't know. And not just anyone. She was the mother of one of those boys. Whatever I said now could hurt her in ways I could barely imagine and that thought scared me and left me incapable of explaining.

And again, it was as if she could read my mind. She looked at me and folded her hands in her lap, a small gesture that made me realize she was composing herself, unsure perhaps of what she wanted to say. All I could do was smile, to let her see I would accept whatever she had to say.

"Listen," she said. "The woman you see sitting here today is not the same woman that endured that loss all those years ago. To lose a child that way changes you. In all the expected ways—the grief, the anger, the sadness—all of that seeps into you. You know that's coming, or you think you do. It's what we all know of grief, the weeping, the wailing, the scrambling around for someone to blame. But it's the other changes which surprise you. It's the things you learn about yourself that change you the most. And for me, the biggest change, the most enduring change, is that I'm no longer surprised by people. The things they do or say no longer shock me. That's not to say I don't get upset, that's not to say I don't wish that people would be better or kinder or more patient or whatever, but it means I'm more prepared for the disappointment. I don't let it touch me in quite the same way it used to. Before Danny was killed, I was often confused by the things people were capable of. I never understood why bad people had to exist. Careless people, the kind who do harm, what purpose did they serve in the world? But now, I can't pretend they don't exist, I cannot wish for the world to be the way I would like it to be. All I can do is try my best not to be like them. And that means being kind. It means listening and understanding and not judging. So, whatever it is you think you need to tell me about Rob, then please, don't feel you need to hold back from fear of upsetting me. I'll listen to what you have to say, and I won't judge you either way."

There was a slight change of tone to her voice, less sharp, gentler. She was encouraging me to speak and so I swallowed and took a breath and began.

"I haven't told you everything," I said. And she nodded, as if she had been waiting for me to open up and tell her what I really wanted to know.

"When I was at the hospice," I continued, "and Rob started talking about Danny, he didn't just mention his name. It was more than that. But I didn't know how to tell you about it, because it was so strange."

"Go on," she said.

"He started talking about a trip he made to the forest where they found your son."

She looked at me with those inscrutable eyes again and I wondered if it was wise to keep on lying to her. But I was getting close to something now, so I had to continue.

"He started to describe it to me. And it scared me, to be honest. It was his tone of voice. The way he described the gulley where they found your son, the small details. It was as if he had been there, had experienced it, and it had terrified him. Dread is the word I would use. The place seemed to have filled him with dread. It was definitely a place he did not want to return to. He was very clear about it. He kept repeating that. 'I never want to go back there, Carla. Never.' And the more I thought about it the more I wanted to know why he had ever been there at all."

"I wouldn't read too much into that if I were you," she said. "The kids back then, they were in those woods often enough. On a long summer day, it's only a bike ride away. They'd do it now and again, take off for the day and head up there. Danny would be gone from morning to early evening some days in the summer and it was only when he came home that he'd tell me where he'd been. Those were different times. Children roamed far and wide back then."

"I see. So you really think my dad was just trying to imagine the place Danny had died?"

"Oh, Danny didn't die there," she said. "He was taken there after his death. Whoever took him there had presumably taken him there to dispose of him."

I shuddered at the thought of Danny lying there, dumped in the woods.

"I'm sorry," she said. "I didn't mean to upset you. But, well, that's the truth of it. That is what they did to him. They took him up to those woods and then left him there knowing he'd be found quickly. Though some say it was to attract the wild animals."

And again I couldn't suppress a shudder. It overtook me and before I had a chance to contain it, I had let out a small gasp.

"My God!" I cried. And I must have stared at her in horror, because she was so calm, so passive, so unmoved by what she had just told me and I found her passivity difficult to confront.

"I've had a whole lifetime to absorb the more gruesome aspects of it all. Don't think it doesn't horrify and upset me, it does, it always will, but I can't cry about it all the time. I don't have that many tears to shed."

"But my dad, though, why would he still cry about all this?"

"You know what I think? I think what you really want is to know who your father really is. You don't know him, and who knows, perhaps you regret the fact that you have been estranged for so long. But if a dying man finds himself overwhelmed by memories from his childhood and you want to know why he's choosing to remember all this. Well, I've already told you, talk to him, ask him. That's it, that's my advice to you."

I couldn't respond. I couldn't speak, I couldn't move. Because when I thought about it, I wasn't sure anymore. Did I want to find out who Rob was? Soon he would be dead. Maybe I should leave it at that. Have that be the end of it. Whatever I learned about him, he would always be a man I could never love with all my heart, not after all he had done to us. So why delve deeper when all that could result from it was that I could grow to hate him more; what was the good of that? That was only hurting yourself. That was allowing him to keep on causing pain. There was no need to do that. To me or to Mom and Gina either, because they would be caught up in all of this, whether they wanted it or not. Any choices I made now, any decisions, I'd be involving them in the outcomes.

"Okay," I said. "I understand."

She nodded and stood up and started walking out of the living room. Our conversation was over.

When she opened the front door to show me out, she held out her hand to me.

"It was nice meeting you," she said as she shook my hand, her tone formal and distant. "If I can offer you one other piece of advice. In a small town like this, you're going to stir up a lot of trouble by opening such old wounds. If I were you, I wouldn't bother anyone else about all this. Me, or Cece or anyone else for that matter. It will only upset people unnecessarily. I'm sure you understand?"

"I do," I replied.

"Good, that's good."

And as I walked down the drive back to my car I felt her watching me. When I waved to her as I drove away she didn't wave back. She just stood in the doorway and watched me, as if she needed to make sure I was gone. Her stance, arms crossed, her brow knitted in a frown, her mouth a thin line of determination, made it clear she did not expect me to return.

CHAPTER NINETEEN

Will already had news by the time I got home. He'd received the autopsy reports for Danny and Adam.

I had slumped down on the sofa, exhausted after my talk with Mrs McIntosh. All I wanted to do was lie there a while and think about our conversation. I had forgotten that Will had mentioned he would be calling in favors, and when he walked into the room and sat beside me and started talking, I didn't listen at first. All I heard was the boys' names and I nodded and stared out the window until he touched my arm and said, "Hey, is everything okay?"

"Huh?"

"Did you hear what I said just then?"

"Sorry, I didn't. I think the conversation with Danny's mom has whacked me out a bit, I'm afraid."

"Oh, right. What did she say? Was she okay about me coming over to talk to her?"

"We didn't get to that, actually," I told him.

"What? But that was the whole reason you went over there."

"I know, but then we got talking, well, I'm not really sure what happened. But, it was clear she didn't want to talk to me about her son…"

"Huh? But you didn't need to talk to her about him. This was just a way to introduce yourself and ask her if she would talk to me."

"Yeah, I know. But it turns out she's a formidable woman still, despite her age. She wasn't happy talking to me. I don't think she trusted me. She certainly made it clear she didn't want me digging into all this."

"Damn, really? Why?"

"Look, I'm sorry I messed it up, okay? I just didn't know how to handle her and it's not that weird that this would upset her, is it? I mean, her son was murdered, I can't imagine that's something she wants to be reminded of, especially not by a stranger."

"Hey, okay, don't worry about it. We can always try and talk to her again when we know more."

"If there is anything to know. I'm beginning to think I've imagined all this. I mean, what do we have? A few newspaper clippings, some diaries. It's nothing, is it? Not enough to start investigating."

He got up from the sofa and headed to the studio where he'd been working all day. "Gimme a second, I need to get my notes."

I stretched out on the sofa and let my head fall back on the cushion. All I wanted to do was sleep a little and let the morning's events wash over me. I was tired of thinking about Danny and Adam and my father. I was tired of wondering just how bad things could get and wrestling with the doubt that I was doing the right thing, because it seemed foolish now. Foolish and impossible.

While I was talking to Danny's mother it had struck me that I was doing something more than just searching for the truth, searching for my father. There was a piece of me that was looking to be some sort of hero. The girl who could help Cece find her son. But sitting there talking to Danny's mother, I began to wonder why I needed to do that. Why it was I thought this was a task that had been laid out for me. I felt stupid and vain when I looked her in the eye and saw what a lifetime of grief had done to her. Despite her energy, despite her resolve, it was visible still, in the creases around her eyes and the sad tilt of her head as she spoke. It had become a part of her, something she had absorbed so that it was present without her being aware of it. Like eye color or the shape of a fingernail. And I thought she had noticed the same sadness in me too and it made me wonder why I thought I was capable of answering the question that had probably haunted her all these years.

Who killed my son? Did I really think I could answer that question?

The more I thought about it, the worse I felt. I had gone there and lied to her for no good reason. All because I had a hunch about something. It was selfish. And it was unnecessary too.

"Hey," Will said when he came back. "Let me tell you what I found out."

"Listen," I said. "Before you do that, can you answer a question?"

"Sure."

"Do you think what I'm doing here is worthwhile?"

"Huh?"

"I just wonder what it is I'm trying to achieve with all of this."

"I thought you wanted to know if your dad was involved in all of this?"

"I don't know if I do now. I mean, what if he is? What if he's …"

But I couldn't say it. Guilty. When put like that, it sounded ridiculous, outrageous even. It was a direct accusation.

"Listen, Carla. Why don't you let me tell you what I found out from the coroner's reports? Maybe that will help you figure out what you want to do."

"Is it awful news?" I asked him.

"I don't know. It's not pretty, if that's what you mean? Autopsy reports never are."

"Okay, then just tell me one thing first. Do they show that, in theory, my father could have done this?"

And he didn't even blink. He remained calm and impassive and looked me straight in the eye when he said, "Yes. In theory, you could draw that conclusion."

*

I needed Will to translate the reports for me. The medical termi-
nology was meaningless in places and only left me gaping with
incomprehension.

"I'm sorry," I told him, when he began to read Danny's report
to me, "but you're going to have to put this in layman's terms if
I'm going to understand it."

"Oh, sorry," he said. "I've been reading things like this for so
long, I forget it can be a jumble of jargon."

He set down the papers and leaned back in the chair, getting
comfortable before he spoke, and I watched and waited as he sat
there thinking, translating the medical facts into something I
could follow.

"Right, so basically both boys died as a result of a blunt force
trauma to the head," he said.

"Okay, and what does that mean?"

"In the case of Danny, the primary cause of death was a fractured
skull, inflicted by something like a heavy tool or implement, like
a hammer, say."

"Primary cause?" I asked him. "So they can't say for sure? There
could have been multiple causes?"

"He'd been dead at least three days before he was discovered
and there were other injuries that may have been secondary. So
the blow to the head is the most probable cause of death, but there
were other injuries that could have contributed to it."

"My God," I said. "Do I want to hear what those injuries were?"

Will let his head fall back against the back of the sofa, looked
up at the ceiling and exhaled. It was an answer in itself. He obviously thought I would be better off not knowing, but at the same
time, he knew I had little choice. If I wanted to pursue this, then
I would have to accept I would be confronted with truths which
were hard to swallow.

"Let me start by saying that I don't think an eleven-year-old boy would have been capable of inflicting such injuries," he said.

"What? Wait a minute, I thought you said it was possible in theory."

"In *theory*, yes. There's a small chance that a child could have done these things. But it's minuscule. Not impossible. But as close to impossible as it can get."

"I don't know if this is helping. If my dad could not have done it, just say so. Then I'll stop what I'm doing and leave it all alone."

"What makes you think your father would have been capable of something this atrocious? Because he was a kid back then, so..."

"You mean, why am I accusing a child of murder?"

"Yeah, basically."

"I don't know. Because I think he had that violence in him? Because I think he possessed it his whole life? I mean, you know the kind of violence some kids are capable of."

"And if he wasn't involved in any of this? What then?"

I just looked at him but couldn't answer.

"What I mean is, maybe you need to think about what it is you're really trying to achieve."

"What do you mean?" I asked.

"I mean, maybe you're just looking for a reason, some sort of explanation as to why your father was a piece of shit."

"I just want to know why he treated us so badly."

"And that's fine. But murder? Seriously, Carla. Is that what you think?"

"I don't get it. When I told you what was going on, you were interested enough to dig into it. You didn't think it was a crazy idea. You can't turn around now and say you think it's outrageous."

"Okay, fair enough. Then let me tell you about those coroner's reports. I'll save you the worst of it, but even the basics are pretty bad. But I swear, Carla, if you hear what happened to those boys, then I don't think you'll think it was your dad who did this. I know

I jumped into this thinking it was possible for a kid to have done it but once I read those reports, I changed my mind."

I nodded, then waited while he gathered up the papers he'd placed on the table, and then coughed before he started to read.

And it was true, I realized as I sat there and listened to him. No young boy could have done those things.

Danny: a fractured skull, a broken collarbone, a broken jaw, bruises to the abdomen and torso.

Adam: a fractured skull, attempted asphyxiation, a detached retina caused by trauma, missing incisors and molars, a broken nose, a broken arm.

Both boys had died from their head injuries, but the trauma they had endured had been caused prior to their deaths. A long, slow accumulation of pain that could only really be described with one word: torture.

When Will had finished listing the injuries, he put the papers back on the table, leaned forward in his seat, with his arms draped across his thighs, and looked at me.

"So?" he said. "What do you think?"

"I think only a monster could have done those things. Someone too cruel to be called human."

"And however bad your father was when you were growing up, that's not the word you would use for him, surely? It's not a word you ever used when you talked to me about him."

"No, it's not."

"There's still a 'but' there, I can feel it."

"It's just a doubt, is all it is. I can't describe it."

"Then let's start at the beginning. A simple round of yes or no. Okay?"

It was an old journalist technique I'd seen him use. When you get stuck, when you reach a dead-end, cut the story back to its essentials, and then see what you have left over, and take it from there. I never imagined I'd be at the receiving end of it though.

"Okay," I said.

But he could see I lacked the energy and the enthusiasm for it.

"I tell you what," he said. "Why don't I get us both a beer first and we can relax a bit before we start. I reckon you've had enough for the moment. Time out?"

I wanted time out for the rest of the day, but I knew he would keep on going now that he had the bit between his teeth. So I nodded and asked him to bring in some snacks as well. I was going to need to hit pause for at least an hour before I could answer his questions.

We sat and drank our beer and ate a few snacks and tried as best we could to talk about other stuff. I told him about Suzie and how I hoped we would become good friends. "I think having someone like her around will make it easier to adjust to living in a place like this." And Will smiled and told me about the neighbor in San Francisco who had got a little dog, some sort of terrier that barked all day and was driving everyone mad. "I swear, you left at the right time," he said. And I couldn't help but look a little sad when he said it.

"Anyway," I said. "Maybe we should get back to work?"

"Yeah," he agreed. "Are you ready?"

I nodded and waited for him to begin.

"Right, then let's start with the basic facts.

"Your dad was eleven years old when Danny and Adam were killed in 1963 and 1964."

"Yes," I replied.

"Your dad was twenty when Jonathan Hutton went missing in 1972. Correct?"

I quickly did the math in my head, then nodded. "Yup."

"Your dad lived in San Francisco when Jonathan Hutton died. Is that correct?"

"Yes."

"The injuries sustained by Danny and Adam could, in all likelihood, not have been caused by a boy of just eleven years old."

"Probably not."

"Uh-uh," he said. "No cheating. Yes or no."

"Yes," I said.

"Okay. So, the chances that more than one person is responsible for this, are small."

"Wait, where the hell did that come from? Are you saying there could have been more than one person doing this?"

"Okay, let me rephrase it. Your dad wasn't here when Jonathan went missing. And even if we assume that he was capable of harming two boys—boys who were older than him, I should add—then what are the chances of a small town like Newcastle producing not one, but two child-killers?"

When he put it like that, it sounded outlandish of course, but he had a point and it was a good one, so what else could I say other than, "None."

"Okay, so if your dad was in San Francisco when Jonathan Hutton went missing, and if one person is responsible for all of this, then this means, whoever it was, it was not your dad. Correct?"

And I could put forward an argument, I could try to contradict it, but with what? I had no arguments. I had no reasoning. The simple facts, the basic logic could only lead to one conclusion.

"Logical," I said.

"Okay, so what that means is this. I think your instinct was right."

"Huh? What? You just said—"

"No, let me finish."

"Sorry, go ahead."

"What I mean is, those diaries, those scrapbooks, I think there *is* something to them. I think whatever it was your dad was trying to do, writing it all down, it was more than just documentation, it was more than just keeping up with an extraordinary local story. There *is* something personal about it. You can feel it in the way he wrote about it. He knew something no one else did. But what I think you got wrong was to think that *he* was responsible for what happened. That he was involved in it all. We know he couldn't have been. Jonathan Hutton is pretty much proof of that. So..."

He paused and took a can of beer from the table and cracked it open, took a long sip from it, then wiped his mouth before continuing.

"So, what I think is that he knew who was responsible. I think he knew the killer."

He stared at me and watched as I absorbed his statement, waiting for me to shake my head and say it was impossible, or to nod in vigorous agreement. But I couldn't react either way. It was possible, what he had suggested. It even made a lot of sense. It would explain the tinge of fear I had sensed in my dad's writing and the weird sense I had had from the very beginning that he had been withholding something in those notebooks. Something terrible and frightening. If he knew the killer, then that would explain it.

"You okay?" Will asked me.

"Yeah," I said. And I leaned across to the table and picked up a beer and opened it, then drank it all down before I felt ready to speak.

"If you're right," I said. "Then what do you suggest we do?"

"I think there might be enough information for us to piece together what happened and maybe find out who was behind this."

I just stared at him. It was impossible, was what I thought.

"What?" he said. "You don't think we can do it? I mean, I thought that was what you wanted to do? I thought you wanted to find out who did this?"

"I did," I replied. "But the more I think about it, the less likely it seems that we can ever know what happened."

"No, you're wrong. I think this is doable."

"Shit, Will, there's no need to get so excited about it."

"What?"

"I just mean, you sense a story here and you want to get moving on it."

"Yeah, so? Carla, I'm a journalist and I'm a damn good one too. You know that. If anyone can help you out here, it's me."

"I know," I said. "Why do you think I asked you to come up here in the first place?"

"So, what's it going to be then? Are we going to do this or not?"

And I realized then what a mistake it had been to involve Will in all of this. Because I wanted to say "No." I wanted to put a stop to it. For the first time since I had opened that box, I understood what I had unleashed and all I wanted was to put it all back inside and pretend I had never opened it. But it was too late now. Will was never going to walk away from this, no matter how much I might want him to. He'd go it alone, if need be, and there was nothing I could do about it.

"Carla?" he said. "Did you hear me?"

"Yeah, I heard you."

"And? Are we doing this? We can find out what happened to them. We can help their parents to lay this to rest forever. I really think we can. So what do you say?"

"Okay," I replied. "Let's see what we can do."

And if he noticed my heart wasn't in it, if he was aware that I didn't share his confidence, then he didn't show it. He simply smacked the palms of his hands on his thighs and said, "Right, then let's do it." While I sat there and tried to suppress the growing sense that what we were about to do was wrong.

*

Adam Peterson, October 1964

I thought he was a nice man. He was friendly. I saw him talking to people all the time. He never spoke to me, or to any of us kids,

I don't think. He was just there, out on the streets. Someone you saw around without knowing anything about them.

My mom said that to me once. She said, "You can never really know who someone is. You can *think* you know who they are. But deep down inside, they can be completely different." I can't remember why that came up in conversation, but it did, and I think about it a lot now. About how right she was.

My dad had taken her to task about it. He didn't shout at her, but he did say, "That's not a nice way to look at things."

He thinks most people are good. And he's right, I reckon. They are, mostly. I know they are. But that doesn't mean my mom was wrong. You can never know for sure. The nice guy on the street, the one who always smiles and says hello. The one who stops for a chat and pets your dog. The one everyone thinks they know. It turns out he can also be a monster.

That nice man? He has hit me and kicked me and hurt me. And I don't know why. I don't know what for. I did nothing wrong. I never did anything to hurt him.

I asked him why. I said, "Why are you doing this?"

And he stopped. He stood over me and looked at me the way you'd look at a dog that doesn't understand why you have given it a beating. It wasn't pity I saw in his eyes. It was more like he was curious. Like he wanted to know why I didn't understand. I could see he thought I was stupid. That I would never be able to understand why I needed to be hurt this way. And he didn't explain it to me. He just stood over me, his face empty of expression, staring at me like I was a strange, alien sort of being. Then he shrugged and turned away from me and walked up the stairs into the house. Turning off the light and leaving me in darkness again. Leaving me to think about things. To think about the reasons why.

But I know now what the reason is, and it is worse than anything my mom could have imagined. It's not that you can never know someone. It's more that some people are unknowable. And they're unknowable because they're not like us. We can never understand them because what they are, are monsters. What they are, is evil.

And Danny McIntosh, he would have learned this too. The man you smile and wave to on the street. The man you trust. He was never a man at all.

CHAPTER TWENTY

"You need to tell me what's going on, Carla."

I opened the door to find Suzie standing on the front porch. She appeared calm, but her voice betrayed her agitation, and she didn't wait for me to invite her inside. She walked straight in and headed to the kitchen and then stopped in her tracks when she saw Will sitting at the table, having breakfast.

"Oh," she said. "I didn't realize you had company." And she turned to face me and took a step back out of the kitchen as if she was making to leave, but I smiled at her and said, "This is Will. We used to... well, anyway, he's up here visiting for a while."

Will stood up and extended his hand towards her and introduced himself with a casual "Hi, good to meet you. You must be Suzie, right?"

Suzie nodded. It was clear, whatever she wanted to talk to me about, she didn't think she could tell me while someone else was in the room. But I could guess what it was. Danny's mom. My latest visit to Rob. I'd promised her I wouldn't upset anyone, and I'd broken that promise. And despite her anger, I could see the disappointment in her eyes.

"You want a coffee?" Will asked her.

"No thanks. I just came by to talk to Carla about something. But it can wait."

"Oh," he said. "Sounds serious. I can leave you guys to it, if you like?"

And Suzie looked at me and nodded that she would be okay with that. But before I could take Will up on his offer he headed over to the coffee pot and poured out two mugs of coffee and set them down on the table for us, then said, "Actually, before I leave, I was wondering if I could maybe talk to you too, if that's okay?"

Suzie looked at him and sat down when he beckoned to her to take a seat. She seemed a little baffled and unsure what to do, and I felt the same. I didn't know what Will was thinking, and a part of me didn't want to know either. But he didn't give me any time to start wondering and worrying.

"I guess you must be here about Carla's conversation yesterday with Mrs McIntosh?"

Fuck, I thought. *Please don't mention that. Please don't go there.*

But it was too late now. Suzie was already nodding as she sat there straight backed and defensive. "Well, that and her visit to see Rob the other day," she said.

"I thought so," Will replied.

"Listen, Suzie," I said. "I thought if I talked to Martha I could keep Cece and my dad out of all of this. I was just—"

"What?" she replied. "Damn it, Carla, where do you think you are? This isn't San Francisco. This isn't some big city where no one knows one another, and no one speaks to one another. Did you really think Martha wouldn't call my grandmother and tell her about your little conversation? Carla, they lost *their sons.* They've been united by this horror for decades. Most of their lives. They talk to one another, Carla. And you can't go over there and start putting out these batshit crazy ideas and expect people to just sit there and take it. What you told Martha was cruel. Your dad? You're telling me you think your dad did this?"

"Okay, okay, wait a minute," Will said.

But Suzie was having none of it. "Sorry but who the hell are you? What has any of this got to do with you?"

"It was my idea to send Carla round to Mrs McIntosh. I asked her to go and talk to her. So if you're angry then maybe you'd be better off taking it out on me."

"Why?" Suzie asked him. "What do you need to talk to Martha about?"

And I knew what was coming. He was going to mention the "book research." He was going to spin her that stupid story and I wasn't going to be able to stop him.

"I'm an investigative reporter for the *Chronicle*," he explained. "I wrote a book a few years back about a case we had in San Francisco. Some teenage boys killed their teacher in a misguided vigilante attempt at justice. When Carla told me about what had happened here, I thought maybe it was a story I could look into, so I asked her to talk to some people, just to see if there was anything to it. But I realize now that it was a stupid thing to do, and—"

"Woah! Okay, give me a second," Suzie said. And she leaned her elbows on the table and fixed her gaze on Will, moving into his personal space so that he knew she was serious and understood she would not be pushed around. "Let me tell you something. People here have put this behind them years ago. They didn't forget about it and they never stopped thinking about Danny and Adam and Jonathan. They never stopped wishing they were all still here with us. But we learned to move on because that was what the families of those boys needed. They needed to live again and find a way to keep their children in their thoughts without having their grief overwhelm them. And you may *think* that it's been so long now as not to matter anymore, at some emotional or psychological level, but let me tell you this. Last night Martha McIntosh called my grandmother, and she was in tears. She's a strong woman, and she has survived many hardships, not least of which was losing her son. It takes a lot to make her cry. It takes a lot to break her down. But that little conversation yesterday, it opened an old wound and you both need to know that. You can't go around hurting people and especially not if it's for a damn book or a newspaper article."

"Oh, Suzie," I said. "I'm so sorry. I never thought for a minute that I was hurting Martha. She seemed so calm, so together. When I spoke to her about all this and about my dad and—"

"I already told you, Carla. We don't want you to open up all this pain again. You need to stop, do you hear me? And it's not just me saying this. Rob sent me over here with a message for you—"

"I just thought I could help you," I said. "I honestly thought I could find out what happened to Danny and maybe also to Adam and Jonathan too. I thought—"

"Just stop, Carla!" and for the first time, she raised her voice at me. "Please, just stop. This is what your dad meant, I guess."

"What do you mean?" I asked her.

"He's dying, Carla, and he's in pain and he is suffering enough. And you went to his bedside and you talked to him about all of this, didn't you? That was why he was so upset? And he wants you to stay away from him now, he—"

"Oh, of course he does. I mean, he's never wanted to—"

"Carla, please. He told me to tell you to wait. That's his message. He wants you to wait until he's gone. 'Tell her she doesn't understand. Tell her to wait until I'm dead.' I don't know what he meant, but that's what he told me to tell you."

"Damn it, Suzie," I said. "He said that? But don't you realize what that means?"

"Carla, I don't care. You pushed him too far and you need to know that I have a duty to protect him and care for him. So please, either back off, or leave."

I looked at Will and he shrugged his shoulders in defeat. If this is what everyone here wanted, if the truth didn't matter as much to them as it did to us, then there was nothing we could do. We would have to agree.

"Okay," Will said. "If that's how it needs to be, then…"

"That *is* how it needs to be," Suzie said.

She looked at me and didn't smile and I felt a pang of remorse. I'd lost a potential friend, someone who had been kind to me and had helped me out when I needed it most. I had hurt her and her family. Unintentionally, but I had.

"I'm really sorry," I said to her as she walked past me. "Please believe me when I say I didn't mean to harm anyone."

"I just want you to mean it this time when you say you'll stop," she said.

I nodded and walked with her to the hall. The door to the studio was open and as we walked past it, Suzie glanced inside and saw the map on the wall with the photos and the plots I'd marked where Danny and Adam had been found.

"What the hell is that?" she asked me. And she walked into the room and stared at the map, then turned to me. "Seriously, Carla, what the hell is this?"

I couldn't speak. What explanation could I possibly give her? In her eyes this map was proof I had been obsessive, that my promises meant nothing. That I had taken this further than she ever imagined and was not to be trusted.

It was a relief when Will interjected.

"I was the one who made this," he told her. And I was glad the shock of his lie meant I didn't react immediately, because once I realized what he had said, I had to look away and pretend I was staring at the wall because if I caught Suzie's eye, she would see immediately what was going on. "I do it when I'm investigating something. It helps me to have a visual aid."

Suzie looked at him and then looked at the wall, then shook her head in disbelief.

"I can't believe this. I trusted you, Carla," she said as she pointed at the map. "You were told not to do this, and you went ahead and did it anyway and please, don't tell me you were trying to help. If someone tells you you're not helping them, then your good intentions don't matter."

Then she turned and headed back to the hallway and left us standing there staring at the map as the door slammed shut.

"Woah," Will said when she'd gone. "Looks like we've opened a can of worms."

I slumped down on the floor, my back against the wall and let my head fall in my hands.

"Shit," I said. "What am I going to do?"

He came and sat beside me and wrapped his arms around my shoulder and pulled me close and I let him, the warmth of his body comforting me and helping to clear my head a little.

"What do you want to do?" he asked me.

"I don't know," I said. "Maybe it's better to leave it for a while. I mean, you heard Suzie, if she had been any angrier she'd have driven me out of town."

He smiled and sighed. "So, cool things down for a little then?"

I nodded. "But that means your dad could die before you sort this out. I mean, he's close to the end now, isn't he?" he said.

"Yeah," I replied. "He is. And despite it all, I'd like to see him again before he dies. If he'll let me."

"I don't think Suzie's the type to keep you away from him. Not at the end."

"I hope you're right."

"Listen," he said. "I can stay for a while, if you like? You know, for when your dad—"

It was a tempting offer and I almost said yes. But the thought of getting close to him again, of needing him. Of leaning on him for that kind of support. I was worried where that would take me and not sure what it was I wanted. To try again with him or to stay here and give it a shot. I'd messed up on both counts and perhaps it was too late to salvage anything from the mess. But one thing was certain, I could think more clearly if Will wasn't beside me to tempt me back.

"Thanks," I told him. "Maybe we should just let this calm down a bit here. Thanks though, you know, for coming up here on this stupid, pointless mission."

"Hey," he said, and he kissed the top of my head. "It wasn't stupid. For what it's worth I think you're right. Something did happen here that your dad knows more about than he admits, and I hope, eventually, you figure out what it was. But it just looks as if, right now, no one here is ready for it, so what can we do? But you did the right thing, Carla, and you did it because you cared, so don't let anyone tell you otherwise."

I was so, so close to asking him to stay or just packing my bag and heading back to San Francisco with him. But I let him go. Watched him drive away, his arm through the window raised in the air in a wave. I waved back, then went inside the house to take another look at that map. Because I was missing something. I could feel it. I'd told Suzie I would stop. I'd told Will I would let it all settle down. I'd promised them both.

But promises—they were made to be broken.

CHAPTER TWENTY-ONE

He was very polite, of course. Apologetic even, but absolutely firm and businesslike.

"Hi Carla, it's Mark Davenport," he said when I picked up the phone, the emphasis on the surname his discreet way of drawing a line. I understood immediately why he was calling. "Listen, I'll try to keep it brief and to the point."

"Okay," I managed to say in the pause he gave me to let me prepare for what I knew was coming.

"I spoke to Suzie this morning and she told me you spoke to Cece Hutton and Martha McIntosh—"

"I didn't mean to—" I interjected.

"No, please, let me finish. Suzie mentioned that you spoke to them about their sons. I don't want to know why you inquired about any of this, but, I'm sure you understand that my business is based on trust and professionalism and I really can't let employees wander around people's homes if I feel they can't be trusted."

"Oh, but I can, I—"

But he ignored me and continued. "Annabelle told me she had the impression you were interested in Adam Peterson. That you seemed overly curious about it all during the house visit. And when Suzie mentioned that a journalist you know was here in Newcastle looking into the deaths of those three boys, well, I don't know what you think you're doing, but I have to let you know that I feel very disappointed. If I had known you had hidden motives for coming to work for me, then…"

He kept on talking but I'd stopped listening by then. I knew what he was going to tell me, that my services were no longer required, that I should think carefully about staying on here, that I had betrayed people's trust.

Damn it, I thought. I had been stupid to visit Martha. This was bound to happen. People rallying round to protect themselves from outside interference.

But it was too late now, we'd broken that trust and I doubted we would ever regain it. I ended the call and sat in the living room wondering what the hell I was supposed to do now. I had started something I felt I had to finish, and I couldn't stop now, because I felt, with Will's help, I was getting closer to the truth. And my dad knew it too. He was frail and sick and dying, but he knew I would never let go of this, that I would need to find out what happened to Jonathan Hutton. He might want to keep his secrets and go to his grave without ever revealing them, but that wasn't an end he deserved. And it may hurt Cece and Martha and Suzie if I delved into all of this, but I was sure if my instincts were right and if I could find that boy, then they would forgive me.

For a couple of days, all I did was sit in the studio and study the map and the pinboard. I lost track of the hours I had spent staring at it in the hope of finding something. It was a vain task I had given myself. A hopeless task. But I needed to figure out how I was going to solve this problem.

On the wall, the smiling faces of Adam and Jonathan looked back at me, innocent and oblivious, and I stood up and walked towards the pinboard, feeling like I needed to get closer to them.

"I'm sorry," I said to them. "I'm sorry I couldn't help you. I…"

But I had no words left. When I looked into those bright eyes staring back at me from the photographs, their expressions frozen in a moment of happiness that had gone unnoticed, I felt ashamed.

One by one, I unpinned their photos. I didn't want to look at them anymore. I didn't want to think of the ways I had failed them. I took them over to the desk and laid them face down.

But when I turned back to the board, the space they left behind was horrifying to look at.

I had a pile of photos stashed in a box on the floor, shots I had taken during my trip to the woods. I clicked open the lid and rummaged among the pile, looking for images I could pin to the board to fill in the gaps that had now been left. When I found what I was looking for, I started to tape them into place, trying to match the seams and create a perfect facsimile of the forest. It felt rather pointless and slightly neurotic, but the simple act of matching the colors and the shapes soothed me, and helped me focus.

When I stepped back from the board to check that everything was properly aligned, I was satisfied with the result but still couldn't accept the missing pieces. The faces of those boys.

I needed something there, I realized, to mark the place where they had been. On the desk I had a jar of pins in different colors, so I took three from the jar, a different color for each boy and then went back to the board to stick in the pins.

First Danny, in the northernmost tip of the forest. Then Adam, found in a hollow to the west. And finally, Jonathan, with no known place. I didn't know where to stick his pin.

I must have stood there for a few minutes staring at those photos of the forest, at the twisted shapes of the trees with their needles and bark, and the convoluted root systems. All that dark, ominously shaded green. And maybe this is the way the human brain works. Maybe you need to empty out your head sometimes and focus on something simple and calming, like the color green, not knowing that it's precisely in moments such as this you will start to make the connections, piece together the component parts, and finally see the whole.

I stared at the places on the map where I'd stuck in pins indicating where Danny and Adam had been found, then looked closely to see if there was an obvious place for Jonathan's pin.

My eye following the contours on the map. The golf course, a rough patch of woodland that skirted the greens, and then rose upwards into the vast expanse of the forest. And there, a name that looked out of place. Lake MacKenzie.

And a shiver ran through me when I remembered those words my dad had written. *Down by Lake MacKenzie.* I looked at the map and sure enough, there it was —Lake MacKenzie, a small lake close to the golf course.

I stuck a pin in the map to the east, close to the lake, because its placement seemed like a natural symmetry and then I stood back again to look at the new configuration, my mind linking the pins together. I felt like I was in a trance when I took a black Sharpie from the desk and walked back to the board, my hand reaching up independently, it seemed, and drawing the line on the map, from north to west to east and then back up to north again, a perfect triangle.

When my arm dropped to my side I stared at the shape and shook my head, not quite believing it. Because it was too neat, it was too perfect, it was too obvious. Someone back then would have surely done the same thing? Mapped out the sites on a board such as this and then seen what was there. But they couldn't have. If they had, then they would have seen it. It was not something anyone could have missed.

On the map I could see that some trails led into the forest and it looked possible to walk to the spot from the parking lot on the road at the start of the trailhead.

What did I have to lose? I thought.

Because he was there, at the spot where I had stuck in my pin or somewhere close. I was sure of it. He was lying there waiting for someone to find him. That was why Rob had told me not to go there. That was why he had lied when I asked him what it meant. *They're not important, Carla. It was just something I wrote when I was a kid.* But those lines on the map told a different story. It was important. Rob was lying.

I grabbed my car keys and headed out the door, jumping into the car without thinking. If I stopped now then I would never go. I would convince myself it was stupid and find a million different reasons not to do it.

The drive over to the trailhead passed in a blur, the streets weaving into each other, the houses and the shops disappearing from view. All I saw was the road and the central line, white and clear, leading me up and out of town and towards the forest.

There was no one around when I parked the car, but in the distance I thought I could just make out the sound of people talking and what I assumed were the swish and thwack of golf clubs striking balls. I couldn't see the course. It was hidden from view by a wall and rows of elegant beech trees. Privacy and exclusivity were the order of the day and I thought then of my dad and all the years he had apparently spent helping to maintain those grounds, keeping them spic and span and well-trimmed, ensuring the wealthy patrons were never disappointed with the smooth undulating greens.

It was strange to think of the manicured perfection that lay behind the wall, because on this side, nature had been allowed to run wild. There was a ditch that ran alongside the wall, presumably dug as part of the drainage system to keep the golfing greens from becoming waterlogged but aside from this the vegetation had sprouted in a mess of tangle and green.

It made me wonder if I had found the right spot. The map indicated a trail ran here, but when I crossed the road and headed to the spot where it should start, I couldn't see a clear path.

I walked a little farther along the road hoping to see an entry point, but there was nothing, so I backtracked and figured I would have to follow the map as best I could, sticking to what was printed there and hoping it would eventually open out into a passable path.

The way through was difficult, a mess of tree roots and undergrowth that slowed me down and threatened to trip me up, but as I moved farther from the road, the tangle seemed to spread out as the woodland opened out a little, and finally, after ten minutes, I was able to walk freely without needing to push my way through foliage.

In a small open clearing I stood for a moment to catch my breath and figure out where I was. The map was as good as useless. With no obvious path to follow and with no clear trail, all I could do was try and get my bearings and keep in mind where the way back to the road lay.

To the left I could see the golf course a few meters below me. Groups of men in bright clothes wandered the greens, followed by their caddies, and the odd golf buggy zipped around silently. It was funny to think that the people below had no idea I was watching them. If they looked up, they would only see trees. I was perfectly hidden, despite being so close by. And it made me shiver to think of that. This forest again, this wild space, so close to humdrum life, yet so different. It was the perfect place to hide away. No one would come here, even with the path on the map. It was a place for animals and birds and out-of-control plants. People were not meant to be here.

But that also made it an improbable spot to bring the body of a child. The tangle of bushes and trees would make it almost impassable if you had a child in your arms.

I walked a little farther, keeping the golf course in view. That way I would know where I was at all times and would be able to find my way back, or, if necessary, climb the wall and find my way onto the greens and then back to safety. If anyone questioned what I was doing I could explain I'd got lost in the woods and had scaled the wall because I was frightened to be out there on my own for much longer. They'd no doubt take one look at me, dressed in jeans and a sweater, with only sneakers on my feet and they would see me for what I was, an ill-prepared out-of-towner who didn't know their way around nature.

As I walked away from the road and deeper into the scrubby woodland, I started to notice how different it was from the wilder, denser woods that lay on the slightly higher ground. The hillside had fallen away towards the golf course and this spot where the trail was supposed to be seemed to have fewer mature trees and more low-level bushes than the rest of the forest. It was brighter and less mossy too, and as I walked on, it occurred to me that the land here had perhaps been cleared and opened years ago. Perhaps it had even been part of the golf course, because it had that feel to it, that it was a former parkland that had been left to run wild, a piece of no man's land between the truly wild forest and the manicured perfection of the putting greens.

And the closer I looked the more I started to notice it—the way the ground undulated in places in an unnatural way. I could see where bunkers may have once existed and stretches of open lawn. This had been a different place once, part of the golf course that for some reason had been walled off from the rest of the grounds and had gone to seed.

And it made no sense. If this had been part of the golf course back when Jonathan had been taken, then there was no way he would have been left here. Not when the two other boys had been taken to the forests and left there so carefully, their bodies to be found quickly, or to de disposed of by the local wildlife. It was as if whoever had left Danny and Adam had understood that they would not be caught while they disposed of the boys in those dark, out-of-the-way places.

But this was different. And now the question arose. If this was where they had taken Jonathan, a place so different from the forest where Danny and Adam had been discovered, then perhaps there was another more important difference I needed to consider. The chance that it was someone else who had brought Jonathan here. That the cases were unrelated after all. Just a coincidence. Two killers. Two people who had escaped justice.

I came to a clearing in the woods and decided to stop and think. The walking was tiring me; the constant struggle through the scraggly bushes and the tripping and stumbling over hidden roots was wearing me down and slowing my progress.

There was a dried-out tree trunk on the ground, and I walked over to it and lay across it and looked up at the sky. It was visible through the canopy here, a bright bird-egg blue that made the forest feel less threatening. I was hoping to clear my head so I could think things through properly, but I had too many questions now and no way of answering them. If Jonathan was buried here then it didn't fit with what had happened to the other boys. And if he wasn't here, then it meant my theory was wrong. I'd simply seen a pattern there on that pinboard because I wanted to see one.

I sat up and straddled the tree trunk and looked around me. It was noticeable now that I was on an old part of the golf course. Not just the undulations in the ground but old brickwork I had failed to spot while I was walking. What was left of some old building perhaps or a wall that had once extended this far into the forest before it was moved. I thought I could see other structures too that had been covered over by plants and mosses and ferns, the outlines of things that lay underneath—outbuildings, perhaps. Old sheds or storage spaces.

Not a place you would bring a dead boy, that much was clear. But if he wasn't here, then where was he? I would head home empty-handed again. No closer to finding him. In fact, more confused than ever.

My phone beeped and startled me, and I fumbled in my pocket to find it and answer it.

Mom.

Damn it, I thought. *I should have checked the screen before answering, this isn't the moment to talk to her.*

But it was too late, she was already chatting to me.

"Hey, Mom!" I said. "Listen, can you call me back? I'm out for a walk in the woods here and the reception is lousy."

"I can hear you fine," she said.

"Okay, but I want to get home and get warm. I've been out here too long and it's getting cold and starting to get dark."

"What the hell are you doing out there then? In a forest, did you say? Carla…"

"It's okay, I know my way around here a little better now, I can manage a walk in the woods."

"If you say so. It doesn't sound like you though. Forests and nature and stuff."

"Well, what can I say? I guess living up in a place like this changes you. Or maybe it just lets you see who you were all along. Who knows?"

"Anyway, I need to talk to you."

"Can't it wait until I get home? I can call you back."

"No need, I'm heading to the airport now. I booked a flight to Seattle this morning, so I'll see you soon."

"Sorry, what? You're coming up here? Mom, why?"

"I spoke to Suzie this morning, that's why. She's worried about you and all this stuff with Rob. Honestly, I had no idea what I was supposed to say. I mean, what the hell are you up to, Carla? Why didn't you talk to me about all of this?"

"Sorry, I meant to call you, I've just been figuring things out and Suzie, well…"

"She's so upset, Carla, even more so since Will published that piece in the *Chronicle* about those boys—"

"Sorry, what? What piece in the *Chronicle*?"

"Why didn't you tell me he'd been up there staying with you? That's so fantastic that you two are still close like that and that maybe you can—"

"Mom! What piece in the *Chronicle*?"

"The one that came out this morning. Listen, Carla, I don't have time for this right now. I'm trying to get to the airport. Why don't you stop running around in a damn forest and go home? It's online, so you can read it yourself. Anyway, I'll see you later, okay?"

And just like that she hung up and left me sitting there in the enclosing gloom of the early afternoon. It was only then that I noticed that the background hum of voices from behind the wall, and the gentle thwack and swish of the golf clubs had subsided. When I looked at the time on my phone I saw I'd been out here for close to three hours, the time passing without me having been aware of it.

For a moment I wanted to stay there, in that calm, quiet clearing where time seemed to have slowed down. I wanted to savor that peacefulness because I knew when I got back to the house, a storm awaited me.

If Cece and Suzie had read that article, and if it detailed the things I imagined it did, then they would be clamoring to get a hold of me.

"Goddamn it, Will," I shouted. "What the hell have you done?"

And in the distance I thought I caught the sound of a bird some place. Hidden in the foliage, observing and waiting. Its call like a warning.

CHAPTER TWENTY-TWO

When I got home, I rushed to get my laptop and turned it on with shaking hands, opening the browser and typing in the address for the *Chronicle*, then scrolling until I found the article Mom had mentioned.

The headline was enough to stun me and leave me close to tears. "The One They Never Found." Something about that word: one, as if Jonathan was nothing more than a number. I couldn't understand why they had gone with such a callous-sounding headline. No doubt the mystery of it was intended to pique the readers' curiosity. Clickbait, nothing more.

I hit the paywall immediately and wanted to scream in frustration as I scrambled around in my purse to find my wallet and credit card. *I'm going to make you pay this back to me, Will Newton*, I thought as I typed in my details and then confirmed my subscription.

Though when I got back to the article, I regretted the decision to read it almost immediately. If the headline was bad then it was nothing compared to the article itself. He spared little detail explaining what happened to Danny and Adam. When they were taken, who had last seen them, when they were found and the traumatic injuries they had endured before their deaths. The spots where they had been found were described and the full horror of what had happened was meticulously presented.

But there was one boy they never found. Young Jonathan Hutton, who disappeared on July 12th, 1972, nine years after Danny

McIntosh was murdered, and eight years after Adam Peterson was killed. In the years that followed their deaths, no doubt a complacency had emerged, the tragedy of the two other boys forgotten in the hope that it could never happen again. But that Wednesday afternoon in 1972, Jonathan Hutton cycled home from school and was never seen again. Taken, everyone assumes, by the same terrible soul that snatched Danny and Adam.

Jonathan Hutton's disappearance is a mystery which has haunted the town of Newcastle over the decades, the name of the lost boy one that every child that grows up there comes to know. The unresolved crime, haunting the children down the years, and serving as a warning: awful things can happen here too.

But now, almost fifty years on, new evidence has come to light, and there is hope that the truth about what happened to the three boys may finally be about to be revealed.

I had to stop reading. I didn't want to know if he had mentioned my name, if he had mentioned my father, if he had spoken about the diaries and the notebooks and had revealed my deepest fears to the whole world.

I couldn't think why he would have done such a thing. To breech my trust this way, all for the sake of a story. Worse, he had nowhere to take it from here. The article had reached a dead-end, the revelations he hinted at, unresolved questions still. I did not know if my father was involved in this or not and I still had no way of proving it. But now he was putting it out there, tarnishing the name of a man too ill to defend his reputation, and for what?

I skimmed the rest of the story, barely able to take it in, my brain registering only the key words and phrases and parsing them into some sort of narrative. This was the first installment in a series, a developing story that, if the investigations based on the new information panned out the way he expected them to, would shock readers across the country.

He didn't mention me by name, nor my father. Instead, there was a reference to an old case Will had come across while researching his book. A crime he had used as an example to show that children were capable of terrible, inexplicable violence. Only now, he seemed to be referring to it as a hint of what was to come in the next installment.

I remembered that case well. Remembered watching grainy footage with Will and crying in disbelief when I understood what was happening on the screen. Two young boys, just ten years old, walk through a shopping mall in England, hand in hand with a small blond-haired toddler. The small boy walks with them out of the mall and nothing about it seems odd, they're just three boys together, kids out and about and causing no trouble. The footage is banal and uninteresting until the truth of it is revealed. The young boy's body found two days later, beaten and battered and discarded on a railway line. Those ten-year-old boys, the youngest children to be convicted of murder in recent British history.

I read the reference in Will's report and understood exactly what was happening. Will wanted to get a lead on the story, to report on it before it became national news—because he knew, once the details emerged, that this was a story that would go around the world. It was a make-or-break scoop for him and he was prepared to go all out to be the first one to run it. This report was just the teaser, the tantalizing first installment in a story that he knew would lead to something bigger, something as horrific and inexplicable as those two English boys and that tiny blond child.

"Fuck you, Will Newton," I said. "I will never forgive you for this."

I thought about calling him but knew it was better to wait for my anger to subside, just enough for me to form a coherent phrase. The doorbell rang. One single press of the buzzer at first, becoming an incessant, impatient ringing when I didn't answer it immediately.

From the hallway I could see through the glass door pane. Suzie. Of all the people that could come by, I reckoned she was perhaps the only one I could not face.

"Carla, open the door. I know you're in there," she said.

And there was no point in hiding away. Sooner or later I would have to face her. I owed her an explanation, in as far as I had one. When I opened the door, she stepped inside, and the image of the newspaper flashed on her phone as she walked past me, waving it in the air.

"What the hell is this?" she yelled.

"Listen, Suzie," I said. "I only read it five minutes ago. My mom called me to tell me about it and I have no idea why he would do this or what he hopes to gain from it. It's *so* irresponsible of him and I'm so mad about it."

"Why would you do this to Cece? How can you do this to her?"

I sat there open-mouthed and incapable of providing an answer. Because what could I say? Will had effectively filed a report suggesting the case of Jonathan's disappearance was about to be resolved. He had no proof of this, he had no evidence he could use to back up his claim, beyond the pieces of the puzzle I had managed to pull together, and none of it amounted to much, none of it could be gathered together to fit the claims he had made.

"Well?" Suzie said. "Do you know what I'm supposed to tell her?"

"No," I said. "I wish I did, but I'm still trying to get to grips with what he wrote."

"What he wrote, basically, was that he knows who killed those boys. Who took Jonathan and maybe even where they buried him. And I swear to God, Carla, what he wrote had better be the truth, because if he's lying about this, in a national paper. If he's going to get everyone's hopes up, based on nothing but a stupid hunch, then I will never forgive him, and you will never be able to stay here in this town. You understand that, don't you? If he's lying, then the blame will fall on you as much as him, because without you, he would never have gone looking. So you need to tell me the truth and tell me everything, because if you don't…"

I pushed my chair back from the table and stood up, not letting her finish.

"Wait there," I said. "There's something you need to see, something you need to read."

And I left the kitchen and walked to the studio to get the box with my father's diaries and scrapbooks. If she wanted to know the truth, then this was all I could give her. And she would have to decide if I was right or wrong.

*

I put the box on the table and took out the notebooks and explained to Suzie what they were. I told her the full story, that I had read them and not understood at first what they were, had mistaken them for something innocent, just the unusual collection of a sad and curious boy. I told her it had taken weeks of contemplation and a trip to the forest for me to understand that the vague feeling of disquiet that had filled me ever since I opened the box, was more than unease. It was a horrible certainty I couldn't ignore. It was the reason why I had persisted, despite my promises to stop.

She listened to me and picked up the books one by one, opening them and flicking through them without reading them. It was only when she flicked past the photograph of Jonathan that had been clipped from the paper that she stopped and opened and folded it down with her hands, and then read the accompanying article.

"My father had already left Newcastle by then," I told her. "Don't ask me why he had clipped out that article. I have no idea why."

"Maybe he was just completing the collection?" she said. "He got the other two, so the third wasn't one he wanted to miss."

I stared at her and waited for her to explain because it was such a strange statement. As if the deaths of those boys, their sad stories, were nothing more than objects to be collected.

"What?" Suzie said when she finally looked at me. "Don't you think he could do that? You said yourself the man you knew was indifferent to suffering."

She was right, of course. I had said that. And I had meant it too. The father I knew was a callously indifferent man. Suffering did not draw compassion from him. And causing pain did not make him doubt himself.

"I need you to read through them," I told Suzie. "Just read them and let me know what you think."

"Did Will read these?" she asked me.

"Yeah," I said.

"And? What did he think?"

"He thought it was possible. That my intuition was correct. My father was connected to all of this in some way, perhaps even directly."

"He thought a child could do such a thing?" she said and shook her head.

"It's not unheard of," I told her. And she looked at me as if what I had said was the worst thing she had ever heard.

So I told her about the book Will had written. About the teenage vigilantes, and about that tiny English child who had been taken from the mall. Sometimes children were cruel. Sometimes they did horrific things. She listened in silence and I saw her eyes close as what I told her sunk in. The full unimaginable horror of it.

"I remember when Will was researching that book," I told her. "He would get this look in his eyes, this glazed-over tiredness. And I'd not be able to talk to him. Nothing would get through. It was as if he was weary of the world and I had never seen him like that. No story ever touched him the way that book did. He'd keep a professional barrier around his emotions, you have to sometimes, in order to stop it getting to you. But with that book, he couldn't do it. It was too awful. It was too much. Kids taking justice into their own hands, kids hurting other kids, you don't absorb a thing like that without getting bruised."

"Is that why you asked him to come up here?" she asked me.

"Yes," I said. "When I realized what I thought might be going on, he was the only person I could talk to about it. The only person I knew who wouldn't recoil, because he knew it was possible. He'd seen it before."

"But you're not as sure as he is though, are you? I mean, the certainty in that piece, he was practically saying he knew who had done it and, worse, he seemed to suggest he knew where Jonathan was, or how to find him at least."

"I know," I replied. "And I need to call him and talk to him about that because there's no way he can write that with so much certainty."

"Did you know he was planning on publishing this?" Suzie asked me.

"What? No, I swear I didn't."

And she looked at me and said nothing for a few seconds, scrutinizing me to be sure I was telling the truth. All I could do was wait for her to decide.

"You must have realized it was possible though? A journalist, confronted with a story like this, they're going to write about it, what else can they do?"

"I guess," I said. "I don't know. I mean, I just wanted to talk to him about it. I didn't know who else to turn to. There's no one here I could have spoken to about this. And I trusted him, as a friend. As an ex."

"What about me? What about Cece? Damn it, Carla, we trusted you, why could you not trust us? Did you seriously think we wouldn't talk to you about this if you'd given us the chance?"

"I'm sorry, honestly, Suzie, I'm so, so sorry. I just thought, well, what did I have to go on? When you look through those notebooks, you'll see it yourself. There's nothing there, nothing that comes close to proof at least. It was just a feeling I had. I read those diaries and I went to the places where the boys were found, I whispered their names in his ear and then…"

"Sorry, what? You went to the places they were found? What the hell does that mean?"

"The way he describes those sites in the notebooks. Read them. They're not just notes he made after reading the paper. The details are so precise. He was there. I know he was. And not as some kid playing out in the woods in the summer. It's different to that. It's no day-to-day diary, no 'what I did on my summer vacation,' this is something else. It's like he was scared of those woods. Scared because he knew what had happened there."

"Everyone knew what had happened there, Carla, that doesn't mean anything."

"I know it doesn't. That's why I only told Will about it. What was the point in upsetting everyone when it could all be nothing? When it could just be me thinking the very worst because it was my father. Because I never forgave him for what he did to us."

"Okay, listen, why don't you leave me to read through these and then I'll let you know what I think? I can't really say anything until I know why you started all this in the first place."

She gathered the books together and stood up and started to head to the front door.

"Where are you going?" I asked her. And she turned and said she was going home.

"I want to read these by myself and then I want to talk to Cece about it."

"Are you sure that's a good idea?"

"Why do you think I came over here, Carla? She read that piece in the *Chronicle* and she needs to know if it's true. She wants to know if there's a chance she can get her son back at last. If she can finally bury him."

And I thought back to the overgrown ground I had visited. The spot on the map where I thought he might be. But I said nothing, because again, it was just a hunch I had. When I'd gone up there, there was nothing to see. He could be there, under that tangle of weeds and roots and shrubs, or he could be miles away in some far corner of the forest I didn't even know about.

So I opened the door and watched her walk down the driveway and head home, then I closed the door and walked into the studio where I stood in front of my pinboard and looked again at that hopeless triangle I had marked out on the map.

Where are you, Jonathan Hutton? I thought. *Show me where you are.*

CHAPTER TWENTY-THREE

I was out in the back and didn't hear the car pull into the driveway. It was only when I heard the gate click open that I realized my mom was here.

"Hey," she said. "I was ringing the doorbell for five minutes, there. Why didn't you open up?"

"Mom?" I said, getting up from the porch stool and walking round the house to the gate.

"Who else were you expecting?" she asked. "I told you I was on my way."

"Yeah, I just didn't think you'd get here so fast."

"Yeah, well, here I am."

She set her suitcase down on the lawn and leaned over to kiss me on the cheek. The case looked heavy and my heart sank a little when I saw it. God knows how long she was planning on staying this time.

"So," she said as she settled in on the sun lounger. "You going to get me a drink?"

I smiled and nodded to her, then left her sitting in the sun, taking her suitcase indoors and up to my father's old bedroom. When I came back out onto the porch with a tray of drinks and some chicken salad, she had already kicked off her shoes and flipped the lounger back into recline, a cigarette dangling from her hand, half smoked. In the ashtray a butt already sat in a pile of ash. She'd managed to smoke two while I was inside and the pack and the lighter sat on the small table beside her, within easy reach, a sign she was upset or nervous about something.

I set the tray of food on the large table between us, then flopped onto the other lounger beside her.

"I thought you might be hungry. Chicken salad okay with you?" I asked her. And she turned and looked at me and smiled.

"Wow," she said. "Fancy."

I lifted up a bottle of Chablis and poured her a glass, then made a jokey show of letting her see the label and offering her the cork to smell.

"I lunch *al fresco* like this every day, as it happens." I grinned.

She smiled and tilted the lounger back upright so she could drink and reach the food on the table. "If I thought that was even a tiny bit true, then I wouldn't worry about you so much."

"Hey, come on. You don't need to worry about me."

"No? That's not what Will says," she said as she finished her cigarette and stubbed it out in the ashtray.

I didn't want to react, but I couldn't stop my voice shaking a little with irritation.

"Yeah, well, do you really think Will knows what's good for me?"

She sighed and gave a little shrug. "I do, as a matter of fact," she said, then picked up her wine glass and took a large sip and forked some salad into her mouth. "Anyway," she continued. "That's not why I'm here. That piece in the paper, is there any truth to it?"

I poured myself a glass of wine and took a sip to try and calm myself and wished I'd had more time to think it over.

Will's article had been pretty truthful, even if it was a shock that he had gone to press without talking to me first or at least warning me of what he was about to print. But there was not a lot in there that I could dispute. The facts of the boys' disappearances and their deaths, that Jonathan was never found, that the perpetrator had never been found. It was all in the public domain. Even the speculative aspects were built on what I had discovered, and the possibility that this new information presented—that Jonathan could be found, and the perpetrator named at last—was perfectly plausible.

"He didn't pluck those ideas out of thin air, if that's what you mean," I told her.

She ate the last of her salad, then reached for the pack of cigarettes, pulling one out and holding it between her lips as she flicked open the lighter and lit it, the movement easy and practiced. She took a long draw on her cigarette, exhaled a plume of blue-gray smoke, then reached for her wine, taking a sip before she continued.

"Yes, well, I assumed it wasn't a work of fiction."

"Listen, I can't prove what he wrote," I told her. "At least, not yet."

She took a moment to flick the ash of her cigarette into the ashtray, then turned to face me, looking me straight in the eye. "So, you really do think your dad was involved in all of this? Carla, come on, that's ridiculous."

I sighed. "Is it?"

She closed her eyes and leaned back in the lounger and for a moment it looked as if she was going to fall asleep. When she spoke there was a weariness in her voice, as if a piece of her had shriveled.

"Rob was just a kid himself back then, you realize that, right?"

"Of course I do. That's why I wasn't sure to start with, when I first found those notebooks and stuff, I didn't jump to conclusions, I was cautious—"

"That's because there was nothing in them. Just a few ramblings from a kid. Where are they, actually? I can't remember what it was he wrote. But if there'd been anything in there that suggested Rob was somehow involved in all of this, I'd have remembered."

"I don't have them," I told her. "I gave them to Suzie. Her grandma wanted to read them."

"You gave them away? Carla, why? If there's any truth in there, any proof, then...?"

"Cece needed to read them. And she has a right to see what's in there." She stared at me, then shrugged, incapable of understanding why I would hand the diaries over so quickly.

"Listen, it's done now," I told her. "And who knows, maybe she'll notice something I didn't. Maybe she'll find something there that proves Rob knows what happened to Jonathan."

"I thought you were already sure of that."

"It's more intuition," I admitted. "Those diaries, they don't prove anything."

"Then why start all this? Why accuse him of this? Why have Will write it all up in a national newspaper?"

"Mom, I didn't know Will was going to write that article."

"Still, you talked to him about it. And you must have told him what you suspected."

"Yeah, I did—"

"And it never occurred to you that a journalist would write it up? Carla, come on!"

"I trusted him, okay, and I… Damn it, Mom, it doesn't matter about Will. You were there at the hospice, you saw the way Dad reacted when I mentioned Jonathan's name. And I know what I saw in his eyes. He was scared of me, Mom. Scared of what I knew. Scared of what I might ask him."

"And that's enough for you? Enough for you to accuse him? The look in a dying man's eyes? Carla, listen to yourself."

"No, it's not enough, not by itself, but… Oh, I don't know. Do you think I'm wrong then? I mean, do you think he's incapable of doing something like this? I know everyone here loves him, but we both know how he can be."

She didn't answer and I saw her shiver and reach for her jacket. But it wasn't the cold, I could tell. It was the memory of him. The man we knew. Yes, he was capable of violence, so why pretend otherwise?

We'd been sitting in the garden for a couple of hours and as the sun dropped behind the rooftops, I started to feel the chill. I tidied up the plates, the wineglasses, and the ashtray, and piled it all on to the tray to take inside.

"It's getting chilly out here," I said. "I'm going to head inside."

In the living room I turned on the fireplace and we sat and watched the gas flames flicker and sway and let the warmth seep back into us. I had a few woolen blankets draped around chairs in the room, and I took a couple and wrapped one over Mom as she curled up in the corner of the sofa, before I settled in a chair facing her and tucked the other blanket around me, then waited to get warm.

"You know," Mom said after a few minutes. "The strangest thing about your father was how unknowable he was."

It was one of those statements that came out of the blue and felt surprising until the simple truth of it settled. I looked at her and waited for her to carry on, unable to reply to what amounted to a statement of fact. Rob was unknowable, this had always been true.

"What I mean," she continued, "is that there was always this... I don't know how to explain it. Like, an aura or something. You know what I mean?"

"I think so," I said. "He always seemed to be thinking about something else. At least, that's what I always felt. He was never really *there*. A piece of him was always off someplace."

"The way he was, with us, I mean. I could never quite figure it out. If it was because of us, something we said or did. Or if he was just simply a bad person."

"You know it wasn't us, Mom. That was just want he wanted us to believe. Men like that, it's what they do."

"I know, but—"

"Bad people exist, that's what I think. Some people are born bad and you don't need to analyze it any deeper than that."

"Since when did you become so cynical?"

I pulled the blanket up around me, instinctively trying to protect myself against that word, even though I knew it was true; I had developed a more cynical side.

I shrugged. "Maybe I've just been thinking about all of this too much, I don't know. But there was something wrong with him, you know there was."

"You make him sound like he's some sort of sociopath or psychopath or something though."

"Did you never get that feeling then? That there was something wrong? The way he could act so impassively, just dish out the pain and then walk away as if nothing had happened, no sorrow, no shame, nothing. I mean, that *is* the word for it, isn't it? It *was* a pathology."

"I don't know," she said. "I'm no psychologist. Does it even need a label?"

"What do you mean?"

"Like you said, maybe we're thinking too much."

"But if he was pathological in some way, if it was something like that, then—"

"Listen, Carla, we won't learn much more about him just by putting a label on it. It won't stop me thinking it was somehow my fault. Something I had done. Some provocation or antagonism."

"Oh, Mom," I said. "You can't still think that, surely?"

"I wish I didn't, but it never leaves. Maybe you're right. Maybe I should look at him as someone who was simply sick. I could just say it was something inside of him. It would make it easier, to say there was never anything I could have said or done that would have changed the outcome. He would have hurt us just the same."

"But you did know that. It's why we left. We knew it was never our fault. We knew it was him."

"Yeah, maybe," she said. Then she got up from the sofa and headed to the kitchen. "You want more wine?" she asked.

I got up and followed her to the kitchen, my legs a little wobbly from the alcohol we'd already consumed.

"Why don't I make us a bite to eat as well?" I said. "If we're going to open another bottle then I need some food in my stomach or I'm going to pass out."

"Fine," she agreed. "What you got?"

"A couple of steaks and some potato salad. Broccoli too, if you want it?"

"Sounds great. Here, let me help you. It'll take my mind off this for a while if I give myself something to do."

We pottered around the kitchen for close to an hour preparing the food and saying very little, save to ask for a pot or some seasoning or to point out where the cutlery was. When the meal was ready we took it to the kitchen table, and I opened a bottle of red and poured us two generous glasses.

"I've got a tiramisu in the fridge too, for later, if you like."

She patted her stomach and smiled and said, "You know, I might just take you up on that. What the hell, eh?"

It was nice to sit in the quiet of the kitchen and eat and say very little. It gave us the time to absorb what we had spoken about and to think about what we wanted to do next.

I knew my mom had not come all the way up here just to talk about Will's article. She had decided, just as I had, that she needed to know the truth about my father, about who he really was and how the events of his childhood had helped form the man we knew.

"Anyway," she said, after she had wiped her plate clean with bread and taken a good sip of wine. "Your dad."

I leaned back in my chair and let my stomach ease over the top of my jeans and decided to release the top button. When my mom started a conversation with "anyway," it was always going to be a long story.

"What about him?" I said, and reached over for my glass of wine.

"That aura I was talking about. That sort of melancholy shadow he had following him everywhere."

"I'm not sure that's how I would describe it."

"No, let me finish. When I first met him, that was how he was. Sad. That's the only word for it. I noticed it immediately, and I wanted to know why. Why was he so sad? I mean, he was young still, what could have happened to make him walk about like that, so apart from the world?"

"Mom, please don't romanticize this, okay? I'm not in the mood for polishing that stone."

She smiled at me. "Creative way of putting it," she said.

"You know what I mean."

"And what *I* mean is I could see something had happened to him, that he was sad for a reason, and when I asked him why, he just straight up told me about his mom and how she died in a car crash when he was just a kid. She was there in the morning when he left for school, and when he came home in the afternoon, there was his father in the kitchen waiting for him with the news. And that was what he couldn't figure, years later. It hit him that his dad had not come to school to collect him. He'd let him walk home from school and then open the door to find Sam sitting in the kitchen where his mom always sat, and he just told him: 'Your mom is dead,' and then left it at that. And apparently, his father sat in his mom's chair every day after that. 'Like he could ever replace her.' That was what Rob said to me. And I could hear the hurt in his voice, you know? The anger too. He never forgave his father for that."

She paused, and I took a sip of wine and tried to imagine my father as a seven-year-old kid, hearing such awful news and then being left alone to figure it out for himself.

"Sounds pretty shitty," I told Mom.

"Yeah, it was," she agreed.

"Why did you never tell us about this?"

"Oh, I don't know…" and she flicked her wrist as if it wasn't important. This childhood trauma of my father's, just another anecdote. "Anyway, what I mean is, a thing like that, something so momentous, well, it scars you, especially if it happens when you're still a kid and you need your mom. That's a hurt that's never going to leave."

I got up and went over to the coffee machine and set about making a pot.

"You want some too?" I asked. "I reckon a break from the wine might do us good."

Mom picked up her half-full glass and emptied it, then poured herself another.

"I guess so," she said. "But I might finish this bottle. It's going to be that sort of night."

I let the coffee sputter through the percolator and stood at the counter waiting for it to finish, then took out two large mugs from the cupboard and filled each one with a spoon full of sugar and a splash of milk and took them over to the table and sat down.

Mom thanked me, but didn't touch the coffee, preferring to stick to the wine.

"Listen," I said. "If all this is too much, I mean, if it's bringing back too many memories or whatever, then maybe we should call it a night and start again tomorrow?"

She looked at me and set her wine glass down on the table, then picked up the coffee and made a point of drinking it down quickly.

"There," she said. "That should sharpen my wits a bit."

I smiled and finished my own coffee, then fixed us both another one. When I sat back down she didn't wait for me to settle.

"Listen, I want to go and see Rob," Mom said.

"I figured as much."

"What? You don't think I came all this way just to talk to you about Will's article, do you?"

"No, it's just…"

"What?"

"Well, they won't let me see him."

"Huh? What are you talking about?"

"Last week, I tried to talk to him about those boys and the things I'd found out, and it upset him so much, they said I can't see him anymore."

She stared at me for a second and I saw she was struggling to process what I had just told her. When she eventually spoke, her voice was sharp and a little higher than usual, as she tried to contain her frustration.

"Damn it, Carla. What did you say to him?"

"Nothing, I just asked him about the diaries and told him I'd been to the forest where Danny was found, and—"

She raised her hand and closed her eyes. "Okay, enough, I can't make much sense of this anymore. Tomorrow I'm going to call Suzie and explain that we need to see him and that she'll have my absolute guarantee that you won't upset him again."

"Good luck with that. She seems intent on protecting him."

"Well, let's see what she thinks tomorrow. They have those diaries now, and they'll have read them, so if they have even the tiniest doubt about him, then surely they'll understand that you were only trying to get to the truth."

"Maybe. All I know is that they think I'm causing trouble and they don't really believe me. But, yeah, let's see."

She sipped the last of her wine and then pulled back her chair and yawned.

"Right, I'm off to bed," she said. "And I suggest you get some sleep too. I think we both need a good rest."

I smiled at her and watched as she left the kitchen, then I took one of her cigarettes from the carton and walked out to the garden to smoke it.

The air was cold and had a heavy damp smell to it, as if the forest was breathing. Exhaling a strange mist that permeated everything with something gloomy and melancholic. Something that could seep through skin. I smoked the cigarette and stared at the apple tree as it glowed in the light from the kitchen, the tiniest speck of light in the nighttime and was surprised by how much comfort it brought. But sometimes that was all you needed to keep the darkness away. A small, bright ember. Hope and truth, they could illuminate the darkness. All you had to do was light the flame.

CHAPTER TWENTY-FOUR

The next morning, I called Suzie and asked if I could come over. She sounded tired on the phone, as if she had been awake all night with worries or nightmares. Maybe she had. When I asked her how she was, that was all she said, "I'm a little beat up, to be honest. Give us a couple of hours to get started with the day and then we can talk."

We headed over to their house late morning, and Mom tried to recall if she had ever met Cece when she visited Sam all those years ago.

"She must have been living here at the time, when your father and I visited, but I can't say I remember meeting her then."

I told her Cece had lived her whole life in Newcastle and that she was a friend of Sam and Rob. So she had to have been here then too.

"Maybe," she said. "But I don't ever remember Rob talking about her."

"Well, he never really talked much about this place though, did he?"

"That's true," she agreed. "And it seems like he had good reason not to."

When we walked up the driveway, Suzie was already at the door, holding it open and inviting us in.

"Nice to see you again, Mrs Allen," she said to my mom.

"Please, call me Sophia."

Suzie squeezed my arm as I stepped inside and said, "Thanks for coming over," and I realized then that the conversation we were about to have was not going to be an easy one.

We followed Suzie down the hallway and into the living room where Cece sat by a chair close to the window. When we entered, she didn't get up or even turn her gaze from whatever it was she was looking at beyond the glass, and I noticed then the slight stoop in her shoulders and recognized it for what it was: grief.

It was stupid of me not to have thought about the impact this would have on her. The way it would force the pain of losing to resurface and become an all-consuming grief again.

Mom noticed it too and went over to the chair and placed her hand on Cece's shoulder.

"I'm sorry," she said. "For what this must be doing to you."

And Cece turned away from the window and looked up at my mother and smiled.

"I'm hoping something good might yet come out of it," she said. And then she beckoned towards the sofa and told us to take a seat.

"Before we start," Suzie said. "I just want to say something, if that's okay?" and she looked towards her grandmother and waited for permission. When Cece nodded, she started to speak.

"I don't know how much of these notebooks and news reports you read?" Suzie asked.

"My mom hasn't read all of them yet," I explained. "I tried to fill her in on most of it, but…"

"It's okay," Suzie said. "It's hard to really get to grips with what's there, I don't think anyone can really explain it. You just have to read them."

She picked up one of the books and flicked through it to a page I now saw was bookmarked with a slip of pink paper.

"There's a whole heap of stuff I could have picked out," Suzie said. "But when we read this, we knew that everything Rob had written down was true. It had to be. Because no one knew about this."

I looked at Mom and then back to Cece and Suzie and felt my stomach pinch with fear. I couldn't think of anything specific in the notebooks that they would have found worthy of bookmarking.

"Read it to me," Mom said. Suzie nodded and then coughed a little, her nerves overcoming her.

"It's a really short note Rob made about a newspaper article. The article was written a year after Jonathan went missing. Cece had asked the paper to print it in the hope that it might jog someone's memory. The anniversary seemed like a good moment."

"I also wanted to make sure no one forgot him," Cece interrupted. "After a year, the story had died down and I was worried that people would forget he was still missing. I wanted them to know that we wanted him home. That we wanted to say goodbye to him properly, give him a proper burial."

I looked at Cece and wondered if I should say anything, but the sharp clarity of her eyes left me in no doubt: she could handle anything I had to say.

"How did you know he wasn't alive?" I asked her. And Mom gasped, but Cece remained calm and said, "No, it's all right. It's a fair question."

And she shifted in her seat as if she needed to prepare herself for what she was about to say.

"After a year, you know your child is never coming back. After what happened to Danny and Adam, I think I always knew, as soon as Jonathan didn't come home, that the same thing had happened to him. You don't want it to be true, of course, but deep down, you know it has to be. I couldn't hope for him to come back alive. But I could hope for him to come home to me. That was something I could hold on to at least. Something realistic. And I still hold on to it. I still want my son to come home so I can lay him to rest with the love and care he deserves."

She let her head fall and I thought for a moment that she was praying, that she was sending up a request to some higher power, asking them to grant her this one, sad wish.

"Anyway," she said, when she raised her head. "Let Suzie finish what she wanted to say. We can talk about this later."

Suzie nodded and then looked down at the notebook and started to read.

She never asks herself: 'what's the mistake he made?' He was headed home from school. He took the same route as always. Ten minutes by bike. The same streets. The same houses. The same people. She knows every one of them. Every street, every house, every person living there. She knows their names. He biked home and someone in one of those houses saw him. Someone in one of those houses took him.

Suzie put the book down on the table, then sat back in her chair and looked up at the ceiling, exhaling and trying to swallow down her emotions. I watched her and waited, not sure what was so important about that note. Why it deserved to be bookmarked and read out loud. Because it seemed so innocuous.

"I'm not sure I really understand," Mom said. And it was Cece who answered.

"It wasn't Jonathan who made a mistake. He did as he was told. He was a good kid. And I always told him to come straight home from school if he didn't already have an appointment or some place to go. I was vigilant. We all were. More than anyone realized. But we tried not to let the kids see it. We let them play, we let them roam. We let them be the kids they were meant to be. But we kept an eye on them. It was a sort of pact we had back then. We all knew about Danny and Adam. We all knew there was someone out there who had taken those boys and killed them. Eight years seems like a long time. Adam died in 1964. It was

1972 when Jonathan was taken. You'd think we'd have forgotten by then. Relaxed and let down our guard. And who knows, I guess in a way we must have, because Jonathan was taken, so…

"Anyway, the thing is, those streets, the route he took. It's true, it was always the same. I can draw a map of it to this day. And I can tell you the name of every household he would have passed. The MacPhersons' and the Montgomerys'. The Reids' and the Boyds'. The Steins' and the Spencers'. The Allens' and the Prices'. It was a network, you see. A face at every window, come four in the afternoon. We watched them come home. It was like we were counting them in. The police did a check, when I reported Jonathan was missing. They knocked on every door along the route he took home and there it was, this checklist of every mom who had seen him go by. Janine MacPherson, Kitty Montgomery, Laura Reid, Amanda Boyd. They all reported seeing him. Janine recalled that he waved to her. And Carole Stein, Nina Spencer, they both saw him go past. And then, Sam Allen—nothing. Donna Price—nothing. Somewhere between the Spencers' and the Allens' he went missing. And the police went down the street, past our home, down the hill, and all across the neighborhood. But no one else reported seeing him. I used to think it was because they weren't part of the network so they wouldn't have been there at their windows waiting to make sure that the kids were counted back home. *What's the mistake he made?* That's what your father wrote. And it struck me, as soon as I read it. I knew what the mistake was. That routine. That route. Everyone watching out for one another. But there's a gap in the route. There's a house where someone is waiting, not looking."

She paused and no one made a move to fill the silence, because we could all sense there was more to come. Then she looked at Mom with those piercing eyes and asked her, "You came up here once with Rob," she said.

And Mom nodded and said, "That's right. He brought me up here to meet his father, Sam."

"But the last time Rob came here, before he moved home, he was alone."

And Mom shook her head. "No, he never saw Sam after that."

"I thought you wouldn't know about it," Cece said. "Anyway, it was around a month after Jonathan went missing. I saw Rob on the driveway, and I remember it really well. I waved and called out to him and I know he heard me, but he turned away, pretended he didn't know I was there. I thought it was strange at the time, but I figured he just didn't want to talk. Everyone knew he and Sam had problems. I figured he thought maybe I was going to try and talk to him about it. That I'd try and interfere and speak up for Sam. But I knew he had heard about Jonathan and I thought maybe he'd come over and talk to me about that. When he just walked up the driveway and went back in the house, I was so disappointed. A few hours later, I saw his car pull out and that was it. Until he moved back here, that was the last I ever saw of him."

"I don't get it," I said. "The link. I can't see it."

"She thinks Sam saw Jonathan that day," Suzie said. "She thinks he saw what happened but decided to say nothing."

"I'm sorry, I still don't follow," I said.

"Sam knew Jonathan's routine," Cece said. "He wasn't one of the watchers. He had no kid to look out for, so he wasn't officially in the network. But he was always home around that time of day, so he helped out, you know? He stood at the window and waved. He made sure everything was okay. He was that kind of guy. Kept to himself but helped out when he was needed. In that respect he and Rob were very alike."

"Okay, but that doesn't mean he saw anything. There's a lot of ground to cover between Sam's house and yours. And he wouldn't have been able to see beyond the next house, maybe as far as a few lawns down, even if he was standing at his window. If Jonathan was taken between the Boyds' and the Steins', then Sam couldn't have seen it," I said.

"*What's the mistake he made?*" Cece said again. And we all turned to look at her.

"It was Nina Spencer who remembered she saw him pushing his bike up the hill. She thought nothing of it. It was steep enough and with a bag of school books and the day being hot, it was nothing unusual. At the time, I remember it made me sad. He was hot and tired. So tired he had to get off his bike and push it up the hill. For years, I wanted so much to have been there for him. To take his school bag, lighten the load. Let him get to the top of the hill and then freewheel down, while I carried his bag home for him. I don't know, maybe it's grief, maybe it's shock, maybe it's because your brain takes a hold of an idea and fixates on it. In any case, that was all I ever thought about, that I should have been carrying his bag. I kept thinking about my own 'mistake.' I wasn't there on a hot day to help him get home. But then I read that note: *what's the mistake he made?* And it was as if I could see him standing right there in front of me. Eleven years old and so stubborn and so strong. He would have kept on going. He would have kept on up the hill. Which meant there had to be a reason for him to have been pushing that bike. Something Nina didn't see. And it can only have been the bike. The bike was broken. A puncture, a loose chain, something like that. He wouldn't have stepped off that bike just because he was tired. He wasn't that sort of kid. And that was the mistake, you see?"

She looked at me, then at Mom, but we both sat there in silence waiting for her to explain it to us.

"That was his mistake. He came home the same route, the same time, and that wasn't the thing that protected him in the end, it was the thing that placed him in harm's way. Because the bike, it was broken. On a normal day he would be through there at speed. Biking as fast as he could. But not that day. That day he was walking. That day he needed help. And that was his mistake.

He needed help with the bike, and someone came across him on the street and offered him help. And instead of refusing it, he said yes. He accepted their help. And that was the last anyone saw of him. Janine MacPherson waving to him from her window and thinking everything was okay."

"Okay," I said. "It's possible. But what's the connection? You think Rob was here that day? You think he just happened to be hundreds of miles from home at that *exact* moment, and that Sam, at that *exact* moment, happened to be watching from the window and saw Rob pick up Jonathan and his bike and take him away?"

"Why not?" Mom said. "After all, he came back here, and never told me about it. He could have been here when I thought he was just on a business trip."

"Yeah, okay. But come on, Mom, the chances of it are what? A million to one? It makes no sense."

"No, you're looking at it the wrong way," Cece said. "I'm not saying it happened deliberately, that Rob had a plan. He was just visiting Sam and maybe he saw Sam keeping watch for Jonathan and that alerted him that there was a boy out there on his way home, someone vulnerable who needed to be watched over. And when Rob looked out of the window, there was Jonathan walking with his broken bike. And so, he walked out on to the street and asked him if he needed any help. And Jonathan, well, maybe he saw Sam here in the house, a familiar face, someone he waved to every day, someone he trusted. And so he said yes. 'What's the mistake he made?' That. That's the mistake he made. He trusted someone he knew. And that's why, when Rob came up here a month after Jonathan went missing, he wouldn't say hello to me when I called out to him. Because he knew. He knew what had happened to my son, what had happened to all our boys."

I looked at Suzie and she knew what I was going to ask her, nodding her head as I spoke.

"We need to talk to him, Suzie. We need to ask him about this. I know you don't want us there by his bedside, but please, we have to be allowed to talk to him, not matter how much it upsets him."

"That's okay," Cece said. "I already told her to call ahead to the hospice and tell them you were coming."

And Suzie stood up then. "I'll go over with you, to make sure there are no problems."

And I looked at my mom, unsure what to do, frozen with indecision now that the moment had arrived. And she stood up and took Suzie's arm, thanked her, then turned to me and said, "Come on, let's go."

CHAPTER TWENTY-FIVE

The nurse on duty was unsure what to do, even with Suzie there.

"He's not been doing so well the last few days," she told me. "I honestly don't think it's a good idea for him to be put under any stress right now." I could tell from her expression that she thought his decline was in some way due to me and that she didn't want me to be in the same room with him after the trouble I had caused the last time.

"Please," I begged her. "We just need a few minutes with him. We need to talk to him before it's too late."

She looked at Suzie for an explanation. "I don't know," she said, "I really don't know." Suzie took her aside into an empty room and Mom and I watched their animated discussion through the window, unable to make out what Suzie was telling her. But whatever she said, it was enough to convince her to let us see him.

"Okay," the nurse said as she approached us. "You can have ten minutes with him, but no more than that, I'm sorry. He's really not in a good way and I don't want to stress him. This is a hospice. He needs peace and quiet."

"It's okay," Mom said. "We understand, and I promise you we won't upset him or take too long. We just need to talk to him, and we wouldn't insist if it wasn't important."

"That's okay, Suzie has explained," she said. "But just be aware that he might not be able to say very much."

We nodded, as if we understood, but it was only when we entered the room and saw him lying on the bed, his eyes closed and his mouth open, the hollow of his cheeks, a clear sign of how close he was to the end, that we understood how far he had deteriorated, and we both gasped.

"We're too late," I said to Mom, and she took my hand and squeezed it. "Maybe," she said. "But let's try, at least. For Cece. Let's try." Yet when I looked at him, I wondered if it was the right thing to do. He was almost gone, anyone could see it, so what use was there in trying to get him to talk to us? Now that I was confronted with the reality of his deterioration, it felt wrong to put him through that and I was about to suggest we leave, when Mom shook her head and said, "No doubts, okay? We've come this far, let's see it through."

We walked to his bedside and sat down, and Mom took a hold of his hand, then wiped his forehead gently. I was surprised at her tenderness, at the way she touched him as though he were a normal man, and someone who deserved such comfort, rather than a man we had come to confront with the most terrible accusation there was.

"Rob," Mom whispered. "Rob, it's us." And we waited for a response, for a sign that he had heard us, but there was nothing.

"Dad," I said. "Can you hear us?" At first I thought it was just an exhalation. A long, drawn-out breath and I took hold of his other hand and started to cry. "We're too late," I told Mom again. "We're too late."

And again, that long breath, only this time, Mom moved closer and put her ear to his dry lips.

"Rob," she whispered. "It's me, Sophia." And his eyelids fluttered and opened very slightly, and we heard it then, a small, pitiful "hey."

For a few minutes we sat there with him, just saying his name and telling him we were there, and I felt him squeeze my hand now and then, the fragility of his grip making me doubt if I could go through with what we had planned.

"We can't do this to him," I told Mom.

She shook her head emphatically. "We have to, Carla. If he knows where that boy is, if he can help Cece to bury her son, then we have to try." And I understood her determination then. The understanding she had, as a mother, that you never gave up trying to do everything possible for your child.

His voice was so faint, I almost didn't hear it. "Jonathan," he said.

I blinked and looked at Mom to be sure she had heard it, because his voice was so faint and so weak and the word itself, that name, sounded again like a strangulated breath. Then he said it again. "Jonathan."

And I stroked his hand and felt him squeeze it back.

"Where is he, Dad?" I said, "You know where he is, don't you? Please tell us."

I felt his grip loosen and we watched as he lay there in silence, his breath becoming more labored, his chest rising and falling at a faster rate now, the gap between inhalation and exhalation becoming longer.

"Look…" he gasped.

"Dad," I said. "Look where?"

And I counted the minutes as they passed in silence. Just the labored rhythm of his breath, and the click of the machines as they drip-fed the medication into his broken body. Then he mumbled something.

"Sorry, what did you say?" I asked him, and I leaned close to him and put my head on his shoulder, but he said nothing.

"I think he said 'box,'" Mom said.

I shrugged, because it was impossible to make out what he had said.

"We found the box," Mom told him. "With your diaries. We found them."

And he squeezed my hand a little more tightly, then turned towards me, his eyes, watery and red-veined. "No," he said. Then he struggled again as if muttering even this one word was too much for him, before he managed another faint sound. "Up… stairs."

"What did he say?" Mom asked me.

"Upstairs, I think," I replied. "Dad, what box? Is there another box?"

And his chin moved ever so slightly, the movement almost imperceptible. But it was there and there was no mistaking it. A nod of the head.

"Where, Dad? What box? Where?"

Then a machine went off. An alarm of some sort and his hand slipped from mine as he struggled for breath. The nurses were suddenly back in the room again and ushering us way. Mom explaining to them that we had done nothing. "We just held his hands. We couldn't even make out what he was saying. He just started struggling."

But they didn't hear us or see us. They set about their work and we were led out of the room where we were left to wait.

In the corridor we sat in silence waiting for the nurses to come back outside, too despondent to talk, neither of us sure what to do. Had we heard him correctly? When Suzie came and sat beside us, I heard her talking to Mom but could barely register what they were saying. Something apologetic, some plea for understanding. And Suzie had nodded and said it was okay. That it wasn't our fault. "He's dying, is all," I heard her say, that phrase clear and cutting through the noise. As if this was how it always was. A man, struggling for breath, squeezing the hands that held his, because, caught between life and death, that was all he could do.

When the nurses finally emerged, they explained they had stabilized him but that we would probably not be able to speak to him again. I heard the words. Sedation. Morphine. Palliative.

But none of it meant very much. There was only one word in my head.

"Upstairs."

And I thought of all the places in the house I had not been, but there was only one space I had not been to. The attic. If there was anything in the house to find, then it would be there.

CHAPTER TWENTY-SIX

The attic was accessed via a creaky wooden staircase. When I pushed against the door at the top of the stairs it didn't shift, and the door handle was stiff and difficult to turn. It took me multiple attempts before I felt it grind far enough to click open the latch and push the door ajar.

It was stiff on its hinges and I had to use the full weight of my shoulder against it before I was able to open it wide enough for us to enter.

"God," Mom said. "I don't think anyone has been up here in decades."

I had noticed the staircase before, but for some reason never dared to take a look at where it led. Now, as I stood in the attic with my mom, I realized why. There was something about a forgotten attic that sparked a childish sort of apprehension. The fear that something terrible was hidden away up there. I had allowed that primal fear to take hold and it had kept me away.

"It gives me the creeps," I admitted to Mom. And she laughed and said, "Well, who isn't a bit creeped out by an attic?"

The space was lighter than I expected it to be. Two skylights let the light pour in at either end of the room, and when I flicked the light switch, a row of overhead strip lighting flickered into life, illuminating every dusty, spiderweb-filled corner.

I had imagined the place would be filled with the usual detritus of people's lives. Boxes full of books and toys. Discarded photo albums. Records and childhood memorabilia. Furniture no longer loved but too good to throw away. But the room was surprisingly empty, which disappointed me. There was nothing here to find. We were on a wild goose chase.

"It doesn't look like there's anything here," I said to Mom. "He must have been hallucinating." And she nodded and started to walk around the room, touching the few things that were there and wiping the dust from her fingers.

I looked around the room and tried to decide where to start. There was an old wooden bureau, its two sides flanked by sets of drawers, four in total. On the far end, where the eaves started to form a sharp angle, stood a large wooden closet. Alongside one wall a stack of crates, around six in total, was lined up beneath the rafters. That was it. The rest of the space was empty, the floor covered in a rug which I could see would once have been expensive. The pattern was one I recognized, some quality English design that seemed so out of place not just in this attic, but in Rob's house, that it made me laugh.

"What was he doing with such a fancy rug?" I asked Mom, and she turned and looked at the floor.

"Whoever bought it," she said. "It wasn't your father, that's for sure." And I had to agree with her. It was so beautiful and so refined. And then it struck me.

"Do you think it was his mom's?" I asked her.

And she smiled. "That would make more sense."

And I thought of the box then. That beautiful walnut wood and the impeccable craftmanship. That would have been hers too. It had to have been.

"What was her name?" I asked, shocked now that I didn't know it. Rob was so young when she died that he had very few memories of her and we were so used to him never speaking about her that we failed to even ask her name.

Mom had to take a minute or two to remember. "A 'C,'" she said. "It began with a 'C.'"

And she walked over the rug and bent down to touch it as she ran through a list of possible names.

"Charlotte, Connie, Cathy, Claire. No! Caroline, of course. That was her name, Caroline."

I looked at the rug, at the intricate floral pattern and the sophisticated colors, creams and blushed pinks and powder blues, a hint of lilac, and I tried to imagine this woman called Caroline and how she came to be the wife of Sam and the mother of Rob. A woman who bought a rug like this, a woman who perhaps kept her jewelry in a beautiful, polished wood box. She didn't quite fit with those men, I thought. She seemed too refined for them. Too delicate and too aware of the importance of beautiful things and the comfort they could bring.

"Just think," I said to Mom. "Rob might have sat on this rug as a kid and played with his toys."

And she shrugged and said, "Maybe, but do you think he would have noticed how beautiful it was?"

"I'd like to think that if Caroline hadn't died, he would have."

And she shook her head and stood up and walked towards the bureau. "Anyway," she said. "We're not here to speculate about who Rob could have been, if his mother had lived, we're here to have a look around. So why don't you take the closet and I'll take the desk and let's see what we can find."

"What is it we're looking for?" I asked her.

"I don't know. But I guess we'll know when we find it."

I smiled at her and headed to the closet while she pulled out the chair from under the bureau, sat down, and opened the first of its four drawers. The truth was, I didn't think we would find anything. It was clear that the space had not been used for storage. If anything, when I looked at the way it was set up, it looked more like a study. A place for quiet contemplation or somewhere to go to deal with basic household administration. I could picture

Rob sitting at that desk, working through some bills or reading correspondence.

The closet had intricate lattice metalwork around the handles, to protect the wood from fingerprints and smudges. Each door had a keyhole, and a key was in one of them. I turned it in the lock, then pulled open the door. It was the side of the closet for hanging coats and clothes. A rail spanned the width of it and four wooden coat hangers clattered on the rail as I opened the door. It was empty but I stretched up and felt around on the shelf above the clothes rail to check if there was anything there. Nothing.

I closed the door and then took out the key and used it in the other keyhole. The door opened to reveal three shelves and below them, three drawers. On each shelf sat a deep red box, each one labeled. Photos. Papers. Miscellaneous.

"Hey," I said to Mom. "I think I've found something."

I heard the chair scrape back across the floor as Mom stood up and walked over to the closet.

"Here," I said, when she was beside me. "Take this." And I handed her the box labeled "Papers" while I slid the two other boxes from their shelves and lifted them down.

I walked over to the rug and set the boxes down, then sat on the floor and opened them. Mom smiled and went over to the desk to get the chair.

"I'm too old and creaky to be sitting on floors," she said.

I tipped out the box labeled "Papers" and sighed when I saw the pile of official-looking letters. As I rummaged through and opened each one, it was clear they were old bits of paperwork related to the ownership of the house, a copy of Sam's will and testament, birth certificates, and health insurance correspondence. An old manila file, which looked promising, turned out to contain school certificates and school reports detailing Rob's progress at school. From a family history point of view, some of it might have made for interesting reading, but it was disappointing, nonetheless.

"There's not much here," Mom conceded. And I nodded.

"What are we looking for though? I mean, what are we expecting? Some miracle piece of evidence that will tie it all together?"

"Yeah," she said. And I laughed at her.

"No, don't laugh," she replied. "Someone took the time and the care to file this stuff away, so you never know."

"I guess so," I said. "It just feels a bit ridiculous, is all."

"Here," she said. "Give me that box there."

She pointed to the box marked "Photos" and I handed it to her, then I put the paperwork back in its box before opening the one marked "Miscellaneous" and tipping the contents onto the rug.

While Mom browsed the photos I tried to make sense of the pile of things on the floor while she interrupted me now and then to show me one of the photos.

"Would you look at this," she said, holding out a faded photo to me. "It's Rob with Caroline when he was just three years old."

I glanced at the photo and smiled at the Kodachrome nostalgia. A tiny child in short pants and a white T-shirt was squinting into the sunlight and clinging to his mother's leg. Rob, a shy and vulnerable looking kid. Caroline was exactly as I had imagined. She was dressed in a light-colored summer dress that buttoned down the front and was belted around the waist; her shoes, red strappy sandals; her dark hair loose and lightly curled and tied back from her face with a glistening hairclip. She looked chic but relaxed, smiling at the camera with one hand laid on Rob's head, a protective gesture that was touching to see.

"They look so happy," I said. "It's sad to think what happened to them."

"Well," Mom said. "It's sad to think what happened to Caroline, I guess. But Rob? Are we supposed to feel sad for him?"

I looked at the kid in the photo and thought of what might have been.

"I just wonder who he would have become if his mother hadn't died," I said. "If there had been someone around who cared for him."

"And maybe Sam would have been a more loving father if Caroline had lived," Mom mused. "We can all imagine things turning out differently, but it doesn't help to think that way. Their lives were the way they were, and in the end they lived them the way they chose to."

"I know," I said. "I just think, looking at him here, that maybe he had it inside him to be someone else. To be kinder, less messed up."

"We can all be kind if we want to be. Each and every one of us. If we decide not to, well, that's a choice, isn't it?"

"Maybe, but life affects us in different ways and not everyone is strong enough to push past the pain."

Mom looked at me and I could see the melancholy in her eyes as she struggled to think of a reply. But there was nothing she could say to counter the basic truth of what I had said. Rob had been hurt in life and he had not been able to process it, and that was not an excuse for what he did to us, but it was something I felt we needed to acknowledge and understand.

"Anyway," I sighed. "Let's have a look at what we've got here."

I sifted through the items I had tipped onto the rug. It was a strange mix of bits and pieces. Some buttons with comic book superhero figures painted on them: Superman, Spiderman, Batman. Boy's things, I figured. And I tried to imagine the boy in the photograph, grown a little, with a button pinned to his T-shirt, heroes he knew from the comics he read at the weekend. There was a yellow wooden yo-yo, and a magnet and a compass. All the sorts of things you could imagine a young boy would need. It was strange to look at them, though, and it took me a moment to realize why. There was something sentimental about it, all these random bits of stuff, boxed away like this, little mementos of a childhood. It was more the sort of thing a mother may do, but I couldn't imagine a man like Sam doing this. Even with the little I knew about him, he didn't seem the sentimental sort and I wondered even if he would have noticed his son playing with a magnet or pinning a button to his shirt. No, the attentiveness was wrong, and I pointed it out to Mom.

"I wonder who boxed all this stuff up," I said. And she looked up from the pile of photographs at the yo-yo I held in my hand.

"Oh, you'd be surprised at the junk parents keep," she said. "I still have a little mirror you had as a kid, that you used to play with. It's a stupid thing, but it's nice sometimes to look at it and remember."

"That's what I mean, though, I can imagine *you* doing that, but Sam? Do you really think Sam would have kept Rob's things?"

She looked at the yo-yo and then started to rummage around in the pile and shook her head.

"No, you're right, it doesn't make any sense, does it?"

From the pile she picked out a small cotton pouch with a draw-string and pulled it open. From inside she pulled a lock of brown hair. It was twisted in a knot and held together with a bobby pin.

"This is definitely something Caroline must have done when Rob was small. Only a mother would take a lock of their child's hair and store it away like this."

I took the lock of hair from her and stroked it. It felt dry and coarse, the years locked away in a dusty attic had taken the softness and the shine from it.

"I didn't realize Rob was so fair-haired as a child," I said. And then I leaned over and rummaged among the photos until I found the one of Rob with his mother.

His hair was visibly darker than the lock I held in my hand, but I checked with Mom to be sure.

"Look," I said. "He's a much darker shade of brown."

She looked at the photo, then took it from my hand to examine more closely.

"It could just be the way the sun is hitting it," she said.

"Sure, but his hair was dark brown when I remember him."

"That happens all the time. Your hair was also a few shades lighter when you were small."

"Still though…" I said.

"Yeah, well, one thing's for sure, whoever kept this box sure liked their mementos."

I stared at the pile on the floor and nodded. Then something caught my eye. Another cotton pouch lay under an old comic book and when I lifted it, I saw that there was another one there. Two more pouches, exactly the same as the one we had just pulled open.

I opened one of them and felt inside, and a shiver ran through me when I felt it: another lock of hair, it had to be. I pulled it out and there it was, a curl of blonde hair pinned with a bobby pin just as the other was.

I quickly opened the other pouch and there it was, a lock of dark hair, this one slightly wavy and a little brittle.

"My God," I said. And Mom looked at me. "What?" she asked me. "What is it?"

"Three locks of hair, don't you see?" And I laid them down, side by side on the floor. Light brown, blond, dark, then pointed to each one.

"Adam Peterson, Jonathan Hutton, and Danny McIntosh. None of these locks are Rob's. They're from the boys. The missing boys. It's their hair, it has to be."

And she looked at the locks of hair laid out on the floor and then began to cry, the sobs shuddering through her uncontrollably.

"No," she said. "That can't be. It just can't be."

"What other explanation do you have?"

And she slumped back in the chair and said nothing, just let the tears flow and I stood up and went over to comfort her.

"This is proof, though, isn't it?" I said. "I mean, they'll be able to test these locks and say for sure if they belong to the boys."

She shuddered, as she wept. "This is why he told us to come up here, isn't it?" she said. "He knew what was hidden here. This is an admission." I wrapped my arms around her and tried to comfort her as she wept. "Oh, God, Carla. Oh, God."

But there was one more secret the attic had to reveal. The final piece of the puzzle that would lead us, at last, to the truth.

*

I took Mom back downstairs and left her in her room to rest.

"I was hoping it wasn't true," she said as she lay down on the bed. "A piece of me was hoping we were wrong. But it's evil, don't you think? I mean, that's the only word for it. Evil, pure evil. Taking locks of their hair, I mean, Carla… I…"

I kissed her forehead and nodded and told her to sleep, then I went back up to the attic.

The locks of hair were strewn on the floor and it was impossible to look at them without a shiver of horror spreading through me. I wanted to push aside the images of the man who had lifted those heads and taken the scissors to the hair and snipped his strange souvenirs. Because that was what they were. They were trophies. A piece of those boys he could keep forever. He could pull the strings on those soft cotton bags and take out the morbid mementos whenever he felt the need to.

And I struggled to imagine my father ever doing this. There was something so meticulous about the way the locks of hair had been preserved, the lack of emotion to it. Each hair curled and pinned in the same fashion, the little bags, plain and simple, as if the contents were something banal. My father was too emotional, too unpredictable to ever be so dispassionate and neat.

I sat on the floor and looked at the things which lay around me. The sweet memory box we had at first imagined Caroline curating now appeared to be something too ghoulish to contemplate. The buttons I thought were my father's, could have been the prized possessions of Danny or Adam or Jonathan. The yo-yo, a favorite toy slipped into a pocket to be pulled out in an idle moment and spooled and unspooled with a deft flick of the wrist. The Spider-man comic book, slipped into a schoolbook in the hope it could be read in secret during a lull in the school day, a dusty history lesson enlivened with color and adventure.

And I felt it then, what had been taken from them. All the small moments, the simple delights, the long-remembered childhood joys. Years and years of this kind of happiness, eliminated. And for what? That was what I couldn't understand, why anyone would want to take so much from these young kids.

I picked up a few bits of paper and tried to decipher what they were. Drawings mostly, in gray pencil. They were startlingly well accomplished. Scenes from around town—I recognized the shop fronts of the main street and the familiar rows of houses that made up the neat suburban landscape. There were other drawings of the forest too, these ones, darker and slightly imposing, the threat of what lay hidden in the shaded depths clearly felt. It took me a while before I saw the name written in small, neat handwriting in the bottom left corner: Rob Allen. And the dates listed too. My father's childhood drawings. I had no idea he was such a good artist and I sat there and admired them and wondered how they had come to be in this box with all the items I had to assume had some connection to the three boys.

And then I saw it. The streets, the houses, the forest. It was as if they were illustrations for the horrible narrative that was slowly unfolding before me. These were the streets where the boys lived, these were their houses, these were the places they had been taken from and the final place they had been taken to.

I took up the drawings of the forests and looked again at the dates: 1963, 1964, and 1972. The years each boy had disappeared.

The forest scenes in the drawings the places where Danny and Adam had been found. And the third drawing? It could only mean one thing—somewhere in that forest lay Jonathan Hutton.

I was about to pick up the drawings and take them to Mom to ask her opinion when something caught my eye. A letter addressed to Sam Allen, a US Postal Service stamp in the corner. I looked at the date and could just make out that it was from 1972. And the handwriting, now that I paid close attention, I could see it was my father's.

There was no need to hesitate or feel fearful. *Just open it*, I thought. And I picked it up and lifted the flap at the back of the envelope and took out the letter.

It was one page, written in my father's familiar scrawl, the date September 14, 1972. I thought back to when Jonathan had gone missing. June, was it? Or July? Certainly in the summer of that year. So my father was writing this, probably knowing already that Jonathan was missing. And it was then that I noticed my hand begin to shake. I closed my eyes and steadied myself and began to read.

Dear Sam,

I cannot call you dad. I cannot call you father. Father means something. Or it's supposed to. Care, love, commitment, things like that. But that was never who you were.

I did not want to contact you, but you have forced me to write this letter, and if I receive no reply, then make no mistake, I will come to you for answers. Because I need an answer. I need to know why.

After eight years, I thought it was over. Though I use that word lightly. It has never been over for me. What you did. What you made me do. How can I forget that? How can I ever get over that? Though you expected me to, didn't you? You assumed

I would walk away, that I would move on, get over it, without any scars, without any consequences. And you knew I would remain silent too. Because who can I turn to? Who can I talk to? How, in God's name, can I explain it to anyone? You know it's impossible. You know you can leave me alone to figure it out by myself without ever having to fear that I will expose you.

I can't say I have been figuring it out. It may look that way to some people. I've got a steady job, and the chance, I hope, to make a life with Sophia. To become a husband and a family man. But, the truth is, I don't know if I'll make it, because the rage I feel some days, when I think back to what you did to me, is overwhelming. You transformed me to such an extent that the boy I used to be, the man I could have become, has disappeared forever. That's your legacy. And whatever it is that is left of me, I just hope it's enough.

The only thing that sustained me was knowing it had stopped. I wasn't there to help you. I wasn't there to disguise who you really were, and without me, you couldn't continue. And you did stop. For eight years, you stopped. Danny, Adam, I thought that would be it. I thought there would be no others.

For eight years, I had a peace, of sorts.

And then I pick up the paper one morning and what do I see? Another young boy missing in Newcastle. The fear that a killer has returned. The story of what happened in '63 and '64 recounted in all its grim detail. Parents terrified again that there is a killer in their midst. Returned or resurfaced, they don't know.

I read this and I knew the truth. The man who had lived among them all this time. The man they all trusted. The man I should have exposed. They were right to fear him. To fear you.

I was a coward then, when I could have done something. I've thought about that a lot. Spent years telling myself that I was just a kid, that there was nothing I could have done. Because what can an eleven-year-old child do to stop a man intent on such violence? Any man that could harm a child could also harm his own son. That was the truth, and I knew it. And you would have hurt me, wouldn't you? You told me so. "One more missing child won't matter. They'll think you were taken by whoever took the other two. You'll just be another victim." And I believed you then, just as I believe you still. Those words have never left me. How can they? You would have taken me into those woods, and you would have left me there, just as you left them.

And so, what now? Jonathan Hutton. I recognize the surname. Cece's son? You would do this to Cece? And how did you lure him to you? Without me there to help you, how did you get him to come to the house? Or was it simply that the opportunity presented itself? That fate stepped in and Jonathan was the poor victim of bad timing?

I'm not even going to ask you if this will be the last time. It has to be. I'll make sure of it. And yes, I know what that means. I will have to tell the truth about what happened to Danny and Adam and my role in their deaths. All I can hope is that people will understand that a fearful eleven-year-old child would not have been able to do very much. I had no mother, no one to turn to. I can ask for understanding and hope for forgiveness. And maybe, because I am prepared to tell the truth, I'll receive it. Repentance, that's what they call it, isn't it?

I don't know. But I can't let you get away with it this time. I can't stand by in silence. I can't be a coward. Because I'm not a child now. I'm a man. And I know what to do and I understand the consequences of it. But I cannot be silent. Not this time.

So call me. Write me. Tell me why. If you don't, I'll come and find you and you better have an answer.

Yours,
Rob

I thought back to what Cece had told me, that strange visit Rob had made to Newcastle, the way he had pretended not to see her when she waved and called out to him.

He had come up here, and now I knew the reason. Sam had not replied, and so Rob had made good on his threat. Only that couldn't have been the case. The truth that was presented in this letter had never been revealed. No one knew what Sam had done. No one knew the way he had coerced his son and made him a party to all those horrible events. It had never come out.

So what had happened? I wondered. Rob had kept his father's secrets after all. But why?

I lay back on the floor and stared at the ceiling, trying to think but getting nowhere.

"Are you okay?"

Mom's question startled me and made me jump.

"Geez, Mom. I thought you were asleep."

"Sorry, I woke up and wondered what you were still doing up here. It's late, Carla. You should get yourself to bed."

"I will. I just need to process this." And I handed her the letter and told her, "It doesn't make for pleasant reading."

She took it from me and read the letter and sighed when she had finished, incapable of reacting beyond this small, exhausted exhalation.

"You know," she said. "I'd often wondered how it was that Sam died so suddenly, so out of the blue. Now I guess I know why."

I looked at her, confused. "What do you mean?"

"This letter, it's from September 1972. Two weeks after this letter was sent, Sam was dead. He shot himself, is what they said. Suicide in any case."

"What? Why did you never tell me this?"

"It's not the sort of thing you talk about, is it?"

"Oh, come on, Mom."

"Listen, Carla, that's just how it was. Sam was dead and life carried on. I figured he'd just had enough was all. But maybe…"

"Mom, Dad didn't kill his own father. You can't be serious?"

"Who knows. Maybe not. Maybe he just gave him a good reason not to keep going, is all."

And I thought about that. I thought about the way Rob would have handled a thing like this. That letter, written quickly, in an emotional hurry. But once he'd had time to think things through, it was possible. He would have come up with a better plan. A way to make his father pay for what had happened in a way that wouldn't damage his own life even further. Yes, it was possible. Mom was right.

"You knew Dad better than I did, I guess," I told her.

"There's just one thing that bothers me though."

"What?"

"Rob would never have left Sam without finding out what he did with that boy's body. He would have wanted to know where Sam took him, I'm sure of it."

"But he can't have known. He'd have told the police. He'd have made sure that they found him. Made sure Cece could bury her son."

"Yeah, maybe."

"What? You don't think he would have done that?"

"I think, deep down, your father is a coward. He may have wanted to know where the boy was, Sam might even have told him, but in the end, I think he would have doubted himself and not known what to do. How to get the information to the police without incriminating his father, or himself."

"I don't know. I don't think he would have withheld a thing like that. I mean you read his letter. He was determined for the truth to come out."

"There's one way to find out."

"How?"

"If he knew where Jonathan was, he'd have written it down. Left it here so we would find it after he was gone."

"You think so?"

"Why else did he keep those notebooks? Those newspaper clippings? This letter? They were all meant to be found after he'd died. That was always the idea. I don't think he really believed we would come back to see him before he died."

"So there's one more thing we need to look for?"

"Yes, but I think I know where it is."

And I stared at her, unsure what she meant.

"Tomorrow," she said. "We need to go and visit Cece."

CHAPTER TWENTY-SEVEN

Cece handed the letter to Suzie and we sat in the living room in silence and waited while she read it.

I watched the expressions shift on Suzie's face, from sadness to horror to anger and then something which looked like relief, the play of emotions on display the same as her grandmother had expressed when she read the letter a few minutes before.

"Sam?" Cece asked. And Mom nodded.

"I'm so sorry, if I could do anything to make this untrue, believe me, I would," I told her.

"No," said Cece. "It's not your problem to solve or wish away. None of this is something you need to say sorry for."

"Perhaps," Mom replied. "But I spent years trying to offer Rob understanding, even love, and perhaps if I had succeeded he would have been able to admit to all this earlier. He could have stopped a lot of suffering if he had. And I could have eased some of his own too, I'm sure of it."

"Please," said Cece. "None of this was your fault. I can accept your sympathy, but you will never need to apologize to me on his behalf. And I don't expect you to try."

"Okay, thank you," Mom said, her voice quiet and small as she held back the tears.

"What are you going to do?" Suzie asked us.

"Take it to the police, I guess," I told her. "Along with the notebooks."

"It won't get them very far, though, will it?" Cece replied. "It's not evidence and it's not going to help me find my son either."

"We found some more evidence in the attic," I told her. "Some of the boys' possessions and…" I had to pause before I could continue because I knew how shocking it was. "Well, there are some locks of hair too. From all three boys, it looks like."

"Oh!" Cece cried. And Suzie took hold of her grandmother's hand, to comfort her.

"There's something I'd like to check if that's okay?" Mom said.

Suzie looked at her, a little agitated. "What?" she asked.

We watched as Mom stood up.

"It's just a hunch and I might be totally wrong about this," she said. "Can you give me a minute just to be sure?"

Nobody understood what she meant so we nodded and told her it was okay, then watched as she headed to the hallway and closed the door behind her.

That was when I understood what she was doing. The hallway was pretty much empty, save for the photographs on the walls. I could picture it as I listened to her footsteps, the narrow space so similar to Rob's, it had stunned me when I first saw it.

Halfway down, I knew she would come to a stop. That was roughly where the photograph of Jonathan hung and that was what she was looking for, I was sure of it.

I heard her stop and I listened as she lifted the photograph from the wall, the metal picture frame clacking against its neighbors as she took it down. There was silence for a moment, and I could only assume she was looking for something there in that photograph, though what it could be was still not something I had figured out.

Then the shuffle of her feet as she turned and made her way back to the living room. When the door opened I could feel the silence as we all held our breaths and waited for her to explain what she had been doing.

"Well," she sighed when she sat down. "I was right."

And she held up the photograph and turned it upside down so that we could see the underside. And there, stuck in the frame, was an envelope, yellowed and crumpled after decades of being hidden away.

She handed the picture frame to Cece.

"All those photographs Rob hung in the hallway. They didn't make sense to me, because it was too sentimental, and Rob wasn't like that. I couldn't understand why it bothered me. Then I saw your hallway and I knew what he'd done. I haven't opened it, but I think I can guess what it is," she said.

And Cece nodded, then sighed and gave the photograph to Suzie.

"Please, you open it," she said.

And once again we sat and waited while Suzie lifted the envelope from the frame and then carefully opened it and read. But after less than half a minute she started to cry and then she tossed the paper on to the floor and let her head fall into her hands as she sobbed.

"My God," she cried. "My God."

I got up and walked over to her and laid a hand on her shoulder.

"Mind if I take a look at it?" I asked. And when she didn't reply, I picked it up and sat beside her on the sofa and read.

It was a crudely drawn map. A few lines and roughly contoured shapes, but there was enough there for me to recognize the setting. The forest by the golf course where I had been a few days ago. Only this map seemed to show the place as it had been years ago, before the wilderness had reclaimed the place I had been to.

Back then the golf course stretched farther and the place I had visited looked to have been part of the green. The map certainly depicted bunkers and lawns and landscaped features. A small lake, a few trees, some sort of pavilion.

And below the map, a few lines of explanation.

You want to find him, it read, *well, here he is. I'm sorry I was never brave enough to tell you. Yours, Rob Allen.*

I wasn't sure at first what it was referring to, where *here* was exactly. The golf course? A body left on a golf course would have been discovered immediately. The lake? Perhaps, but it was no longer there, so if it had been drained, then Jonathan would have been found.

"I don't get it," I said. "He can't be there. They'd have found him. It's too public a place."

"What?" Cece asked. "What is it?" She stood up, walked over to me and took the map and stared at it, taking her time before it hit her and she understood what she was looking at.

"Is he here?" she asked me. "My God, is my son here?"

"I don't know," I said. "I really don't know."

Suzie lifted her head and wiped away the tears that smudged her face.

"He has to be there though, doesn't he? Otherwise what's the point of hiding this in that picture frame for all this time? Unless your father was fond of sick jokes?"

"No," Mom said. "This isn't a joke."

"What is it then?" Suzie demanded, her voice pinched with anguish, her energy taut as if she was about to burst into a frenzy of rage at any moment. "Why the hell did he put it there? And, now I think about it, when? When would he have done this?"

"He always helped me out," Cece said. "Every time the place needed sprucing up. Some painting, repairs, that sort of thing. He could have done it when he was painting the hallway or something like that. He was good that way, always helping me out."

"Good?" Suzie shouted. "How can this be good?"

Cece walked back to her chair and slumped into it and let her head fall back as she closed her eyes. "I don't know," she said. "I just meant that was when he could have done it, don't ask me why he thought this was the way to go about it. How can I possibly know? He's a coward, I guess. He's simply a coward."

"Listen," I said. "We have to take all of this to the police now. We're not going to get any further along with this without them. If Jonathan is there, then we're not going to be able to find him. We need help."

"He's there," Cece said, her eyes still closed. "I can feel it."

*

The officer at the station didn't know what to make of us. Four women descending upon him with a story he had trouble following. He had taken us into an interview room at the back and left us sitting there while he called a superior.

"I just work the front desk," he told us.

Cece had smiled and told him not to worry. "We can wait."

Ten minutes later, two officers came into the room and they nodded at Cece as if they recognized her.

"Mrs Hutton," one of them said, and Cece looked up at him and smiled.

"Well, Andrew Scott, nice to see you."

The other officer introduced himself as Detective Carter and they both sat down at the table and looked at us as if we were a confusing sight.

"So," Detective Carter began, "if I understand it correctly, you seem to be suggesting you've found Jonathan."

Cece pushed the map towards him, and the letter Rob had written to Sam.

"We think we know where he's been buried," she said.

Detective Carter opened the letter and unfolded the map and read, his face impassive, as if the contents were the sort of thing he dealt with every day, then he handed them to his colleague.

"Why don't you start at the beginning and explain it to me. What am I looking at here, and why do you think it proves anything?"

For over an hour we recounted the story to him. How I had found the notebooks and the newspaper clippings. Rob's delirious ramblings. The trips I had made to the forest. My seemingly pointless trip to the golf course and then the discovery of these letters and the lockets of hair in the attic and in Cece's house.

The detectives listened and questioned us as we spoke. Why did you not come forward sooner? Why would Rob have kept such a secret for so long? How could the original investigation have missed Jonathan if he was somewhere on the golf course?

"That's why we're here," Cece pointed out to them. "We can't search the golf course on our own, we need your help."

"And we can't search golf courses without reason," Detective Scott explained.

"I know that," I told him. "But surely these documents are reason enough?"

"Perhaps, but I'll need to follow procedure, is what I'm saying. If there is enough evidence to warrant a search, then we'll conduct one."

"But how long will that take?" Suzie asked.

"Could be a few hours. Could be a few days. Could be weeks before a search order comes through."

"What?" Cece said. "Why so long?"

"I'm sorry," Detective Scott said. "I need to follow procedure. I can't promise anything."

"You mean a search may not be granted?" Cece asked him.

"It's a possibility," he agreed. "Evidence is needed, and I'm not sure you have enough here."

"I see," Cece said.

And to a casual observer I guess she would have appeared defeated and tired. She had waited so long, had been disappointed for so long, that she could not be expected to react anymore. But I caught it, though, the look in her eye, something determined and focused. I didn't know what she had planned, but it was

clear to me that she was going to make damn sure that the search
went ahead.

It was late afternoon when we drove back across town. All the
way home I struggled to stay quiet and not ask Cece what she
was planning to do. I just focused on the road and tried to push
away my thoughts. I was hoping she wasn't thinking of some sort
of independent action. Gathering a team of locals to dig up the
greens and scour the nearby woodland in defiance of the law.

Turned out, I needn't have worried. Cece's mind worked in far
subtler and more effective ways.

When we pulled up outside her house, she told me to park
up the driveway and come inside because she had something she
wanted to ask me.

"A sort of favor," she explained. And Mom looked at me,
uncertain and a little afraid.

"That's okay," I replied. "Whatever you want, if I can help out,
then you know I will."

Suzie had laughed as we stepped out of the car and walked to
the front door. "I've seen that expression on my grandma's face a
thousand times. She's not asking you, believe me."

And I saw Mom smile as we walked inside.

"So," Cece said when we were in her living room again. "I
need you to talk to that friend of yours, the one at the *Chronicle*."

"Will?"

"Is that his name?" Cece said. "In any case, you need to call
him and tell him I want to speak to him."

"What? Now?"

"Yes," she said. "Do you have a cell phone?"

"Sure," I said, and I took it out of my pocket. "But what do
you want me to say to him?"

"Nothing, I just want you to say I need to talk to him and then hand me the phone. I'll do the talking."

I dialed the number and when Will picked up I told him there was someone who needed to speak to him. When he asked me who, I said nothing and handed the phone to Cece. If I told him who it was he might have panicked and hung up, figuring Cece wanted to talk to reprimand him about the article he had written.

"Is this Will?" Cece asked, and I mouthed to Suzie that she should take the phone and put it on speaker so we could all hear the conversation.

"Yeah, this is Will. Sorry, who am I talking to?"

"I'm Cece Hutton, Jonathan Hutton's mom."

And we heard Will take a sharp intake of breath. It was a few seconds before he could speak.

"Right," he said. "Listen about the article, I—"

"I don't want to talk to you about that," Cece said, and I smiled as I imagined Will reacting to her stern tone. If he thought he was dealing with a vulnerable old lady, he was going to be in for a shock.

"We need your help," Cece continued. "I've read those notebooks Rob kept and there's some new developments I want you to write about now."

"Okay," Will said.

"We think we know where Jonathan is, but we need to push the authorities to go out and search the area, and right now they're not convinced."

"Wait, how the hell do you know where he is?" Will asked.

"We found a map," Cece explained. "And it corresponds to the area Carla searched a few days ago. We're pretty sure it's where Sam took him."

"Sam? Who's he?" Will asked.

"He's my grandfather," I said.

"Carla?"

"Yeah, sorry, we put you on speaker, we're all here, me, Suzie, and my mom."

"I see. Okay, then listen, tell me what happened so I can put something together."

I related the whole story of the map and our morning at the police station and explained why we were convinced that Jonathan was buried on or near the golf course.

"One other thing," Cece said when I had finished. "We need to make this a big thing. Like a nationwide story. Can you do that?"

"If everything you told me is true, then I'd say there was no way we could stop that from happening," Will explained.

"Good," Cece said. "But make sure it happens, okay?"

"Don't worry, you can count on it," Will replied.

We ended the call and each of us stared at Cece, awed and impressed by her ingenuity and tenacity.

"You think it will work?" Suzie asked.

"We're about to find out," Cece replied.

CHAPTER TWENTY-EIGHT

It's hard to describe a media frenzy when you are in the middle of it. That's what we provoked, though, a full-blown national news storm. Will was right, the story had too many ingredients for it to be ignored. A lost boy, a cold case, a mother waiting to bury her son at last.

The day Will's second story ran in the *Chronicle*, Gina called me, her voice stammering with indignation and disbelief.

"Why the fuck didn't you tell me about any of this?"

"Sorry," I said. "Everything happened so fast."

There was silence at the other end as she absorbed what I said. Then I heard her sigh.

"Sam, really? I mean it's impossible."

"Gina, I can't talk about all of this on the phone. Just get up here as soon as you can, okay?" I asked her.

"Tomorrow is the earliest flight I could get."

"Right, I…"

"What?"

"It's just, I'm not sure how long Dad has. I got a call from the hospice an hour ago. Apparently, he's really close now."

"How close?"

"I don't know, it could be hours. Maybe he'll hold out until tomorrow. But I don't know if we'll get a chance to say goodbye to him."

"Fuck."

"I thought Rob had done this," I said, my voice breaking as I tried to fight back the tears and the guilt. "I thought he'd killed those boys. And I told him that. And I don't want that to be the last conversation we had. I just want him to know that we found his letter to Sam, that we know the truth. He was just a kid and his own father put him through that. I can't…"

"No, Carla, listen to me. What Dad did was wrong. I need you to know that. He could have told the police about this years ago. He could have stopped Sam. He could have even saved Jonathan. But he didn't. Think about that."

"I know, it's just—"

"You can't change what he did, Carla. So please, don't beat yourself up about it. And whatever you do, don't watch the fucking news. You don't want to know what they're saying about him."

"What? What are they saying?"

"Please, Carla. Just wait for me to get there tomorrow. If we're lucky, then it won't be too late and we can see him one last time, okay?"

"Yeah, okay."

"And remember, don't turn on the TV."

It was the first thing I did, though, after she hung up; I went into the living room and turned on the TV, then flicked through to the news channel.

We had asked for this, I knew that, but still, it was difficult to take in the full impact of it. There, on the screen, under a relentless ticker tape of ghoulish headlines, was a photo composite of my father and my grandfather, their faces staring out of the screen, eyes menacingly vacant. The message clear: these were not men, they were monsters. These were the bogeymen every parent feared. The evil presence in their midst. It was open season, everyone was free to say what they wanted, to theorize at will on the whys and the wherefores. To analyze the mindsets and dig into the backstory. It was unbearable to listen to the voice of the TV anchor as he stared into the camera and asked: "How did a town hide such monsters?

How did a family manage to keep such terrible secrets?" and realize that he was talking about my father and my grandfather.

It would only be a matter of hours before they came knocking, demanding our side of the story.

"Was that Gina you were talking to?"

"Damn, Mom. Don't sneak up on me like that."

"Sorry."

"Yeah, she saw the news on TV this morning and freaked out."

"It's already on the news?"

"Don't watch it," I warned her. "It's grim. Truly grim."

"Why, what are they saying?"

"Oh, that Dad and Sam are monsters. That we protected them all these years. That the police have cordoned off the golf course and are out there now, with Suzie and Cece, searching the area. There was even a helicopter flying overhead, tracking the teams combing the greens. They brought a digger. I mean, what are they planning on doing? Tearing up the whole course?"

"If that's what they have to do, then that's what they'll do, Carla. If that boy is lying under those greens, then they have to find him. They have an obligation to Cece. We all do."

I tried not to think about what Cece must be going through. That she had the energy to be out there watching and waiting was astonishing. She knew, I reckoned, that they would certainly find him, if not today, then very soon.

"Maybe we should go over there and help her?" I suggested.

"And do what, exactly?"

"I don't know, just stand by her. Bear witness to it, maybe."

Mom sat on the sofa and pursed her lips. "Did you make any coffee?" she asked.

I nodded and went to the kitchen and poured us both a mug and took in a plate of small Danish pastries.

"What are these?" she asked me when I set the plate down beside her.

"I like them in the morning. Something sweet with coffee but not too filling."

She took one and bit into it. "Fancy," she said.

It felt strange to be sitting there eating sugar-coated pastries and drinking coffee while the police combed the golf course and the forest trying to find the place that Sam had indicated on the map. Thinking about Jonathan lying there alone and his elderly mother walking around in the cold morning air, hoping for a miracle, was too much.

"We have to go over there," I said to Mom. "We can't sit here eating cakes while they endure this. It's wrong."

"Fine," she said. "But just tell me first why you want to go."

"We should be there. It's the right thing to do."

"Is it? Or is it just that you want people to see us there? To see us, what was it you said? *Bearing witness.* Do you really think that will make people absolve us?"

"Absolve? Mom, what does that even mean?"

"I mean, I just don't want to go over there if it's only to be seen to be doing the right thing. To be standing shoulder to shoulder with Cece when they find her son, so that we can show the world we are as horrified by all of this as they are. To show them we're here to help Cece."

"But that's ridiculous! We *are* horrified. We *are* here to help her. Why do you think I took those notebooks over to her in the first place? I knew what they were, I knew what they meant."

"Carla, I know that. Of course I know that. I just don't want to be, I don't know, what's the word?"

"Performative."

"Is it? Is that a word?"

"Oh, Mom, who cares? We should just go there. It doesn't matter what other people think. Cece will know why we're there. And she'll want us there, I'm sure she will."

"I tell you what, why don't you call Suzie and ask her? Instead of charging over assuming they want us there, why don't we just ask? That seems like a better way to go about it."

"Okay," I said. And I picked up my phone and called Suzie.

I knew what the answer was going to be before I asked her the question. This was something they had to do alone. Cece had waited years for this moment, and we had no right to take a place at her side.

Mom had been right. I'd just wanted to show the world that what they were saying about us—that we had to have known somehow that Rob and Sam had committed these crimes—was a lie. I wanted to stand in front of the world and let them see that Rob and Sam had also harmed us, that we had endured pain too.

But this was not the right way to stand up to the world. I'd have to find another way to let people see who we were and what Rob had done to us—what he was still doing to us.

I was lost in thought when the doorbell rang, and I walked down the hallway and opened the door, without thinking, my vigilance weakened by worry and stress.

The light of the camera made me flinch and as I tried to blink it away, I became aware of someone talking to me, their voice harsh and slightly manic. They spoke so fast it took me a moment to understand what was going on. A television crew on my doorstep, the images beamed live into millions of homes while I stood there, bewildered and dumbfounded, dressed in my pajamas and looking for all the world like a disheveled and untrustworthy fool.

"Did you know Sam Allen was a murderer?" I heard someone ask.

"Did your father help him?" they continued.

"Do you have anything to say to Cece Hutton?"

The barrage of questions was too much, and I simply stood there staring at the camera and allowing the face of the reporter to come into focus. A young blonde woman with impeccable hair and glowing makeup, dressed in a powder-blue coat. She looked too neat, too nice, to be standing on my doorstep demanding answers and I found it impossible to speak.

It was Mom who rescued me. I felt a squeeze on my shoulder and heard her say, "Who are you? What is it you want?"

"We're from NWRT," the woman said. Which meant nothing. "We just want to talk to you about the search for Jonathan Hutton and your family's involvement in the murders."

I don't know how Mom managed to remain so calm, where she found the strength to keep her head cool and make a quick decision, but her steady tone and reasonableness had the effect of relaxing me and clearing my head, as if the shock of the confrontation had been neutralized by the sound of her voice.

"Why don't you give us ten minutes to get ourselves ready and then we can talk calmly about this without all this shouting?" she said.

The reporter saw her chance and grabbed it.

"Great! Ten minutes. We'll be ready."

Then Mom closed the door and turned back to the living room.

"Mom," I said. "We can't talk to them. What the hell are you playing at?"

"Carla," she said. "I have no intention of talking to them. I'm not stupid. But I got the door closed and bought us some time. If they're still here in an hour we can call the police and have them escorted off our driveway."

I had to give it to her, it was quick thinking.

"So," she said. "I'm going to take a shower and get dressed and then make some proper breakfast. Why don't you get cleaned up and we can eat together? I'll make sure to keep the blinds drawn so we get some peace."

I went upstairs to the bathroom and left the water to run for a while until the room steamed up, then I stepped under the shower and let the hot water wash over me. I wanted to stay there all day,

cocooned in the hazy heat of the vapor, distanced from the world
by this misty cloak.

It hadn't really hit me until then that there was a piece of me
that wanted to run away from it all. I had started out on this
search without stopping to think about the impact. What it would
mean for me, for Gina and Mom, and for the families of those
three boys, to learn the truth. I imagined truth was good in itself,
that it could cause no harm, do no damage. But there had been
something else I'd been hoping for too, something I would need
to explain to Mom and to Gina. I'd been denying it, but now I
had to talk to them about it, because it was a part of the story
that needed to be told. Maybe not now, but at some point, even
if it was only something we told to each other. It was necessary,
because it may just heal us; that was what I understood.

Yesterday, coming back from the hospice, I'd had a small pang
of regret which I had immediately suppressed. I told myself it was
the stress of the moment. But seeing Rob lying there, medically
removed from the world already, it was difficult to understand why
I still felt the need for reconciliation and forgiveness.

But what I'd been looking for was to hear him say it first: *I'm
sorry.* And faced with the impossibility of it, I had been forced to
accept that we were not the sort of people who could forgive and
forget, the sort of people who could talk to one another. I had
left the hospice filled with the same unresolved emotions I had
arrived with. Rage, confusion, frustration.

But reading the letter he had written to Sam had softened some
of that rage. I think we had all known something had been done
to him and that the damage had been unfathomable and now we
understood the reason why.

But if this was his story, if this was the truth he had been forced
to keep secret his whole life, then surely we needed to acknowledge
that in some way? Surely the right thing to do was to accept that,
as a child, he had been forced to endure something so unbearably

awful, he should never have been left to recover from it in silence. It didn't undo the hurt he had caused us, but it did allow us the opportunity to understand him. It wasn't quite forgiveness as such, but it was a way forward. And it would heal us, I was sure of it.

When I went down to the kitchen, Mom was already putting breakfast on the table, something more substantial than my pastries, but the sight of the food left me a little nauseous.

I sat across from her and sipped the coffee she had poured for me and declined her offer to *eat up*.

"You've still got to eat," she said, as she lifted some scrambled egg onto her fork.

"I know, I'm okay with coffee for now and the pastry was enough to keep me going."

She frowned and continued eating and all the while we tried to ignore the sound of the doorbell and the voices from the driveway.

"Wait," I said, when I couldn't stand it any longer. "I know where the power cable leads to. I can turn it off."

I headed to the hallway and found the box for the doorbell hanging on the wall and took a chair from the living room to stand on so I could reach up and disable the switch. I was visible through the glass pane in the doorway and I could see the reporter as she peered in and called out to me. When I had disabled the doorbell and returned to the kitchen I sent Gina a text message explaining the situation. She'd have to fight her way inside, I figured.

"So what do we do now then?" I asked Mom.

"They'll go away soon enough. They won't want to miss whatever's happening over at the golf course. We're not so interesting."

The phone rang and I saw Suzie's name flash on the screen and picked up immediately.

"Are you okay?" I asked her.

"They've found some remains," she said. "They've found him."

"What? Where?"

"In the woods next to the golf course, where you went looking the other day."

"But I don't understand, there was nothing there."

"Turns out there was. An old water well that used to be some sort of decoration back when this spot was still part of the greens."

I didn't recall seeing a well, but no doubt they had been more thorough than I could have been, and would also have had detailed maps of the place as it had been back then.

"Are they sure it's him?" I asked Suzie.

"They'll need to do some tests. It'll take a few days. But it's a child. It's a boy. So…"

"Oh, I'm so sorry, Suzie. I'm so sorry."

"No, it's good. We have him back. Finally, we have him back."

I ended the call and turned to Mom.

"So, that's it," I said. "They've found him."

"Are they sure?"

"Pretty much."

She stood up and walked over to me and wrapped her arms around me and we held one another as tightly as we could, relief and sadness overwhelming us so much we couldn't speak, or even cry.

"We should let Dad know," I said. And I felt her embrace loosen as she let out a long, exhausted sigh.

"Shouldn't we wait for Gina to get here first, before we go and see him?" she asked me.

I shrugged, and I wanted to explain to her that we had no time. He could die any moment, die without knowing that he had helped us in the end. He had led us to those mementos in the attic, to his letter to Sam, and now Cece was reunited with her son at last. He should know what he had done. Know that we understood what he had gone through, and that we forgave him.

"I know he probably can't hear us," I continued. "I know that maybe it's too late now, but we can try. I think we should try, don't you?"

And I don't know what her answer would have been because the phone rang. It was the hospice calling to tell us he was gone.

"Did he know?" I asked the nurse. "Did he see the news? About Jonathan? They found him?"

She paused, unsure what to say, her silence in that split second the true answer. But I accepted her tiny lie in that moment. I took the solace where I could find it.

"Yes," she said. "The television was on. We thought he would have wanted to have known what was happening."

"Thank you," I told her.

"That's okay, you're welcome."

I left Mom to call Gina with the news, unable yet to say those words—he's gone—because it was a truth I was not yet ready to acknowledge. Then I went to find the photograph of Rob with his mother. The small boy before all this hell started. The man he could have been. The man he truly was. I stared at his smiling face and hoped that somehow, he could hear me when I told him it was over. The past could not be altered. The damage could not be undone. But something had been set right today. Something important. And it was because of him.

"You did it," I whispered. "You did it."

And I looked at his eyes, bright and innocent and kind, and I made a promise to myself that this was the man I needed to think of, the man I needed to remember. This was my father.

*

She knew pretty much everything from the newspapers and the television, but I could see Gina was overwhelmed as I told her what had happened.

When I finished, she got up from her chair and came over to sit beside me, then pulled me close in an embrace, calling out to Mom to join us. We sat there, the three of us, holding each other and comforting one another in silence.

Then Mom pulled away and leaned back into the sofa, releasing a deep and exhausted sigh.

"You know," she said. "I always knew that something more had happened to him. He always brushed it away when I asked him, said it was just the way it was for a child who lost his mother at a young age. I knew it was more than that. The way he could retreat from the world for days, the long silences and then those bursts of rage, the violence. That was more than just abandonment. But I stopped asking him. He never answered me and in the end, I knew better than to force it. His fists were strong and the punches he dealt hurt too much. And they were real, the pain he caused was real. So I let it be. But maybe—"

"No," Gina interrupted. "You did the right thing given what you didn't know at the time."

"If he'd just spoken about it, it might have changed things."

"How?" Gina said.

"We could have found help for him. We could have gone to the police even, before Sam died. We could have had him arrested. Those parents, they could have had justice."

"No, Mom," I said. "Let's not go there. We'll end up blaming ourselves for not doing something we had no control over. Dad never told us the truth, and he had his reasons and we just have to live with that. There was nothing we could have done."

"Why though," Gina said. "That's what I don't get. Why did he never tell anyone? Why protect Sam like that?"

"Gina, he was eleven. Who knows what else Sam said to him back then to force him to keep quiet? The threats he made. Rob had no one to go to, no mother, he was powerless. And besides,

Sam was his father; an eleven-year-old boy won't betray his father. He'd have been scared."

"Yeah, maybe. I don't know…"

"Gina, I'm not making excuses for him, but think about it. A kid that age."

"But he was an adult too, don't forget that. When Jonathan was killed, Rob knew it had to be Sam, and still he did nothing."

"That's not quite true," Mom said.

"Huh, what do you mean?" Gina asked her. "He never went to the police, he never told you, he never—"

"Let me explain," Mom said.

And we sat and listened.

"That time when Rob came back up here, the last time he saw Sam. It was a few months after Jonathan went missing. I don't really remember him telling me where he was going. I think I thought he was gone for some work thing or whatever. But I've been thinking about that trip ever since Cece spoke about it because something was bothering me. I don't know what went on between your father and Sam over the course of those few days, but I remember they called each other a few times after Rob came home and it was always the same, an argument and Rob slamming the phone down and never telling me what was going on. And then we got the call to tell us Sam had died. Just like that.

"When the report came back that it was suicide, I couldn't get Rob to talk to me about it. Even at the funeral, we came up here and he was so quiet, so accepting of it. I thought it was just grief, just shock, but now I'm not so sure. Because during those telephone calls he'd scream at Sam and didn't care who heard him. *You know what to do. Just do it. That's the only way this will ever stop. End it, damn it! End it.* I thought it was some argument about money or something. And even when Sam died, I never thought about those calls, other than to tell Rob that he shouldn't regret that their last conversations had always ended in these fights. I told him he wasn't to know that his father would choose his own way out.

"And he'd always look at me and smile, and pat me on the shoulder, like I was a little child and say, *Don't worry about it, you don't need to bother yourself with any of this.* But the thing is, I think I understand now, what Rob meant when he said, *You know what to do.* He meant suicide, didn't he? That's what he meant?"

I looked at Gina, but she didn't take her eyes from her lap, she just looked down and kept her head bent, and I leaned over and touched her arm and asked if she was okay.

She looked up and shook her head and managed a small, uncertain smile.

"I remember asking him once," Gina said. "When I was maybe ten or thereabouts. I asked him to tell me about Sam. We never knew him, and I wanted to know. And I didn't understand what he meant when he told me never to ask him that again. I was shocked and couldn't really believe he meant it, so I asked him again and he grew impatient. I thought he was going to hit me, I remember bracing for it, but instead he said, 'In the end he was a good man, in the end he did the right thing.' I didn't understand what he was talking about. I only remember it because it was weird. But he came up here and he made sure Sam understood that he would not let him get away with it this time. I mean, that has to be it, doesn't it? It has to be?"

"I think so, yes," Mom said. "We'll never know for sure, but I think that's what happened."

"So what does that mean then?" I asked them. "That we think Rob did the right thing in the end too? I mean, you understand what you're saying here, right? That he told his own father to kill himself?"

"Yeah," Gina said. "And it was the right thing to do. He did the right thing."

I had no reply for that and when Mom sighed and got up and said she was going to call it a night, I realized how tired I was too.

"Good idea," I said. "The next few days are probably going to be crazy. We should get some rest. If you need something to eat, Gina, the fridge is full. Can you fix yourself something?"

"I'm fine, I ate on the plane. For now, sleep sounds like a good idea."

That night, I lay in bed and tried to sleep, waiting and waiting for it to come, and finding it at last only when I thought of Will. Just days ago it would have tormented me to lie in bed and think about him, but tonight, I had to admit that it would have been nice to reach out across the bed and touch his arm, feel his skin, say goodnight.

*

The casket was simple. Plain oak, with a white cloth interior, nothing fussy or extravagant, a simplicity which seemed appropriate. This would be a quiet ceremony. Private and away from the clamor of scandal which had followed us following Jonathan's discovery.

We stood around the casket, each of us momentarily lost in our own grief, and stared at Rob.

He was dressed in white, his hands clasped on his chest and that same serene expression on his face, the one he had when I last saw him in the hospital.

He looked innocent and strangely pure, and Gina gasped when she saw him and muttered something barely audible, "He looks so peaceful," or words to that effect. And something about the tone of her voice, the trace of sadness it contained, whisked me back to a long-forgotten summer. A rare holiday we had all taken together to Lake Tahoe. It had been so hot the day we'd driven over from San Francisco and the air in the car was thick and heavy with the smell of sweat and cigarettes. I remembered Gina whispering to herself, her voice quiet and low because she wanted no one to hear.

But I had listened carefully and realized she was listing the things she saw as we drove by. Things she liked and wanted to take note of, the sort of miscellany no one notices—the pale blue awning of a gas station, a car bumper sticker from Disney World, the red stripe of a motorcyclist's helmet. It was as if Gina was taking mental snapshots of the road trip, composing her own internal photo album, like those photos I had seen once and really loved. America through the lens of Stephen Shore. An unseen place that existed on the periphery of your vision and yet somehow, in your heart, became home.

And I wondered why Gina needed to document the journey in this way. Surely, it was the destination that mattered most. Why focus on the drive? It was only later, a few days into the holiday, when the veneer of rest and relaxation had started to crack, and the first signs of tension had filled the air, that I understood. Gina wanted this moment to be the overriding memory. This quiet, happy anticipation. If she laid that down, then Rob could not take it away from her. It was hers and hers alone.

And now, here we were, standing over Rob's casket and Gina was whispering again, trying to fix this last image of Rob in her head, his serenity, the peace he had achieved.

"Are you okay?" Mom asked her.

And Gina nodded. "Yeah, I'm fine. I just wish we could have…" But it was too much to wish for what we could have said to him, the farewell we now all wished we could have had.

"Who wants to say something?" Gina asked. "I don't know if I have the right words."

I didn't either and I wondered if there was anything we could say at that moment which would feel right or seem fitting.

"It's okay," Mom said. "I don't think we need to say anything."

"Sorry. We can also say that, can't we?" I asked.

And Mom looked at me and asked, "For what happened to him as a child, you mean?"

"Yes, and for not being there in the end. For not getting there in time to tell him we found Jonathan. I'm sorry for that. I wanted him to know that."

"Well," Gina said. "We're just going to have to live with that, I guess."

I thought we were all done, but Mom had one last thing she needed to do. I watched as she turned away from us and leaned over the casket, brushing Rob's hair with her fingertips and caressing his cheek. There was a tenderness there that she could not suppress. And the grace of it, the decency of it, was almost too much to bear.

When she brushed a kiss on Rob's forehead and whispered a sad "goodbye" to him, I heard the door click shut. The intimacy was not something Gina could bear to witness. Though I thought perhaps she should have seen Mom's face as she leaned over the casket. There was a relief there, a looseness of her jawline and her forehead that hadn't been there for years. It was as if all the tension of the years had been lifted by this one gracious act.

And I had leaned over the casket myself then and said my own goodbye. Touching my father's face one last time and kissing his forehead.

It was strange to say goodbye to him this way, with no one there and no ceremony of sorts. Just the morticians nodding as we left the room. But it would have felt wrong to have a proper funeral. That was something we needed to preserve for Jonathan.

But I could feel it already, the space opening up within me where the pain and the rage had once been. A space I could fill now with something good, something better.

CHAPTER TWENTY-NINE

The whole town turned up for Jonathan Hutton's funeral, the mourners spilling out of the churchyard and onto the streets.

When the hearse drove past the crowds lining the street outside the cemetery, people bowed their heads, some threw flowers, and the soft low sound of sobs filled the air.

The television crews kept a discreet distance, but I was aware of them as we drove into the churchyard behind the family cortège. Cece had insisted we have a place in the church and during the ceremony.

"Without you, I would not have got my son back," she told us when she came round to visit and hand us the funeral card. "I want you all beside me."

When Cece took to the lectern, she smiled as she looked down at the coffin, acknowledging her son's presence there in the church, and waited for the congregation to settle before she commenced.

The sight of her standing there, so small and so alone, caused Mom to choke away a tear and I felt her take my hand and grip it tight. When I looked down, I saw she had taken hold of Gina's too and was squeezing it with equal vigor. And we sat there, hand in hand, and waited for Cece to begin.

"Well," she began, addressing the casket, as if the room was empty and there was no one else listening, "I never imagined I'd be making a speech like this. Mothers aren't supposed to say goodbye to their children this way. In my mind, you are still a little boy. The son I never saw grow up and build a life for himself. The son I have waited my whole life to have returned to me. I have imagined your life, the one that was taken from you. I have sat at home and thought of the people who loved you and all the ways you could have shared these years with them. The things you would have done, the family of your own you would have had. I have even seen you some days, walking down the street towards me, as if you never left. And you never really left. This place was home to you all these years we've been waiting. You were here in our hearts and we never gave up on you. We knew that one day, you would come home. And though it took you years to find your way back to me, you are with us again now, and I am thankful for that."

She paused, letting everyone absorb her words, and I could hear faint muttering in the chapel as the funeral guests expressed their agreement with what she had said.

I had no idea who they were. Save for Suzie and a few doctors and nurses I recognized from the hospice, I recognized no one. A couple of months in town had not been long enough for me to familiarize myself with the faces of the neighbors and the shopkeepers. I didn't know which child belonged to which adult or which dog to which house. This place was home to them, but it never could be for me. I understood that now.

When the mutterings subsided, Cece continued. Addressing the congregation this time. "I know there are those of you here who will disagree with me and who are not for forgiving, and so I want to say this. Rob was a flawed man, but he was also a good man and, in the end, an honest one. It will take time to process all that has happened and to find space in our hearts to understand, but we will. Because we have to if we are ever to move on. But I have my son back at long last and, for now, that is all that matters."

There was silence for a moment, broken only by soft whimpers and gentle sobs. I watched as Cece made her way from the lectern back to her seat next to ours, Suzie standing up to help her, taking her elbow and setting her down safely in the low wooden pew.

He was a good man.

Cece's words rattled around in my head and drowned out all other talk, the rest of the ceremony a blur of movement and noise that went unregistered.

She had looked over at us as she said this, her voice steady, her words slow and precise, because she didn't only want us to listen, she needed us to understand. Rob was a good man. That was what she wanted to tell us and that was what she wanted us to understand. We should think of him this way. And we should know that this was how she would think of him. That the good he had done, in the end, outweighed the rest.

And I had caught her eye, that sharp, penetrating ice-blue sphere, so intelligent and fierce, undiminished by old age, and I had held her gaze and smiled, letting her know I understood.

At the cemetery, as we watched as Cece finally lowered her son into the ground where his father lay, I thought I saw her lean more heavily on Suzie, as if she had finally decided she was ready now, to let the weight be carried by others. She had been burdened for so long, and now, at last, there was a release.

EPILOGUE

For a year, the house stood empty and the sale sign on the front lawn attracted no one. Everyone knew its story, and no one wanted to buy a property with such a gruesome history. When the agent eventually suggested we tear it down and sell the land as a plot we agreed.

I went up to watch as the crew ripped it apart and found it strangely comforting to witness the destruction.

"So, what are you going to do now?" Suzie asked me.

"I don't know. If the land sells, then I want to use the money to get a small place close to San Francisco."

"Oh, so you're definitely leaving?"

"I can't stay here, Suzie. I thought I could, but this place, everything that happened here, my family, it's just—"

"That's okay, I get it, you don't need to explain it to me."

"Come and visit me though, yeah?" I said.

"Sure, you know I will. And let me know how it goes, okay?"

"With what?"

"With everything. Starting again. You and Will."

"Me and Will?"

"Hey, don't give me that. You and Will. Enough said."

I smiled, "Well, you know, these things take time."

"Only if you let them."

Suzie dropped me at the bus station and waved me off as I boarded the bus back to San Francisco.

"Why don't you just fly?" she asked me.

"Nah, I like it this way. It gives me time to think on the journey. Figure things out while I stare out the window."

"You sure are different, Carla Allen, you know that?"

"Yeah, so they say."

"And come back and visit us. You promise?"

I smiled and told a lie. "I promise."

I think she could see in my eyes that I didn't mean it, but she let it go and waved as the bus pulled out of the station and turned out onto the street.

I let my head fall against the window and watched as Newcastle dwindled into the distance. At the other end, the future was waiting for me. And this time, I was ready to embrace it.

A LETTER FROM JENNIFER

Dear reader,

I want to say a huge thank you for choosing to read *The Vanishing Child*. I hope you enjoyed reading it as much as I enjoyed writing it.

For an author, there is nothing more inspiring than knowing there are readers out there in the world reading, and hopefully enjoying, your work. If you want to keep up to date with all my latest releases, please sign up at the following link. Your email address will never be shared, and you can unsubscribe at any time.

www.bookouture.com/jennifer-harvey

If you did enjoy reading *The Vanishing Child*, I would be very grateful if you could write a review. I'd love to hear what you think, and it makes such a difference helping new readers to discover one of my books for the first time. Thank you!

I love hearing from my readers—you can get in touch through Twitter, Goodreads, or my website.

Thank you,
Jennifer Harvey

@JenAnneHarvey1

www.jenharvey.net

ACKNOWLEDGMENTS

I wrote the first draft of this novel in the first half of 2020 as the pandemic took hold and lockdown measures came into force across Europe.

It felt as if life had been turned upside down in the blink of an eye. Suddenly, the future seemed to be not only a strange and rather vague idea, but also a daunting and uncertain prospect.

It was a strange time to be writing a novel because in many ways my day-to-day writing life remained the same. I sat at my desk, as I always did, and I put words on the page. But each word set down felt like a commitment to the future. The story would be told, the book would be published, and this was a future I could will into existence. Writing, in a way, became an optimistic and defiant response to the pandemic.

For a while, it was an effective response. Every day, I could "live" within the world I had created and try to keep thoughts of the world beyond at bay.

But the true weight and extent of the pandemic is something no imagined world can suppress and as I pushed on with my writing, I found myself relying more and more on the people around me for support and encouragement.

No writer ever writes in splendid isolation and no book sees its way into the world solely on the efforts of the writer alone. In 2020, this support network became more important than ever.

Cara Chimirri, as always, has been a wonderful source of support and inspiration and her clear editorial guidance has improved this novel immeasurably. Thank you so much, Cara. It's a true pleasure to work with you.

The community of writers I have met along the way in my writing journey has been an invaluable source of support in these strange times we are living through. So many writers have helped me, day to day, simply by writing their books and their stories or managing and editing so many wonderful literary magazines.

In particular I would like to thank: Neema Shah, Haleh Agar, Stephanie Scott, Charlotte Levin, Cathy Ulrich, Janice Leagra, Alva Holland, Steve Campbell, Pat Foran, Melissa Ostrom, Penny Haw, Jeanette Sheppard, and Carla Kovach. You have cheered me on and lifted my spirits so often.

Special thanks too to Joe Melia and the team at the Bristol Short Story Prize. Your continued championing of the Bristol Prize short story writers is wonderful and so appreciated.

Thank you too to Laura Gerrard, for her insightful comments and suggestions during the edits of this novel and for helping to make the prose flow so well.

As always I wish to say a huge thank you to all the book bloggers and readers who take the time to read and review my novels. Your support makes it all worthwhile and I value it enormously.

Thank you as always too to Kim Nash and Noelle Holten for their exciting and fantastic marketing and promotion support. You are both terrific.

My heartfelt thanks go to all the hospital staff, and key workers in education, transport, social care, and essential retail, who have worked so hard to help people through this pandemic.

My admiration for the scientists who developed a vaccine so quickly is boundless. We now have a way forward towards a better future thanks to the wonder of science.

Last, but not least, thank you to my friends and family, for always being there and helping me through the highs and lows, especially during this strange and momentous year.

Here's to the future.